The Visible World

Books by Mark Slouka

LOST LAKE

GOD'S FOOL

THE VISIBLE WORLD

The
VISIBLE
WORLD

Mark Slouka

HOUGHTON MIFFLIN COMPANY

Boston   New York   2007

For information about permission to reproduce
selections from this book, write to Permissions,
Houghton Mifflin Company, 215 Park Avenue South,
New York, New York 10003.

Visit our Web site: www.houghtonmifflinbooks.com.

Library of Congress Cataloging-in-Publication Data
Slouka, Mark.
    The visible world / Mark Slouka.
        p.   cm.
    ISBN-13: 978-0-618-75643-8
    ISBN-10: 0-618-75643-4
    1. Heydrich, Reinhard, 1904–1942 — Fiction.
2. Czechoslovakia — History — 1938–1945 — Fiction.
3. Domestic fiction. I. Title.
    PS3569.L697V57 2007
    813'.54 — dc22   2006023705

Book design by Melissa Lotfy
Typeface is Fairfield

Printed in the United States of America

MP 10 9 8 7 6 5 4 3 2 1

Portions of this novel previously appeared in *Harper's Magazine*
("August") and *Granta* ("The Little Museum of Memory").

The author is grateful for permission to quote lines from "As
I Walked Out One Evening," copyright 1940 and renewed in
1968 by W. H. Auden, from *Collected Poems* by W. H. Auden.
Used by permission of Random House, Inc.

For my mother and father, Olga and Zdenek Slouka,
who lived the years and half the story,

and for the seven who died on June 18, 1942,
in the church of Sts. Cyril and Metoděj

I would like to thank Leslie, Maya, and Zack for all the years of talk and laughter around the dinner table, for their support, their love. And Tina Mion, our twenty-first-century Goya, for the inspiration of her genius. On a different scale, I am grateful to the Guggenheim Foundation for helping me hold off the world just a little.

The glacier knocks in the cupboard,
The desert sighs in the bed,
And the crack in the tea-cup opens,
A lane to the land of the dead.

—W. H. AUDEN

THE
NEW WORLD

A Memoir

I

ONE NIGHT WHEN I WAS YOUNG MY MOTHER WALKED
out of the country bungalow we were staying in in the Poconos. I
woke to hear my father pulling on his pants in the dark. It was
very late, and the windows were open. The night was everywhere. Where was he going? I asked. "Go back to sleep," he said.
Mommy had gone for a walk. He would be right back, he said.

But I started to cry because Mommy had never gone for a
walk in the forest at night before and I had never woken to find
my father pulling on his pants in the dark. I did not know this
place, and the big windows of moonlight on the floor frightened
me. In the end he told me to be brave and that he would be back
before I knew it and pulled on his shoes and went searching for
his wife. And found her, eventually, sitting against a tree or by
the side of a pond in her tight-around-the-calf slacks and frayed
tennis shoes, fifteen years too late.

My mother knew a man during the war. Theirs was a love story,
and like any good love story, it left blood on the floor and wreck-
age in its wake.

It was all done by the fall of 1942. Earlier that year, in May,
Czech partisans had assassinated Reichsprotektor Reinhard
Heydrich in Prague, and the country had suffered through the

predictable reprisals: interrogations, purges, mass executions. The partisans involved in the hit were killed on June 18. In December of that year my parents escaped occupied Czechoslovakia, crossing from Bohemia into Germany, from Germany to France, then south to Marseille, where my mother nearly died of scarlet fever before they could sail for England, and where my father and a small-time criminal named Vladek (who had befriended my father because they were both from Brno) sold silk and cigarette lighters to the whores whose establishments tended to be in the same neighborhoods and who always seemed to have a bit of money to spend.

They were very young then. I have the documents from the years that followed: the foreign-worker cards and the soft, well-worn passports with their photos and their purple stamps, the information (hair: brown; face: oval) filled in with a fountain pen . . . I have pictures of them — in Innsbruck, in Sydney, in Lyon. In one, my father, shirtless and glazed with sweat, a handkerchief around his head, is standing on a chair, painting a small room white. The year is 1947. The sun is coming through a curtainless window to the left. My mother is holding the can of paint for him. Behind him, the unpainted wall above the brush strokes looks like the sky above a mountain range.

I was born, three years later, into a world that felt just slightly haunted, like the faint echo of an earlier one. We were living in New York then. At night, high in our apartment in Queens, my mother would curl herself against my back and I would smell her perfume, her hair, the deep, cave-like warmth of her, and she would hum some Czech song or other until I pretended to be asleep. We always lay on our right sides, my head tucked under her chin and her left arm around me, and often — it's the thing I remember most clearly about her now — her fingers would twitch against my stomach or my chest as if she were playing the piano in her dreams, though she wasn't dreaming, or even asleep, and had never played the piano in her life.

• • •

4

Half a lifetime after the night my father left our cabin to look for my mother, long after they were both gone, I met a man in Prague who told me that the city I thought I'd come to know actually lay four meters under the earth; that the somewhat dank, low-ceilinged café we were sitting in at the time was not the first story, as I had assumed, but the second. To resist the flooding of the Vltava, he said, the streets of the Old Town had been built up with wagonloads of soil — gradually, over decades — and an entire world submerged.

He was a tall, well-dressed man with a crown of gray-white hair and a rumbling baritone voice, and he sat at the tiny glass table sipping his tea with such a straight-backed, sovereign air, such a natural attitude of authority and grace, that he might have been an exiled king instead of the retired director of the Department of Water Supply, which he was. In some of the buildings of the Old Town, he said, pausing to acknowledge the slightly desperate-looking waitress who had brought him a small cup of honey, one could descend into the cellars and find, still visible in the pattern of the brick, the outlines of windows and doors: a stone lintel, a chest-high arch, a bit of mouldered wood trapped between a layer of plaster and brick.

In the course of his work, he said, he had often been called to this building or that where some construction had accidentally unearthed something, and found himself wondering at the utter strangeness of time, at the gradual sinking away of all that was once familiar. He smiled. It could make one quite morbid, really. But then, if one considered the question rightly, one could see the same thing almost everywhere one looked. After all, twenty minutes from where we sat, travelers from a dozen countries stood bargaining for ugly gewgaws on the very stones that only a few centuries ago had been heaped with the dead. Certain things time simply buried more visibly than others. Was it not so?

The waitress came over with a black wallet open in her hand like a miniature bellows, or something with gills. She had scratched herself badly on her calf, I noticed, and the blood had welled through the torn stocking and dried into a long, dark icicle. She seemed unaware of it. My companion handed her a fifty-crown note. And then, before I could say anything, he wished me a good day, slipped on his greatcoat, and left.

I walked for hours that night, among the crowds and up into the deserted orchards and past the king's gardens, still closed for the winter, where I stood for a while looking through the bars at the empty paths and the low stone benches. Along the far side, between the stands of birches whose mazework of spidery branches reminded me of the thinning hair of old ladies, I could see a long row of waterless fountains, like giant cups or stone flowers.

I was strangely untired. A fine mist began to fall, making the cobbles slippery, as if coated with sweat. I looked at the stone giant by the castle gates, his dagger forever descending but never striking home, then walked down the tilting stairs to a place where a crew of men, working in the white glare of halogen lamps, had opened up the ground. As I passed the pit, I glimpsed a foundation of some sort and what looked like a sewer of fist-sized stones, and struck by the connection to the man I had met in the café, for whom these men might once have worked, after all, I started for home. Everywhere I looked, along the walled streets and narrow alleys, above the cornerstones of buildings and under the vaulted Gothic arches, I saw plaster flayed to brick or stone, and hurrying now through the narrow little park along the river, I startled a couple embracing in the dark whom I had taken for a statue. I mumbled an apology, my heartbeat racing, and rushed on. Behind me I heard the man mutter something angrily, then a woman's low laugh, and then all was still.

That night I dreamed I saw him again in a house at the end of the world, and he looked up from the glass table to where I stood peering in through a small window and mouthed the words "Is it not so?" I woke to the sound of someone crying in the courtyard, then heard pigeons scuttling on the shingles and a quick flurry of wings and the crying stopped.

And lying there in the dark, I thought, yes, that's what it had been like: beneath the world I had known — so very familiar to me, so very *American* — just under the overgrown summer lawn, or the great stone slab of the doorstep — another one lay buried. It was as though one morning, running through the soaking grass to the dock, I had tripped on an iron spike like a finger pointing from the earth and discovered it was the topmost spire of Hradčany Castle, or realized that the paleness under the water twenty yards out from the fallen birch was actually the white stone hair of Eliška Krásnohorská, whose statue stood in Karlovo náměstí, and that the square itself — its watery trolleys, its green-lit buildings, its men forever lifting their hats in greeting and its women reining in their shining hair — was right there below me, that an entire universe and its times, its stained-glass windows and its vaulted ceilings and its vast cathedral halls, were just below my oars.

But I could never go there. All I could do was peer from above as the people went about their day, unaware that with every step, every kiss, every tram ticket tossed to the curb, they were constructing the world that would shape my own.

2

WHEN I WAS A BOY WE LIVED IN A FIFTEENTH-FLOOR apartment in Queens, like an aerie above the world, and at night my father would read to me from a thick yellow volume of Czech fairy tales. In the book was a page with a kind of tissue over it. Under it was a picture of a beautiful girl in a dark forest. She had thin arms and she wore a white dress like one of my mother's scarves. She was leaning back against the trunk of a huge, mossed tree as though trying to protect it, a hunter's arrow buried deep in her breast.

I would look at that picture when I was alone. At the thin fingers of her left hand splayed like a starfish, grasping the bark. At the blood-red fletching, the stub of the wooden shaft. At the place where it disappeared — right there, just above that small, painful arc, that indescribable, exquisitely painful arc. There was a look on her face, caught between the strands of black, blowing hair, that I found shameful and disturbing and mysterious. I could never look at it for long. A look of shock, of course. And pain, yes. But something else, something I could not understand then — can barely understand now. A look of pleading, of utter renunciation, of love. Of love beyond all song and argument.

. . .

No one could tell you about my father without first telling you something about her. She made him, you see, shaped him, turned him into the man he was. She changed the course of his life as easily as a hill turns a meadow stream. And though you might think that, given enough time, the stream will move the hill, or cut it through, it's the stream that will twist in its bed, alter its course. The new comes to feel natural. Detour becomes destiny.

For twenty-six years, Antonín Sedlák was like every other mother's son in the city of Brno, Czechoslovakia — four rows up, three over — running his own particular course to the sea. Then he ran into her, and nothing was ever the same for him again.

What can I say about my father that isn't bent out of truth by hindsight, misshapen by love? My father was a good and decent man, I think, a man capable of outrage over the world he happened to have found himself in, but someone whose faith in reason, like some men's faith in God or love, remained intact long after his life had made it ridiculous. He couldn't help it. His every gesture departed from that well-lit station, and though he understood how quaint this was, he was powerless to change it. It was his nature, and he wore it with dignity, like a childhood hat one has long outgrown but can't remove for the rest of his life. And somehow I could never bring myself to hold it against him.

I have a small, square photograph of him I've always liked for some reason I can't quite explain. There he is — already tall at thirteen, handsome enough, seemingly comfortable in a collar as high and stiff as a whiplash brace — looking straight on. Not smiling. And yet there is something there — a touch of amusement perhaps, a calm recognition of the absurdity of the proceedings — that seems like a smile.

Everything that he accomplished in his life was a violence against that almost-smile. Against its generosity, its good-humored reasonableness and decency. Against his very nature. And that, too, the smile seems to anticipate, and accept for the irony it is.

I see him clearly now, like a house revealed by fallen leaves. My father, who fashioned himself over the years into a kind of load-bearing joint, braced up to his burden, and died two years after being relieved of it. Who didn't know how to be in a world so suddenly lightened. I remember the bumps of blue veins on the backs of his hands, the mole on his cheek. I can see him, his big warm forehead, his way of listening while lighting a cigarette or taking a slow sip from his glass, that gesture of his — a slight backward tilt of the head, an open hand — at once wry and unresigned, as if to say, So, what would you do? I see him sitting in the chair by the long, low bookshelf, his bow and his violin propped against the wood next to him. Clean shaven. The flat planes of his cheeks. It embarrassed me to kiss him in front of my friends. I can see him smile. When he reaches for his glass or turns toward where I am kneeling, hidden in the wall, spying through the crack in the door behind my bed, the lenses of his small, rimless glasses turn into coins.

It was my father who told me about Pythagoras. I was seven years old. Pythagoras, he explained, besides doing some very nice work on triangles, which I would someday have to learn about, had believed that the essence of all things was a number, that our souls migrated like finches from life to life until we were liberated from the cycle of birth, and that eating beans was a form of cannibalism. He had come to this last belief, he said, because a cut-open bean looked, and still looks, very much like a human embryo. My father lit a cigarette. And so, he said, since human beings must act on their convictions and, whenever they see a tragedy unfolding, throw themselves headlong under the wheels of history, Pythagoras did what his conscience demanded, and banned the eating of beans. As a result, in Crotona during those few years, among the Pythagoreans if no one else, beans were accorded the respect they deserved.

Which would have been poignant enough, but no, history could never resist the extra step, the peacock's turn — it would always sign with a flourish. Which was why, on a cloudy afternoon at the end of the fifth century before the birth of our lord and savior Jesus Christ, Pythagoras, fleeing Magna Graecia with a mob at his heels, came to the edge of a vast bean field sleeping peacefully under the sombrous sky and, rather than run through this tender nursery of souls, stopped, and was beaten to death with short sticks.

A sad story? Not at all, my father said. A story of courage and conviction, sacrifice and love. Pythagoras was a hero. He took a sip from his glass. A hero for our time.

3

I DON'T KNOW THAT THERE WAS EVER A TIME WHEN I didn't know their story. It was always there, like a ray of light cutting into the room. It had been there before me. I simply walked through it in my time.

When I was young, of course, I didn't understand exactly why they had hidden themselves in a crypt, which I knew to be a kind of basement in which people were buried. Or what had happened to them there exactly. I only knew that there were seven of them, that they were Czech soldiers, parachutists, and that they had done something very brave. That they'd been surrounded. That they'd fought to live.

Like the Alamo, I said to my father. Not at all like the Alamo, he said. They were fighting for their own country.

In the afternoons, when my mother was in the kitchen, I would secretly play parachutist (my men would sit on the back of a gray model airplane like cowboys on a horse and sail down into occupied Czechoslovakia on tiny blue parachutes I'd found in a shop on Canal Street), and for a long time, whenever I sat at my desk, I would play "hidden soldiers," setting up my GI Joes in the partly open drawer that held my pencils and erasers so that they could shoot at the Wehrmacht battalions (GI Joes with their helmets painted black) arrayed along the edge of my shelf.

The soldiers, partisans and Germans alike, stood on a flat base, like a skateboard, holding their flexible green rifles. Every now and again I would find one with a tiny bit of plastic still clinging to him — a remnant of the mold from which he had been stamped, a kind of factory placenta — and I would take this bit of stuff webbing the crook of an elbow, say, or linking chin strap to chest, and carefully tear it off with my fingernails.

I would study their faces: the flat green planes of their cheeks, the slight indentations that were their eyes. I wasn't sure, early on, whether the men in the crypt had lived or died, so sometimes I'd let them live, flying up to the top of my desk like armed angels. Other times they'd be killed, and I'd knock them down with my finger. I continued to do this — killing them one time, saving them the next — even after I knew what had happened to them.

Like all children, there were many things I didn't understand. I didn't understand why it was that the roses of Karlovy Vary, when dipped into a bucket of mineral water at the cost of ten crowns a stem, would grow streaked with gray and green deposits and harden to stone. I didn't understand the story I'd overheard of twenty-year-old Robert Nezval, the poet's son, whose mother had walked into the family parlor one winter afternoon to find him playing the piano with both his wrists slashed.

But some things I knew. I knew there had been a war. That all the people we knew had gone through it in one way or another. That Czechoslovakia, the country my parents came from, had been taken over. That some had fought back, and others hadn't.

I knew other things. I knew that once upon a time there had been someone for whom my mother had cared very much. Who had gone out hunting in the rain one morning and never returned. Who had lost his way in the forest. Or leaned too far over the water. I knew this the way children know things, and knowing it didn't trouble me. It had to be that way so that things could be the way they were now. So that in the early mornings my father could draw me whales with his fountain pen instead of working on his dissertation — three quick strokes made a spout; a single touch of ink, a backward-glancing eye.

In the winters, when we were still living in the old apartment above 63rd Road, my mother would braid vánočka for Christmas Eve. She tried to teach me, but I was a hopeless case: my hands seemed to have been made for the express purpose of tearing dough or turning it into glue. Year after year I would stand beside her and watch her roll out four perfect ropes of yellow dough, press their ends together with the heel of her floured hand, then twine the separate plaits into a pattern of triangles, all the while dipping her fingers into a hill of flour spilled on a piece of curling wax paper. I understood nothing. She worked quickly, almost carelessly, with the kind of rough familiarity I had seen in expert gardeners, centering the flour into a flat-planed hill with her palms, wrecking it, building it up again. And suddenly it was done and she was painting the finished braid with egg yolks, making it shine.

I still remember those winter afternoons, with the perfume of the dying pine drifting in from the next room and the early dark coming on outside. The decorated balconies on the buildings opposite ours looked like small, multicolored candies. We laughed at the baggy constrictors of dough I produced and the great doughy highways I wove out of them, and one year she stuck big gecko pads to the ends of her fingers and chased me around the living room. I can still hear her laughter now and then, as if it had been trapped somewhere, and when I do, I'm once more in that kitchen with her, high above the world and separate.

After we were finished, I would watch her wiping the table down with short, sharp strokes, rinsing out the rag in the sink, pushing back her hair with her forearm. She would usually begin cleaning the sink immediately, sweeping around the edges with her hand, and I'd watch her scrub at the sides with blue cleanser, turning tight little whorls, miniature hurricanes. And suddenly — this is how it always was — something would change, and it would be as if there were someone else in the room with us.

"It doesn't matter," I heard her say once as she was rinsing her hands. "None of it matters."

She turned off the water. For a few moments she leaned both hands on the sink, deciding, I thought, what to do next.

"Daddy should be home soon," I said.

She was still thinking.

"Can I go play in my room?" I said.

My mother began wiping her hands on a dishrag decorated with pine trees and ornaments.

"Why don't you go play for a while," she said. "Daddy will be home soon."

And there he would be. Placing his black hat carefully on the peg. Giving his heavy coat a shake before hanging it on the rack. My mother would come out of the kitchen holding a wooden spoon or an open cookbook and give him a quick kiss and then I'd be in his arms and he'd carry me down the hall and into our narrow living room, and after dinner he'd pull a chair to the side of my bed and read to me. The yellow shade of the pirate lamp made a small circle. My father would sit at the edge of it, holding the book in his left hand as though giving a sermon, always touching two fingers to his tongue before turning the page.

Once upon a time, he would read, there was a small village, and in that village lived a humble farmer and his wife. And to this couple one happy day there was born a son. They named him Otesánek. *What does Otesánek mean? It doesn't mean anything. It's just a name.* The farmer and his wife were very happy. Otesánek was a fat, healthy baby with small black eyes. *See?*

Here's Otesánek in his mother's arms, and there's the father, and there's the horse, looking on from the stable. Is that their dog? I should think so. All the neighbors came by to congratulate them. Look at those arms, said the tailor. Look at those legs, said the cobbler's wife. What a healthy baby, they all said. Just look how he eats!

Otesánek ate and ate. He ate like no other baby had ever eaten before — *not like you, arguing with your* kašička *every morning* — and he grew like no other baby had ever grown before. The cow couldn't give enough milk. The chickens couldn't lay enough eggs. *Here he is, sitting on the floor. Look at all those pitchers of milk, all those loaves of bread. Is that his father? It sure is. Look how small he is. He doesn't look very happy.* Otesánek's mother and father ran all around the village buying food. Otesánek's father carved him an extra-large spoon to eat with. But it wasn't enough. Otesánek would eat whatever they put in front of him and scream for more.

Otesánek grew and grew. Soon he was bigger than his father. Soon he was bigger than a cow. He grew so big that he couldn't fit into his parents' little house anymore. He had to sit outside in the yard. One day a chicken wandered by, pecking at the dirt. Quick as a flash, Otesánek grabbed it and stuffed it in his mouth. The family goat came next, and the pigs, and the dog with the pink tongue. Otesánek ate the sheep in their hot, woolly coats. He ate the white geese that walked by the pond, and the carp that lived under the lily pads. *What are those, Daddy? Those? Those are the hooves of the cow.*

Soon he was bigger than a house. When he ate the plow horse, his mother and father came out to plead with him. Otesánek, please, they said, we will have nothing if you keep this up. When will you stop? Quick as lightning, Otesánek grabbed his mother and father in each of his huge, pudgy hands. When there is nothing more to eat, he croaked, and he stuffed them head-first into his mouth.

Otesánek ate the whole town: the cobbler and the cobbler's wife, the tailor and the carpenter, the shopkeeper and the teacher and all the little children. One by one. And he might have gone on eating forever except for a little girl whom he had swallowed as she sat at her sewing holding a pair of rusty scissors. Down she went, down into the hot red room of his stomach. When she realized where she was, she took the scissors and cut a hole in Otesánek's belly. Out she came. Out came the cobbler and the cobbler's wife, the tailor and the carpenter, the shopkeeper and the teacher and all the little children. Out stepped the plow horse and the goat, the chickens and the geese. Out jumped the dog with the pink tongue. And out came Otesánek's mother and father. They were happy to be alive. They danced and sang and carried the little girl around on their shoulders. And they all lived happily ever after.

I can still see him, the crease of the page cutting him vertically above the elbow and the knee. Dimpled knees arched across the road, he has just snatched his father and crammed him head-first into his mouth. He has a single tooth, as big as a dictionary. Black holes for eyes. To plead for mercy is absurd. There is no mercy here. He is the force that consumes, and he will keep on until the world — the narrow roads, the great square fields, the church itself, whose steeple pokes up like a child's toy just above his thigh — is empty of man and beast. A grave under the sun. And only he is left.

They're dying in the red room. All of them. Gesturing like bad Shakespearean actors, like swimmers fifty fathoms deep. The children turn slowly, uncomprehending, their schoolbooks paging in the hot tide.

A quick flash of inner pain, like gas, passes over the monster's face. Something sparks on the white wall of his skin, like a diamond birthing itself from his heart. You can see it, there! — a tiny blade, spotted and fine. Now he is clawing at his stomach, thrusting his own fist down his throat, as though devouring himself. He is in agony. There is nothing he can do about it. He is as big as the sun, and he can't stop it. To get at what's killing him, he'll have to tear himself open. Either way, he'll die from within.

There she is, stepping through the thick door of his flesh into the morning air. The monster lies slumped against a hill, still in his diaper. She is holding the scissors by her side. She has long black hair and a sad mouth, and of all the people dancing in the square, she is the only one who isn't smiling.

4

MY MOTHER HAD BEEN BORN IN 1920 IN RAČÍN, A VIL-
lage in the Vysočina highlands of Moravia. When I was a child
she would tell me Račín looked very much like the pictures of
Czech villages in my book *České pohádky*, and I would sit on my
bed and look at them and imagine her there, hiding in the black
shadow of an open door, or below the undercut bank of a stream.
It seemed to me that if I looked closely enough, deeply enough,
I'd make out her outline, a deeper dark within the shadow's
wedge, or recognize that bit of light between the blades of grass
as the topmost curl of her hair.

When I visited Račín in 1979, I discovered that it was, in fact,
just like the pictures in my book. A cluster of slate roofs. A tangle of close, muddy gardens and tilting fences. The requisite
small, swift stream, thick with nettle, cutting under the road. An
odd feeling. It was as though I had found myself inside my own
storybook. No one seemed to be about that hot July afternoon —
even the butterflies along the roadside seemed drugged, their
wings opened wide across the blooms — and I wandered down a
dirt road past a stagnant pond to the shade of a forest dotted
with mossed stumps and thick tufts of grass, and all the time I
had the strange but not unpleasant feeling of being watched.

At some point I remember sitting down on a pile of fresh-cut pines that someone had left by the wayside. The white circles where their branches had been lopped off made them look spotted. They were bleeding dark trails of sap from every cut — the air was rich with it. Large brown-and-purple butterflies I recalled from one of my childhood books moved in and out of the trees along the edge of the field; a small group fanned at the graying edge of a puddle a horse had left in the road. In my book, I remembered, the cardboard cutouts of the butterflies had slid in and out of invisible slots in the stems of flowers, opening and closing their wings as I opened and closed the book.

Back in the village I found the house — fourth down from the pond — without too much trouble. I had an old photograph, taken before the war. It hadn't changed. I looked at it for a while, with its slate roof and stuccoed walls. At the end of a goat-eaten yard was an old barn, half stone, half brick. A sheep with bits of leaves and sawdust in its wool was lying in its shade. No one seemed to be at home, and after a minute or two, when the sheep hadn't moved and the strangely familiar face of a six- or eight-year-old girl had not appeared in the double windows to stare at me — as I had half believed and feared it might — I went on my way. If there had been someone to warn, someone to tell of the things to come, I might have stayed.

She had been the third child born, and the first to survive. There had been a brother who came after her, she told me, though he had lived only a few hours, like a moth, and had been buried in a down-filled box hardly larger than a loaf of bread. My mother remembered that morning — the morning they buried her little brother — as one of the most precious moments of her childhood. She couldn't tell me why. Sometimes there are things you love and can't explain, she said.

A cold morning. A fresh wind roughed the grass along the road; the flowers shook their heads and nodded. Her father, she said, held her hand as they walked, his calloused palm as hard and warm as a piece of wood left in the sun. On the way, she remembered, he told her a wonderful story about a *trpaslík* — an elf — who knew the path to a stone door, no taller than a hammer, that led to the other world. The one below the pond. From there, her father told her, you could look up and see *this* life, see everything — the trees, the separating clouds, the fishermen pulling at their earlobes or folding up their wooden stools — all this, just slightly distorted, like a face behind poorly made glass or a pane of new ice. These glimpses of our world were very precious to those who lived below; they could gaze at a dog's pink tongue lapping at the edge of the sky for hours, and on those rare afternoons when the children leaped from the clouds, spearing down toward the silted roofs of their world clothed in white sheaths of bubbles, they would gather in great swaying crowds, their clothes fluttering about them, and weep.

I begged her to tell me what happened after that, how the story ended, but she had forgotten. It didn't matter. There were some things my mother wouldn't tell me — I was used to that. But the story bothered me. I wondered what the pond people did in the winter when the sky above their heads stiffened and their world went dark; how they could see or play, and whether they had great watery fires to keep them warm.

And so, for some time after my mother told me her father's half-story, whenever I found myself alone with one of my parents' friends, I would ask them — Mrs. Jakubcová, for example. Mrs. Jakubcová had never had any children of her own. She had calves as big and smooth as bowling pins, and she always sat on the sofa with her legs to one side as if glued at the knees, and smelled sweet and sad, like a dusty pastry. One day I asked her about the people who lived under the pond, and while I was at it, why the young man had played the piano instead of calling for a doctor, and who the men in the crypt had been. And she tented a napkin over her finger and touched it to the corners of her lips two or three times — a few yellow crumbs and a chalk line of powdered sugar had stuck to her rose-colored lipstick — and told me that as far as she knew the people who lived in the pond slept a kind of half-sleep, like bears, waking fully only when the ice had cracked apart and light came into their world again, and that she didn't know but that perhaps the young man had cared for his music more than he did for himself, and that the men in the crypt had been heroes. Czech patriots. Those had been hard times, she said.

Some weeks later I tried Mr. Hanuš, who walked with two canes because he had lost all his toes in a town I thought was named Mousehausen, but when I asked him one evening after he'd hobbled into my room to say good night to me (for he insisted on this), he didn't seem to know anything about the pond people sleeping through the long winters. Sitting on the edge of my bed — I couldn't have been more than six — he told me that the winters were the times of storytelling, when they imagined what they could not see and entertained themselves with long, complicated tales in which all the things they had glimpsed the year before played a role. I asked him about the young man who played the piano. Robert Nezval hadn't wanted to live anymore, he said. Picking a big, gray picture book off the floor (it was a book of Greek myths; I have it still), he began to page through it absent-mindedly, past the picture of the herd of cows that Hermes stole from Apollo, with their bright yellow horns and blushing udders, past Athena being born from the head of Zeus, and Persephone being dragged into the earth by Hades. I wanted to show him the small wooden brooms that Hermes had tied to the cows' tails to erase their tracks, and the four sleeping pigs, pink as newborn mice, falling into the dark with Persephone, but he was moving too quickly. Sometimes people just didn't want to live anymore, he said. It happened.

As for the men in the crypt, he said, it had been a bad time and they had done a brave thing, as true and just a thing as one could imagine, and thousands had died because of it. That happened too.

"What did they do?" I asked him.

"They killed a man named Reinhard Heydrich."

"How?"

"How?"

"How did they kill him?"

Mr. Hanuš sighed. "They tried to shoot him but the gun didn't work, so they threw a bomb which wounded him and later he died. This all happened long before you were born, in 1942."

"Did he wear a black helmet?"

"Heydrich? No. A kind of cap. Some of his soldiers did, though."

"Why did they kill him?"

"He was a cruel man. He deserved to die."

"Why?"

"Why? Because he killed a great many people who did not deserve it, and sent many more to places that were very bad."

"Like prison?"

"Worse."

"Did you . . . ?"

"So who is this?" he asked me, pointing to a picture of Selene gazing down from the moon at sleeping Endymion, who lay, vaguely smiling, surrounded by strangely wild-looking sheep. He looked at me over the tops of his half-glasses. "I get to ask some questions too, you know," he said.

So I told him how it was Selene, the moon, who had seen a shepherd named Endymion and fallen in love with him and had asked Zeus to grant him the gift of eternal sleep so that he might remain forever young and handsome, and that that was why she was looking at him from a hole in the moon. "I see," said Mr. Hanuš. "And who does this huge hand with the grasshopper belong to?" That, I said, was the hand of Selene's sister, Eos, who had also fallen in love with someone, maybe another shepherd, I wasn't sure, but had made the mistake of asking the gods for eternal life instead of eternal sleep — a big mistake — and so had been left with just a grasshopper in her hand.

Mr. Hanuš looked at the picture thoughtfully. "I like the sheep," he said. He closed the book with a gentle clap. "If I were you, I would stay away from sisters like that. And the gods too, maybe. Now go to sleep, quickly — until morning will do — or your mother will be angry with me."

I lay down on my pillow and he pulled the dinosaur blanket up to my chin and petted my hair once, and I let him because I knew that this was important to him. "I'll tell your mother and father to come give you a kiss," he said, reaching for his canes. "Now sleep."

And I slipped down as though pulled from below, and in my dreams that night the things I'd been told and the things I hadn't mixed and blurred and Selene looked down over 63rd Road and SS troopers in their low, rounded helmets stood arrayed along the roof of Alexander's department store watching as, far below, a silent herd of cows with yellow horns and brooms tied to their tails moved like a sea of humped, ridged backs through the unlit canyons toward Queens Boulevard, erasing themselves, while far, far above them in a dark apartment very close to the sky a young man sat in a wash of light as blue as ice and played the piano — beautifully, perfectly — until he fell asleep.

5

MY MOTHER AND FATHER MET IN BRNO IN 1939, FOUR
months after the occupation began, when my father wrote her a
love letter he had composed for someone else for a fee of ten
crowns. He did this regularly, he told me, and did quite well by
it. It was nothing, he said: a few particulars, a handful of ripe
clichés, and the thing was done. This time, however, when he
delivered the letter for his client, things went badly. "Honza
didn't write this," the young woman who would be my mother
declared almost as soon as she began reading it. She laughed,
then read aloud: "'. . . in the empty rooms and courtyards of my
heart'? Oh, God." My father started to say something. "Stop,"
she said. "Honza's a sweet boy, but he wouldn't know a metaphor
if it ran him over in the street." She looked at my father. "What
kind of man writes love letters for other men?" she said. "A poor
one," my father said.

They began to talk, and by the time he walked out of the
pastry shop on Zapomenutá Street, where he had found her sitting with her girlfriends (the two of them had moved to a table
near the back to talk privately), she had agreed to meet him the
following day for a walk. There were reasons for this. He was
handsome. He was not a fool. There was a kind of sad lighteart-
edness about him; he seemed not to care very much how he ap-

peared to the world. And he had nerve. The day after they met, he found Honza in the locker room of the gymnasium after soccer practice (the schools had not been closed as yet) and gave him back the letter. He had decided to go out with the girl himself, he said. And when Honza, not entirely unreasonably, took offense at this turn of events, and with two of his friends gave my father a sound beating, my father, wiping the blood off his face with his sleeve, somehow managed to get up and pull a ten-crown coin out of his pocket. "Here," he said, throwing it on the locker room floor. "A full refund."

They saw each other all that summer and fall. He would meet her outside the steel railroad station and the two of them would walk arm in arm up the street that used to be Masarykova ulice but was now Hermann Göring Strasse, then across the square and down the small, quiet streets to Špilberk, where they would lose themselves, along with all the other lovers, in the vast grounds of the castle. I can picture them there, lying on the grass, my mother looking up into the deepening blue, my father, propped up on an elbow next to her, recounting some small thing or other, smiling in that way of his, turning the story like a candlestick on a lathe.

I like to think of the two of them there, wandering arm in arm up the paths and away from the town like newlyweds entering for the first time the house they would live in the rest of their lives, walking from room to blissfully empty room as though they could simply walk away from the gathering of things, as though they could still find a place — up this flight of stairs, maybe, behind this wall, in this room-sized garden — where time could not find them.

It was on one of those days that my parents accidentally took the second set of stairs leading down from Špilberk Castle instead of the first, and so found themselves walking past the entrance to the crypt of the old Capuchin monastery. My mother had never been there. The crypt would be closing in fifteen minutes.

A watery-eyed old woman with long white hairs on her chin was sitting in a chair at the top of the stairs, next to a rickety card table and a bowl with three coins. They were the last, apparently. The school groups, if there had been any that day, had left. The tourists who had once crowded the stairs to view the bodies of the monks, centuries dead, had dropped off with the war. The place felt oddly deserted. The old woman might have been waiting there for years.

"*Je tam dole zima, děti,*" she said, looking at them. It's cold down there, children. "*Oblečte se teple.*" Dress warmly.

And indeed they could feel the dank, subterranean chill breathing up out of the stairwell. My father put his arm around my mother's shoulders. The woman handed them two yellow tickets.

"*To vám nepomůže,*" she said, smiling. That won't help you.

My father took the tickets, though there was no one to give them to, and together they started down the steep, turning stairs. They were halfway down, laughing about something or other, when they heard her call down the shaft after them: "*Musíte spěchat, děti.*" You have to hurry, children. "*Není moc času.*" There isn't much time.

Perhaps it was the change from the upper air, or the sudden silence of those dim, low-ceilinged rooms, or the clayey smell. Perhaps it was something about the short, unlit halls, where my father had to duck his head as he led my mother by the hand to the next candlelit room. Or something else altogether. It was nothing, after all. In the outside world the universities had been closed, the factories turned to the business of war. Up above, the newspapers listed the names of the dead in thin black rectangles, like advertisements for faucets or shoes.

In the first, main room, where generations of schoolchildren had giggled over the poor mummified body of Franz Trenck, they stopped to look through the glass-topped coffin at the black, jerked flesh, the finger-thick cable of the neck, the nail emerging from the cuticle. In the second room a prison-like cell dug out of the wall and closed off by iron bars was filled with small brown skulls. They lay jumbled, one on top of the other, cheek to cheek, jaw to neck, some facing this way, some that. Some seemed to be laughing. The bars had been set into the stone.

My father asked my mother if she was cold. She was fine, she said. They read the brief biographies framed on the walls — the dates, the names — and walked on.

In the fourth and last room, apparently, there was a row of caskets arranged along the wall like basinets on a nursery floor. In each was a shape that had once been a human being but was now just a pelvis, a skull, a few fraying ropes of tendon. Here and there, hipbones tented bits of desiccated cloth. So much death, so neatly arranged. Walking from one to the other, my father told me years later, gave one the uneasy feeling of being asked to choose something.

All the caskets were open. Next to each, at the end of a curved metal stem like a rectangular flower, was a sign that gave some information about the body next to it. It was a bit of a jolt, my father said, to learn that some of the dead had once been women, but once one knew, it was possible to imagine one could see it. And not just in obvious things — a wider pelvis, perhaps, or a thinner chest — but in other, frankly impossible things: in the girlish bend of an elbow or the inward tilt of a knee. In the demure, almost coquettish turn of a chin. They began to try to guess in advance.

She was in the ninth casket in the row of eleven. It was obvious right away that she had been buried alive, my father said. Unlike all the others, who seemed more or less at rest, with their arms and legs laid straight out and their chins tucked almost thoughtfully into their throats, she was all rage and fury. Her caramel-colored skull, with its few pitiful wisps of hair, had bent straight back on the spine, so that she appeared to be arching up on her head. Her mouth was still open, caught in mid-scream.

Worst of all, though, were her hands, or what remained of them, which lay palm-up by her neck like birds' feet, still clawing at what had long ago given way.

A tiny bell sounded from the stairwell, and they turned and left the abbess in her coffin, walking past the rows of sleeping dead and the tumbled skulls and Franz Trenck in his glass-topped coffin, then up the narrow stairs to the street where they found the sun already fallen behind the body of the church and night coming on.

6

AMERICA WAS MY FOREGROUND, FAMILIAR AND KNOWN: the crowds, the voices, Captain Kangaroo and Mister Magoo, the great trains clattering and tilting west, pulling out of the seam in the summer wall as my father and I sat waiting in the DeSoto on Old Orchard Road. Behind it, though, for as long as I can remember, was the Old World, its shape and feel and smell, like the pattern of wallpaper coming through the paint.

My father loved America, loved the West — the idea of it, the grandness and the absurdity of it. It was a vicarious sort of thing. To my knowledge, for example, he never watched a baseball game in his life, yet the thought that millions of men cared passionately for it, that they had memorized names and batting averages, somehow gave him pleasure. The time we drove west, my mother in her sunglasses and deep blue scarf looking like Audrey Hepburn in *Breakfast at Tiffany's,* he was nearly stunned into speechlessness by the vastness of it all: the sheer immensity of the sky, the buzz of a bluebottle under that huge lid of sun, the oceanic valleys stretching to the horizon. The little two-lanes and the sleepy motels thrilled him; every menu was an adventure, and he'd study the gravy-stained paper through his reading glasses as if it were a letter from some distant land, which I suppose it was.

I have a memory of him standing in the open door of some small motel room in New Mexico, leaning against the doorframe, smoking. Swallows or bats are dipping under the telephone wires. It's dusk, and the land on the other side of the road opens into endless space — bluing, vast, lunar. It's as if the room, the motel, the gas station down the way could tip into it at any moment and snake like a necklace into a well. My mother lies on the bed under the light, her legs crossed at the ankle, reading a magazine.

"My God, Ivana, you should come and see this," my father says. "I could fit half of Czechoslovakia into the space between the road and those cliffs out there."

"I'm sure you could," says my mother.

The West, my father liked to say, especially after he'd had a glass or two of wine in the evenings when we had friends over, was the great solvent of history. It dissolved the pain, retained the shell: "Paris, Texas; Rome, Arkansas . . . Just try and imagine it the other way around," he'd say. "Chicago, Italy? Dallas, Austria? Unthinkable." No, the funnel was securely in place. Everything was running one way. Eventually all of Europe, all the popes and plagues, the whole bloody carnival, would be a diner somewhere off the highway in Oklahoma.

"Here he goes," someone would say.

"Think of it," my father would say. "The Little Museum of Memory. The Heaven of Exiles. Entertainment for the whole family."

On a train out of Grand Central one March day, many years later, I ran into a man I recognized vaguely from childhood. He sat by the window in the winter light, busy with shadows. A sculptor from Prague, older than my parents, he had come to our apartment half a dozen times in the late 1950s, then disappeared. He was in pharmaceuticals now. He had a house in Rhinebeck.

And so how were my parents? I told him. He had liked them, he said, he had liked them both very much, they had been very kind to him when he had arrived in this country. And yet every time he had come to our apartment he would get the feeling that everybody there was slowly suffocating, but too polite to mention it. At some point he just couldn't stand it anymore.

"It was a new world out there," he cried as small ice floes on the river behind him disappeared into his head, passed through the back of the seat, and reemerged on the other side. "All they had to do was take it. And what did they do? They sat there, even though they were still young and full of . . . possibilities, mourning what was lost. Reading the old books. Singing the old songs. *Kde domov můj?* — Where is my home? I'll tell you where it is — right here," he said, slapping the cracked leather seat next to him.

"In Rhinebeck," I said.

"Yes, in Rhinebeck," he said. "Or in Riverdale. Or Larchmont. But *here*. In America." He shook his head. "But your father understood all this. He had a poetic phrase for it — *sklerosa duše*. Do you know what that means? Sclerosis of the soul. We all suffer from a kind of sclerosis of the soul, Vašek, he would say to me, brought on by a steady diet of fatty songs, one too many rich regrets . . . but here, have some wine, they say it's good for these things. Laughing at it. Making a joke out of it. Nostalgia, he'd say, was the exiles' hemophilia, though contagious rather than hereditary. Oh, he could be charming, your father. And your mother, so lovely."

He'd never forget them, he said, but at some point he'd realized he could have nothing more to do with them. Why? Because they understood the trap they were in but did nothing to get themselves out of it. And not only did nothing to get out of it, but spent their days caressing it, polishing the bars, so to speak. Sad, really. A tragedy, in its way.

The train had stopped. It had been nice to see me again, he

said. And giving me his card, for some reason, he picked up his coat from the rack and hurried out into a snow flurry descending from a clear blue sky.

When I think back on that close little apartment with the Kubelius sketches in the hallway and the bust of Masaryk by the door and the plastic slipcovers on the new sofa, it seems to me that even when the living room was full of people eating *meruňkové koláče* and drinking, they were somewhere else as well. I don't know how to describe it. They seemed to be listening to something . . . that had already passed. And because I loved them, I grew to love this thing, this way of being, and listened with them.

As a child, my bed was pushed against the wall, blocking off a door to the living room. A matter of space. My father unscrewed the doorknob and covered the hole with a brass plate and then, because the frame of the door looked so ugly rising up behind my bed, my mother hung a bamboo mat over it to hide it. It was this makeshift curtain, which smelled like new-mown grass, that I would move aside so that I could spy on them as they talked: the Jakubecs and the Štěpáneks, Mr. Chalupa and Mr. Hanuš with his two canes . . . It's odd for me to think, simply by adding the years, that they must be gone. Only pieces of them remain: a genteel, tremulous voice; white fingers tightening a bow tie; a musty, reassuring smell, like cloth and wool and shoe polish, which reminded me, even then, of the thrift shops on Lexington Avenue . . . How quietly, like unassuming guests, they slipped from the world. How easily the world releases us.

Mr. Štěpánek was a small man who always sat very straight on our couch, as though hiding something behind his back; he had a lot of opinions about things and got into arguments with people because he thought a lot of things were funny. His laugh was like a little mechanism in his throat: a dry, rapid-fire cackle — ha ha ha ha ha ha ha — that always went on a second or two too long. He and my father had been childhood friends — they had grown up in adjoining buildings in the Židenice district of Brno — and perhaps for this reason he irritated my father in that close, familiar way that only old friends can irritate each other.

I loved Mr. Hanuš best, but it's Mr. Chalupa whom I remember most clearly. I'm not sure why. He never brought me things. Or talked to me much. Or came into my room and sat on the edge of my bed, as Mr. Hanuš did, and looked at the pictures on my wall. It was never "Uncle Pepa is here, look what he brought you," just "Say hello to Mr. Chalupa, where are your manners?" and I never minded much because I couldn't imagine him any other way. He wasn't interested in me. He'd show up at our door every Friday, carrying his violin case and a bottle of wine in a kind of wicker net and a white paper bag with a loaf of the Irish soda bread my father liked, and say, "Here, take them, take them," as though they were an itchy garment he couldn't wait to shed, and my parents would smile for some reason and take the things from him, and my mother would say, "Say hello to Mr. Chalupa, what's the matter with you?" and he'd say, "How are the Beatles, young man? How are the Fab Four, eh?" — in English, as though he didn't know I spoke Czech — then sink into my father's chair, which used to be by the long white bookshelf in the living room, and tell my parents about the troubles he'd had on the F train out from Manhattan. And that would be it for me.

I remember him well dressed, in a suit and tie, a slim man of average height who wore a hat and who always seemed somewhat put upon, as though the world were a vast, willfully cluttered room he had to negotiate — and quickly — because the phone was ringing on the other side. When I dreamed of him, nearly forty years later, he was sitting in my father's chair on an African beach at nightfall, still dressed in his suit and tie. A huge, still lake, backed by mountains, lay before us; behind us, white dunes of shells rose to a distant ridge on which I could see rows of fires and the silhouettes of men and monkeys. He was sitting there with that look on his face, staring irritably at the sand in front of him, ignoring me. I was about to say something to him when a tall wooden ship, far out on the water, spontaneously burst into flames. He seemed unsurprised. He looked up at the thing — the blazing masts, the spar like a burning sword, the beating wings of the sails — and, shaking his head slightly, turned his hands palms-up without raising his wrists from the armrests then let them fall as if to say, "Well, that's just fine."

I would spend hours spying on them through the blocked-off door behind my bed. I found that by turning off the light and pushing over the curtain a little, I could see nearly half the living room through the crack between the door and the frame. When Mr. Chalupa was there, my father would always sit on the sofa directly below me. Kneeling on my bed in the dark, barely breathing, I'd look over the smooth sloping shore of his balding pate to the white bookshelf on the far side of the room. Mr. Chalupa sat to the right, his violin and bow laid neatly across his lap or leaning against the bookshelf. My mother, whom I could see only half of unless she leaned forward to get something from the glass table, usually sat next to my aunt Luba (who wasn't really my aunt) on the small sofa with the hole below the left cushion in which I used to hide Sugar Daddies before I was discovered.

There was nothing much to see, really. They'd talk and laugh and drink, and eventually the guitars would come out of their cases and the violin bows would be rosined up and the men would take off their jackets and loosen their ties and Mr. Chalupa, who played the violin better than anyone else and knew every lyric to every song, would roll up his sleeves and the singing would begin: "Pri dunaji šaty prala," "Mikulecke pole," and "Polka modrých očí" — Slovak and Moravian folk songs — and when enough wine had disappeared, dance tunes like "Na prstoch si počítam" and "Keď sa do neba dívam," and on and on till two or three A.M. Sometimes I'd wake up deep in the night and hear them leaving, saying something about their coats or bumping into things by the door, shushing each other and laughing. And it seemed to me in those moments that their voices were all that was left of them, that they were good-natured spirits the hours had made insubstantial, and lying in bed I'd listen to them gathering their instruments, whispering, joking, joining in part of a refrain until, stepping through our apartment door, they disappeared as abruptly as the voices at the end of a record.

Mr. Chalupa had escaped from Czechoslovakia in 1948, like most of them, then spent some years in Salzburg, some more in Toronto, another in Chicago, before coming to a temporary rest in our apartment in Queens. The year was 1956. I was six years old. We put him up for a few weeks, during which time he slept in my room and hung his pants over the back of my chair while I slept on a mat on the floor of my parents' bedroom. When he found a place somewhere on the Upper East Side of Manhattan, I moved back to my room. For the next year and a half he continued to come by our apartment every week or two, to play his violin.

I saw him for the last time (though I didn't know then that it would be the last time) on a night in January 1958, when he broke a bottle of red wine against the corner of a shoe rack while taking off his coat in our hallway. It was one of those huge bottles, my father said later, that looked as if it had been bought from a Spanish peasant for a kilo of cheese or a length of rope, and it soaked everything. Chalupa looked at the mess he'd made — at the small red lake at his feet, at the wine spattered knee-high up the wall, at the neck of the bottle still in his hand — and shook his head. Everything breaks, he said.

No word of concern, no apology. My mother picked up the ruined rug and hung it over the outside railing where it rained

36

wine onto the leafless hedges fifteen floors below, and eventually others came by with more wine and everyone forgot about it. The group spent the evening singing as always, and late that night, when they were all leaving (Chalupa was the last to go), my father said we would see him in two weeks and Chalupa said he wasn't sure, and when my father asked why, he shook his head as though he had heard that the F train would be out of service on that day, and said, "Melanoma, old man."

"I saw him once or twice more in the hospital," my father said, "but that was that. Between the toes, Antonín," he said to me. "That's where they found it. Absurd."

I didn't hear the story for a long time, and when I did, it came as something of a shock to realize that Mr. Chalupa had been dead all those years. I had always assumed for some reason that he had simply left New York, that he had been playing in some other circle — picking at someone else's *bábovka*. I could see him there, in that other apartment, leaning back stiffly in someone else's reading chair or drumming his small white fingers on the neck of his violin while waiting for the others to return from the kitchen.

For a while, the knowledge that he had died a full ten years earlier troubled this picture I had of him, like wind on water. But then the picture re-formed itself, and though I knew it was a lie, it still felt truer than the one that had replaced it. It was as if the fact of his death had left a space — like the chalk outline of a body — in the shape of the thing that had gone. The easiest thing was to bring back the body. It fit best. There he was again, back in that other apartment, in Baltimore or Chicago, playing his violin.

It was not until many years later that I learned that Mr. Chalupa, who had once slept in my room, had also worked for the Gestapo.

I had arranged to meet an old couple I was working with at

the time in an outdoor café on Londynska Street in the Vino-hrady district of Prague. At the last moment the wife couldn't make it, and so it was just me and the old man. It was late May and the cobbles were wet from the rain and the branches dripped water on the umbrellas over the metal tables. Except for a young couple with a miserable-looking dog, we were the only ones there.

We talked for a while about the translation project we were collaborating on, and then the conversation turned to what it had been like growing up in New York in the Czech exile community, and Chalupa's name came up.

"Miloš Chalupa?" the old man asked.

"You knew him?" I said.

"Everyone knew him," he said. "Or of him. He was some kind of accountant before the war, though I'm not sure what he accounted for, or to whom. During the war he was an interpreter for the Gestapo."

At that point the waitress, who had been staying inside because of the rain, came out with a rag to wipe the tables that weren't covered with umbrellas. *"Dáte si další, pánové?"* she called to us from across the small patio. Would we like another? *"Ale dáme,"* the old man said. A low rumble sounded in the quiet street. It seemed to come from over the train yards to the south.

"You're saying Chalupa was a collaborator?" I said.

"Who knows?" the old man said. "They say he was approached by the Resistance sometime in 1941, around the time the RAF dropped those paratroopers who were to assassinate Heydrich into the Protectorate. He told them he couldn't help them."

"So he *was* a collaborator," I said.

"Listen," the old man said, "if only the heroes were left in Prague after '45 — or in Warsaw or Leningrad, for that matter — there would be fifty people left between here and Moscow."

The waitress placed two glasses of wine in front of us and went back inside the café.

"Maybe he did it to keep himself above suspicion," the old man said. "So that they would trust the picture he gave them."

"You believe that?" I said.

"I believe it's going to rain," the old man said as the first fat drops began to smack down on the cloth above our heads. He leaned over the table to light a cigarette, then dropped the match into a glass on the table next to ours. "I saw Heydrich once, you know. I was waiting for the tram in front of the National Theater. They stopped everything, cleared the street. I saw him get out of the limousine. Very tall. I remember he moved his head like this, like a bird."

"What happened?" I asked him.

"Nothing happened. He walked into the theater. I walked home."

It was raining hard now. Everything around us had turned gray. The old man was quiet for a while; I saw his head shake very slightly, as if he were disagreeing with something, though it might have been simply a tremor. He ran his fingers over the back of his hand. "You see, it wasn't always easy," he said. "To tell. To know who was who. Now take the boys who assassinated Heydrich in May of '42. A heroic act, a just act, and eight thousand died because of it. Entire towns were erased from the map." He shook his head. "Don't fool yourself; I suspect your parents knew who Chalupa was. We had all heard the stories about him. In the end we just had to choose which one to believe."

He was quiet for a moment. "Are you dry over there?" he said at last.

"I'm fine," I said.

"Here's an ugly story for you," he said.

He couldn't tell me what Chalupa thought, he said, or what he believed. He could only tell me what he had done, which was really all that anyone could say about anyone. There were some facts: After the uprising in 1945 Chalupa hadn't been shot as a collaborator. He'd been at such and such a place at such and such a time. X number of witnesses had confirmed that this or that had been said. It all amounted to little or nothing. The interrogation had focused on a single, well-known event — I could read the report if I wanted. Obviously his questioners had given him the benefit of the doubt, because he'd lived to play the violin in my parents' apartment in New York.

The basic story, the old man said, began and ended with a woman named Moravcová, who lived up in the Žižkov district with her husband and their sixteen-year-old son, Ota. "You'd have had to see her," he said. "A real *hausfrau* by the look of her — thick legs, meaty face, all bosom and bun. She was one of the most important figures in the Prague underground during the war — the anchor. No one did more, or took more chances. Nothing got past her. Nothing. When one of the paratroopers sent from London approached her for shelter in the fall of '41, she supposedly brushed him off at first, even threatened to turn him in to the authorities, and so convincingly that for a few hours he thought he had approached the wrong person, simply because there was something about him that had made her suspicious. London had to confirm, and a second code had to be arranged, before she would take him in. Couldn't risk endangering her boys, she said. And they were all her boys: the paratroopers — two of whom stayed in her apartment posing as relatives looking for work — their contacts . . .

"She washed and ironed their clothes, went shopping for them. Basically, she did everything. She'd bring parcels of blankets and clothing and cigarettes to the safe houses, traveling by tram, holding them right there on her lap, right under their Aryan noses. Not once or twice, you understand, but dozens of times, knowing all the while that if any one of them demanded that she open the package, she'd never have time to get to the strychnine ampoule she carried like a locket around her neck. On certain days she would go to the Olšany graveyard to receive and send messages, lighting a candle or pruning back the ivy on her mother's grave, maybe exchanging a few words with someone who might pause at the adjoining plot or tip his hat to her on the path. She was rational, smart, tough as an anvil. What made her special, though, was that she was apparently terrified the entire time. Rumor had it that she took to wearing a diaper, as if she were incontinent, for the inevitable accidents. That after Heydrich was assassinated, when everything was going to hell, she'd pretend to be nursing a toothache and travel with the ampoule already in her mouth — which, if true, was simply madness. The point is that she knew what she was risking, and she risked it anyway."

The rain had begun dribbling between the two umbrellas I had crossed over our heads, and the old man moved his wine out of the way.

"In any case, after Heydrich was hit — it happened right up here in Líbeň, though it looks quite different now — things happened very quickly. They carried him out across Charles Bridge at night, torches and dogs everywhere, and before they got him to the other side, SS and NSKK units were sweeping through the city, searching neighborhood by neighborhood, block by block. Combing for lice, they called it. They were very good at it, very thorough. Wehrmacht battalions would seal off an area, five or six city blocks, and then they'd go apartment to apartment. It's all television now, really. I barely believe it myself. I'll give you an example. Right after Heydrich died, Wenceslas Square was filled with half a million Czechs swearing their loyalty to the Reich. People were hysterical; they knew what was coming. I saw this with my own eyes, and I still don't believe it.

"Anyway, after Heydrich's death, the underground freezes. Moravcová somehow manages to get her family out of Prague. The boy goes to the country, the husband to stay with an army friend in Královo Pole. Moravcová herself hides in Brno, which is hardly better. After a few weeks, when nothing happens, all three return one by one to their apartment in Žižkov, who knows why. Maybe they're worried that their absence will be noticed. Maybe they just want to come home.

"Which is where Chalupa, the translator, comes into it. He gets a telephone call at four-thirty in the morning, is told to be ready in five minutes. He doesn't know that the paratroopers hiding in the crypt of the church on Řesslova have been betrayed, that they will die in that crypt early the next morning, June 18 — that the whole thing in fact has begun to crumble. He only knows that something is wrong.

"You have to picture it. Three cars are waiting in the dark. A door opens, he climbs inside. He has no idea where they're going until he hears the name. Some woman named Moravcová. An apartment in Žižkov. He just sits there on the leather seat, holding his hat on his lap like a truant. What else can he do? No one speaks to him — they don't trust him, naturally, and his ability to speak German only makes things worse because it means he's neither one thing nor the other, hammer or nail.

"It's a quick trip. The city is almost deserted at that hour, and the limousine races through the intersections, crosses Bulhar Circle, then turns left up that long hill there. He knows they'll be there in three minutes, then two, and then they're there and Fleischer, the commanding bastard that morning, is already pounding on the door, swearing, when it opens and a bent, tiny woman appears, like a hedgehog in a fairy tale. '*Schnell, wo wohnen die Moraveks?*' Fleischer yells as they shove past her, and Chalupa begins translating when the hedgehog calls out at the top of her lungs, as though she's suddenly been struck deaf, 'Would you like to take the stairs or the elevator, *mein Herr?*' but they don't notice because they're already rushing up the stairs and it's too late for anything at all.

"By the time Chalupa gets there, they're all three standing with their faces against the wall, the father and the boy still in their pajamas, Madame Moravcová in a housedress, as though she's been awake all night. '*Wo sind sie, wo sind sie?*' — Where are they? — Fleischer is roaring as the rest of them pour into the other rooms, as the sofa and chairs are tipped on their faces and pulled from the walls, and Chalupa begins to translate *Kdo, já nevím . . .* — '*Wer? Ich weiss nicht . . .*' and then stops because Fleischer has her by the throat and is striking her face, hard and fast, back and forth: '*Wo — sind — sie, Wo — sind — sie, Wo — sind — sie.*' She sinks to the floor. '*Steh auf!*' She stands. 'Please,' she says, 'I have to go to the bathroom, please.'

"Chalupa looks at her husband and son. They are both barefoot. There is the smell of shit in the room. The husband's hair is standing up; his right leg is trembling as if he were listening to a very fast song. The boy is looking into the wallpaper. In the transcripts Chalupa claimed he never saw such terror in a face in his life. 'Please, I have to go,' Moravcová says again. She doesn't look at her husband or her son. Chalupa translates: '*Sie sagt, dass sie aufs Klo muss*' — She says she must go to the bathroom . . . and now he understands. Fleischer is striding into the other room, still looking for the paratroopers. '*Nein.*'

"So there you have the basic situation. A wrecked room. Three people lined up against a wall. A single guard. 'Please, I have to go,' Madame Moravcová is pleading, over and over again, 'please.' Perhaps she realizes that their lives are over, that life is simply done. Perhaps not. Suddenly someone is yelling from the hallway outside: '*Zastavte! Zastavte!*' — Stop! Stop! Though maybe it's just '*Václave! Václave!*' — The name. Who can tell? They sound alike; anyone could confuse them. And Chalupa — here's the thing — supposedly translates the first and the bastards run out, thinking the paratroopers have been flushed into the open, and in the five or six seconds before the guard remembers himself and rushes back in, Moravcová sees her chance and takes it, and by the time they push past her fallen body blocking the bathroom door from inside it's too late for the water they pour down her throat to do them any good. So, *zastavte* or *Václave*, take your pick."

"She left her family?" I said.

"Indeed."

"She must have known what she was leaving them to."

"I doubt she imagined the particulars. Supposedly they broke the boy the next day when they showed him his mother's head in a fish tank."

"Good God."

"Doubtful," the old man said. "But we should get to work."

I remembered Mr. Chalupa. He'd slept in my room. I could see that irritated look, the way he would lift his violin out of its case with three fingers, the way he would sink into my father's chair. "How are the Beatles, young man?" I could hear him say. "How are the Fab Four, eh?"

7

THIS IS HOW THINGS WERE IN MY HOUSE.

One afternoon when I was perhaps seven years old, no more, I asked my mother whether she had ever had a dog. I wanted one myself. She told me she had, in fact, had a dog once, but that it had been very long ago. He'd gotten lost, she said. She would tell me about it sometime.

So I asked my father. I found him in his office, which looked down into the canyons between the apartment buildings to the little playground where I played. He first asked me what my mother had said, then sighed and capped his pen. "Move those papers over," he said. And then he told me about my mother's dog.

As a young girl, my father said, my mother had spent her summers with relatives in the Valašsko region of Moravia. In those days, he said, the *cigáni*, the Gypsies, could still be found camped along a river or on some empty ground. One minute there would be just a field, a dirt road, a stand of birches; the next they would be there: the men unhitching the horses, the women beating down the weeds for fire rings or yelling at the dogs, dirty-faced children with hair as black as ravens staring as though they'd never seen a person in a wagon. There were poplar trees along the fields, and their small leaves would twirl like decorations in the wind. And if you happened to be the person in the wagon, you'd look up and see them — the old ones — already half a kilometer down the road to town, their huge black skirts with the loops and the hooks sewn into them dragging in the dirt.

In any case, my father told me, my mother spent a lot of time in the company of an old man named Mr. Koblížek who lived two houses down and who was something of a storyteller. He had a square block of a head silvered by stubble and ears like miniature lettuces, and he'd sit on a bench on the south side of his house in his tattered slippers smoking a short black pipe.

No one had quicker hands than a *cigánka*, Mr. Koblížek told my mother. No one. You could watch her all you wanted, but it wouldn't matter. "The *cigáni* were not like other people," he said. They knew things. Oh, they could mumble and scrape humbly enough, but if you threw stones at them, they would turn in the middle of the street and curse you so vilely even the dogs would turn away. He himself, Mr. Koblížek said, had once seen a *cigánka* put a spell on a dog who had bitten her, so that the poor animal couldn't open its mouth to eat or drink, but went about slobbering and rubbing its head in the dirt, trying to push its tongue through its clenched teeth, until its owner finally realized what was happening and killed it.

No, the *cigáni* were not to be trifled with, Mr. Koblížek said, waggling a great square finger at my mother. The suffering of our Lord Jesus meant nothing to them. They never went to church or prayed for their souls. He'd heard it said that the old ones could see the dead walking down the road or resting in the shade of the trees at noon. That they could catch the reflection of the moon in a pot and carry it under the trees, where it would glow all night like a white lantern.

Anyway, my father said, it was during one of those summers along the Bečva that my mother got a dog. She found it in a corner of a neighbor's stable — a squirmy brown pup, fat with worms, struggling to reach a teat — and somehow convinced her uncle to let her keep it in the barn. It could not have been easy, my father said. You have to remember, he said, these were country folk — practical, unsentimental people; that same afternoon the rest of the litter was probably put in a sack with a stone and tossed in the river.

My mother, my father said, had never had a pet before, and she loved the thing dearly. Soon it grew into a small, brown, wormy dog who followed her about everywhere and who would sit waiting for her on the bank of the Bečva, looking worried, whenever she went swimming in the afternoons. She made the dog a bed of rags in the hay. Sometimes she would lie down next to it and pet it on its brown nose while it slept, my father said, which was probably how she came to have worms.

That August, when the Gypsies were encamped a kilometer down the road in a fallow field by the river, the dog disappeared. He'd probably been eaten, her uncle told her — the Gypsies ate dogs sometimes. He was very sorry. He had been growing attached to the little mongrel himself. My mother just stood there, runny-nosed and barefoot, ugly with grief, sucking her upper lip to keep from crying. Pulling her closer, her uncle wiped under her nose with the edge of his thumb and then, with the other edge, made a wide, flat smear across her cheek. They would try to get her another dog, he told her.

But that was not the end of the story, my father said.

"Another child would probably have cried in her bed that night," he said, "or lay awake listening to the wind, looking for things in the garden, or dreaming of what she would do to those who could do such a thing. Your mother got up to get her dog."

She went barefoot. In the house, everything was still, as if under a spell. As she closed the heavy wooden door behind her, she could hear the clock start to whir and then chime, twice. To avoid waking the village dogs she cut back through the garden, then up through the fields to the road. Everything was moving as though under water, the clouds rushing over the fields and the road and the white trunks of the birches. The moon flew across the sky, its reflection leaping among the trees.

She knew where she was going. She had passed the field where they were camped at least a dozen times before with her uncle. When she came to the crossroads, she turned right toward the river, walking on the soft dirt along the side, stepping over the briars and their shadows because it's impossible to tell one from the other in the moonlight. Even before she saw the wagons lined along the road by the side of the field, she could see the firelight on the trunks of the trees and hear the yelling of the men.

"Now you have to understand," my father said, looking at me. "This was a very foolish thing to do." The *cigáni* were not like the people my mother knew in the village, he said. He himself had once seen a group of *cigáni* in the Tatra Mountains dig half a horse out of the earth and eat it. They had a game they played. Four or five men, sitting around a wooden board, would wrap rags around their hands. These would be tied off at the wrist, leaving their fingers just enough flexibility to grasp the handle of a knife. Everyone would be very drunk. Bets would be made, drinks taken from jugs standing in the dirt, another log or board tossed on the flames for light. Then, when all were ready, my father said, their elbows on the board and their bandaged arms raised and the crowd yelling and shoving for a better view, the ear of a hare would be thrown into the center of the board.

"An unpleasant business," my father said. By the time someone emerged from the fray with the ear pinned on the tip of his blade like a slice of sausage, the rags would be stained black as if splashed with paint. And sometimes things went wrong. A friend of his had seen a *cigán*, furious over some real or imagined slight, slowly force another's arm to the wood and then, with a tremendous blow, as though killing a wolf, drive his knife through the bones of the other's hand, pinning him palm-down to the board.

"Anyway, it probably took them a few moments to notice the little girl on the other side of the fire," my father said. "It probably took them a few more to realize she was real."

Co tady chceš? — What do you want here? — said a voice like a crow. *Běž domů.* Go home.

I want my dog, said my mother.

A man snorted like a boar; a few people laughed. Let's get on with it, someone said.

Ztrať se, a number of voices yelled. Get lost. Go back where you belong. From somewhere under the trees a pig was grunting quickly. A huge gust of sparks rose into the branches.

What makes you think we have your dog? said the voice like a crow.

Horses neighed from the dark. An old woman in a wide, colored skirt was coming toward my mother, making sweeping motions with her hands as though pushing away an unpleasant smell. *Maž, maž. Tady tě nikdo nechce.* Go. Nobody wants you here.

The men were getting on with their business, wrapping their hands in rags, tearing at the cloth with their teeth. When the *ciganka* got to the edge of the fire, my father said, my mother stooped and picked up a branch that was sticking out of the flames.

The crowd burst out laughing. Why would we take your dog? they yelled. Go home, you little fool. Someone said something she didn't understand and the crowd howled with laughter.

Give her the dog, called the crow, and a tall, powerful-looking man in loose cloth pants stepped out of the smoke. The crowd quieted. He had long black hair and a thick black mustache and his skin was as brown as the bark of a tree. He looked at her for a few moments, then began slowly unwrapping the rags from around his hands.

Get the dog, he said, and instantly the dog was there, led by a boy about my age. The dog seemed well fed, my father said, and he had a short length of woven horsetail leash around his neck.

49

He seemed glad to see her. The *cigán* nodded. And without another word my mother took her dog and walked home to her uncle's house and led him to his rag bed in the barn. Finally she returned to the house, and lifting the heavy wooden door so it wouldn't creak, crept past the ticking clock up the stairs to her room. As she lay in bed she could see the dark frame of her window against the lightening sky. It was almost morning.

He had to work now, my father said. He had only told me this story about my mother and her dog because, he said, he wanted me to know something about my mother.

I nodded. But Mommy said her dog ran away, I said.

And so he did, said my father. Later. Personally, he'd always thought he'd returned to the Gypsies, where life was good for a dog.

And that was the end of the story.

A year or two later my parents bought me a dog. And one day that dog disappeared. We had moved to the suburbs by then, to a small house in Ardsley with a cracked driveway and a mimosa tree that dropped pink blossoms all over the yard. Perhaps he'd been stolen, my father said. Or run over by a car. We hunted around in the thin woods at the end of the road, calling his name, and hung up signs on the telephone poles asking whoever had found him to give him back to us, but no one ever called. In all honesty, I'd never really cared for the dog — a purebred boxer with a streak on his nose — but I'd gotten used to him, and when he disappeared, I missed him for a while. And then one day when my mother was driving me somewhere, we saw him in the back of someone else's car.

It was a rainy day in late fall; gusts of wind shook the car and smeared the water across the windows. My mother tried to get the attention of the people in the other car, waving and tapping on the glass with her wedding ring, then followed them off the highway and through the tolls, mile after mile, down roads we had never been on before, to some part of Queens I didn't know. After a long time we crossed a bridge over a big river to a world of factories where tall chimneys poured smoke into the rain while others burned like giant candles.

When it was almost dark the car stopped in front of a smudged little house and a family with two small children got out. It had stopped raining. They were frightened at first, and the man kept waving his hands and saying What do you want? What do you want? but when my mother explained, he apologized and said that he was very sorry but that the dog was theirs and that he and his family had come from Pakistan a year ago, and then he went into the house and brought out some papers. I talked to our dog, meanwhile, but he didn't recognize me. Eventually we got back in our car and went home without him. I remember looking out the window as we drove back over the bridge. One black cloud was lit up from behind, and I could see the water and the factories.

It'll be all right, said my mother. It doesn't matter. And she laughed to herself and shook her head.

Later I remembered the flames and turned around quickly in my seat, but the road had taken a turn, and they were gone. And so the story stopped again, balanced on one foot, so to speak.

Twenty-five years later, on an October afternoon in 1985, I was working at my desk at a cabin I'd once lived in with my parents when I heard someone calling a hello and found an old couple I vaguely remembered from my childhood standing by the stone wall. They had been driving in the area, they said, and had suddenly remembered visiting my parents years ago at a cabin on a lake, and had decided on a whim to see if they could find it. They were very proud of themselves, and though I didn't particularly want to, I invited them in for a glass of wine and we talked of this and that and they asked me if any of the other Czech families they had met in that earlier time still lived at the lake.

They remembered Reinhold Černý very well, they said, and the Kesslers, whom they had met once or twice in the city. Černý had passed on years ago, I told them, as had Kessler. Kessler's wife, Marie, I had heard, was living somewhere in North Carolina. And the Mostovskýs? Their children were two cabins down, I said.

At which point my dog, waking from where he'd fallen asleep in the shade of the small wrought-iron table around which we were sitting, knocked against one of the legs and spilled some wine. They begged me not to scold him — it hadn't been his fault, after all — and explained that they had three dogs at home who were just like children to them, and how they had both felt sick, absolutely sick, to read in the paper, what with all the news about China and everything, that the Chinese still ate dogs. It was barbaric, absolutely barbaric, they said, and to think we could do business with these people. The whole thing had reminded them of my poor mother.

How so? I asked.

But surely I knew the story, they said — both my parents had spoken of it. A terrible thing for a child to go through. How my mother's dog had been stolen by Gypsies one summer and how my mother, who could have been no more than seven or eight years old at the time, had crept out of her grandparents' house in the middle of the night and walked miles and miles to a Gypsy camp and demanded her dog, only to be given a flour sack that might have held a rabbit, or a small carp, and how she had walked all the way home, the small dear, and buried the remains in the garden before returning to bed. Surely I remembered it now.

I told them I did.

This was a nice place, they said, looking around. It was odd, really. They hadn't thought about my parents for years before they'd read that report about dogs in the paper, and yet, hardly two weeks later, here they were. Of course, it was probably be-

cause the article had started them thinking about my mother —
though they hadn't realized they were thinking of her at all at the
time — that they had remembered our cabin and decided on a
whim to try and find it.

They wouldn't have been surprised, now that they thought of
it, if my parents hadn't told me the story of my mother and her
dog. A terrible thing to tell a child. How she must have suffered,
the poor dear, walking all those miles with that sack at her side.
Still, they agreed, the story said something about her character.
How strong she was. They nodded, agreeing with each other.
The Lord only visited those who could bear it, they said.

8

SHE HAD BEEN BEAUTIFUL. I HAVE A FEW PHOTOGRAPHS, favorites I salvaged after my father died from the shoeboxes I found piled in the basement by the folded ping-pong table: one of a black-haired tomboy standing by her bicycle in the Vysočina forests, looking at the photographer as if wondering whether he's going to try to take it away from her; another of a young woman on a windy corner in Brno, too impatient to be fashionable, pinning her hat to her hair as the statue of a dead saint, behind her, points to an escaping trolley; a third — overexposed — of my mother against a white sea of cloud in the Tatras, the hand of a companion — not my father — visible at her waist.

And then there's the one of him, or so I have to assume. I've looked at it closely. At the overlong sleeves of the sweater — the left pushed partway to the elbow, the other almost covering his hand. I've studied the cigarette, like a tiny stub of light clamped between the tips of his fingers, protruding from inside the wool. There's nothing to see. A man standing in the snow, squinting into the glare. Not particularly handsome. The snow on the hill behind him has partly melted.

I don't know what he meant to her exactly. Or how he died. I only know that his face, the sound of his voice, never really diminished for her. That she simply refused to give him up.

There are people like that, after all — individuals who resist the current, who hold out against that betrayal. Who refuse to take their small bouquet of misremembered moments and leave. You'll run into them at the deli counter, or while waiting in line at the theater, and they'll say, "I had an acquaintance many years ago" or "I once knew someone who I cared for very much who also hated sauerkraut," and suddenly, standing there waiting to give the butcher your order, or clutching your paper ticket, you can see them leaning into the current's pull, hear the rocks of the riverbed clattering like bones.

It wasn't a matter of jealousy or fear. My parents never slept in separate beds or took vacations with "old friends" or hurt each other more than husbands and wives generally hurt each other. It was subtler than that. My mother respected my father's strength, his endurance, was grateful to him for taking on the role he had for her with such tact, but hated him for it too. And because she recognized the injustice in this, she loved him — or tried. And because she knew he recognized it too, she failed.

And my father? My father saw it for the perfect thing it was, appreciated it the way a master carpenter will appreciate a perfectly constructed joint, the tongue mated to the groove like an act of God. Kafka would have understood: he would do the right thing — the only thing — and be hated for it. Inevitably. Even justly.

9

ONE DAY WHEN I WAS SEVEN AND HAD BEEN GOING TO
school for a year or so, my father asked me what I was learning
(he was sitting in his favorite chair by the long white bookshelf
in the living room; my mother had gone out, to do some shopping, she said), and I told him about reading and spelling and
math. I'd written a report on volcanoes, I said.

My father nodded. "The Greek philosopher Empedocles dove
into a volcano to prove he was a god and burned to a crisp," he
said. "What do you think of that?"

I said I thought it was silly.

"Smart boy," my father said.

He looked at me for a moment, sitting on the sofa, skinny legs
dangling like a ventriloquist's puppet, then took a small sip from
the glass on the shelf next to him. "We need to supplement," he
said.

For years afterward the Greeks tasted like Ovaltine, because
every time my father decided to supplement, he would let me
make a cup and sip it while he talked. And for years that taste
was all I retained from our sessions in the living room — that
and the memory of him sitting in his chair, talking to me as if
I were older than I was, as if I knew why he was smiling or

why he had run his hand over his head that way or why he'd looked out the window over Queens Boulevard as if suddenly remembering something, some appointment he'd missed.

He told me many things; I don't remember them all. He told me about Empedocles and Parmenides and Anaximander, Heraclitus and Thales. He liked their names, and he would make me repeat them and seem pleased when I got them right. "Say Empedocles," he'd say, "say Anaximander," and I'd say Empedocles or Anaximander and he'd chuckle as if there were someone else in the room with us and say, "That's good. That's very nice."

Parmenides, he said, had worried a lot about reality because he'd noticed that what his senses told him didn't make sense. "Which didn't really make sense," my father said, "but never mind." Parmenides, he said, went on to claim that reality could be understood only by thought, which was a disastrous thing to say if one thought about it — a bit like saying that a nail could only be hammered with a tomato — even if it *was* true.

The rational mind was a terrible tool for the job, my father said. It thought logically, or tried to. It sniffed after justice where there was none. It insisted on looking at *everything,* even when that was clearly a bad idea. It had this notion, which it clung to, that the truth would save us, though it was quite obvious that precisely the opposite was often true. "The fact is that many things are true," my father said, "but we have to pretend they aren't."

"Why?" I said.

"Because the truth would confuse us and make us sad," my father said. "Take Empedocles — can you say Empedocles?" "Empedocles," I said. "Good boy," said my father. Empedocles, he said, believed that there were only two basic forces in the world — love and strife. Love brought things together and strife

57

pulled them apart. All very logical. Empedocles claimed that this explained how things could change and yet the world could stay the same. My father looked at me. "Now let me ask you. Which do you think is easier, to keep things together or to pull them apart?"

"Pull them apart," I said.

"Exactly," said my father. He smiled. "Maybe that's why Empedocles dove into the volcano," he said.

In any case, he'd never liked Empedocles much, my father said. Thales, who lived on the coast of Asia Minor and who could navigate ships and reroute rivers, was much more interesting. Thales, a bald-headed old man with hairy ears, said the world floated like a log on endless water — which it very well might, said my father — and that all things were full of gods — which they were. Of course, the problem with the second part, my father said, was that when people thought of the things that were full of gods, they always thought of death and sunsets and Niagara Falls, never doorknobs.

The Greeks were full of wisdom, my father said.

But I wanted to know when Mommy was coming home — it may have been the first time my father called me in to ask me about my schooling; it may have been some time after that. I don't remember.

"Heraclitus was fun," he said, not hearing me. "Heraclitus, you see, was bothered by the fact that nothing in the world stayed the same, that everything changed. That the world was always rushing on, whether we noticed it or not. And he tried to explain this constant changing and decided that since fire changed everything it touched, fire was to blame." My father looked out the window. "According to Heraclitus, everywhere we look, the world is on fire, burning invisibly, changing before our very eyes." My father paused. "Of course, some things never change, never mind how long they burn. So, so much for Heraclitus."

But I wanted to know when Mommy was coming home. I was getting hungry and my Ovaltine was gone.

My father was looking out the window over Queens Boulevard. In the far distance, a small brown plane was turning toward La Guardia Airport. "Soon," he said. "Very soon, I'm sure."

10

BY THE TIME I WAS NINE WE HAD LEFT THE CITY, THE asphalt playgrounds, those inland seas, I'd played on, the loaf-shaped hedges and shadowed continents of lawn, and moved to a small, flat house in the suburbs. The house had a fireplace that didn't work and a basement and a sliding glass door which let out onto a porch that overlooked a scrubby patch of woods. In the spring, when the mud had finally thawed and the huge, ridged leaves of the skunk cabbage had sprung out of it, hiding the trash, I would catch red-backed salamanders there.

That summer, at the Memorial Day picnic, my father broke his glasses trying to catch a football which slipped through his hands. My mother hadn't wanted to go. Mr. Kelly, who was from South Dakota, and who pitched to the kids on the block every Saturday from the foot of his driveway, aiming at a square he had drawn on the garage door with a piece of chalk, had thrown it to him from across the street. He felt bad afterward, and helped my father look for the pieces, and my father, who as a schoolboy in the summer of 1937 had run eight hundred meters around a cinder track in two minutes and one second, setting a national junior record that lasted for nine years, smiled and said that from now on he believed he'd stick to balls that didn't have points.

It was not long afterward that we got into the DeSoto and drove north to visit the Jakubecs at a cabin they rented on a lake.

The cabin stood on the top of a grassy meadow under some big trees and smelled wonderfully of Mr. Jakubec's pipe. All the familiar people were there — Mr. Štěpánek with that laugh of his, and Mr. Chalupa and Mr. Hanuš, as well as some people I didn't know — and Mrs. Jakubcová served coffee and strawberry *táč*, and later we all went swimming, everyone carrying towels and mats and drinks out into the hot sun, and my father and a man who lived on the lake named Mostovský made their arms into a kind of chair and carried Mr. Hanuš down through the grass to the water because the meadow was tilted and his canes stuck in the soft ground. As they carried him down through the long grass in their bathing suits Mr. Hanuš yelled to me to get him a rose from the hedge, and when I handed it to him he put the stem between his teeth and looked at my father and said, Kiss me, Sedlák, I feel just like a girl again, and my father laughed and told him to kiss Mostovský instead, that he deferred to the better man, and the two of them staggered on, sweating, to the water's edge, where they set him gently down on the boards of the dock so that his feet, which looked like closed fists, could dangle in the water.

We stayed for five seasons, renting a cabin just down the shore. Years later, remembering our summers there, I returned alone.

There was a sort of softening that occurred to people there, an involuntary easing of something very much like pain. I don't know what it was about the place exactly. Perhaps it was the sun, or the water, always busy with some kind of invisible midges, or the strange pleasure of seeing the dark prints of their bodies evaporating off the wooden dock. More likely, for people who measured everything by its similarity to the world they'd known before, it was that it was so close to the original they'd lost — a reasonable facsimile.

And yet it was this very closeness, which invited the heart to play, and which would find them staring at a line of light slanting through the leaves, or watching their own white feet sweep back and forth through the water . . . it was this very familiarity that brought out every difference like a thorn, that made the place more excruciating than New York City could ever be. It was so close, this small pond with its screen-door *chatas* smelling of cedar and smoke, and yet . . . the birds sounded different here, and the water was warmer than it should have been, and the air did not smell of chamomile and pine and moldering loam and *hříbky* with caps of dirt on their velvety heads, but of other things.

Of course, even if everything had been precisely the same, it wouldn't have helped. Nothing could match what they'd had, for the simple reason that they couldn't have it again. It was not that what they'd lost had been better or more beautiful than what they'd found here, just that it had been theirs, and it had been lost. Not even the war had done that. They could no more substitute for it than a mother or father could substitute for a lost child by adopting another who shared the same features or spoke in the same voice. And yet, though they knew this, they couldn't help being drawn to that other, newer child, listening to it, running a hand over its hair.

Even my father, who at best tolerated this kind of sentimentality, was not immune. In the mornings I would find him sitting on a chair he'd carried out to the shore, tracing the corners of his mouth with his fingers like a man smoothing a mustache, the slow waves of light from the water moving up his shirt.

"It's not that I don't understand," he said to me once.

I'd sat down in the grass next to him. My parents had had an argument the night before over some movie I didn't know, and my mother had gone into the little wooden bedroom next to mine and slammed the door.

He waved his hand to indicate the black water, the trees, the last slips of mist being dragged up into the bluing sky. "I do," he said. "It's just that it does no good."

I didn't miss the city, particularly. I missed driving in on summer mornings, when a kind of bruise-colored fog obscured the buildings and only the tallest skyscrapers rose above it, flashing their sides one after the other like great, silver-scaled fish, and I missed the coconut custard pie and milk my mother would buy for me at the Chock Full o' Nuts with its clean, curving counters, and the *obst-torte* with the glazed strawberries we would share at the German pastry shop on Second Avenue. But that was all, really. Our friends still visited us at the lake in the summers, and my father still brought home Irish soda bread in white paper bags as he always had, and though I missed my room in the apartment on 63rd Road, what I really missed, I see now, was not the room itself but the feeling of being a child there. For a while after we moved I would wake up in the dark and think I was still there, and that the door to the hall was behind me rather than to the left, and it would take me a few moments to move things around, so to speak, to reconcile where I was with where I'd been.

A year after we moved to our house in the suburbs I dreamed that I was walking through our old apartment. It was dark and yet I could see all of our old things: the low white bookshelf in the living room and my child's desk and my bed with the pirate lamp and the chair my father sat in whenever we had guests, all of which we had left behind. And though I could see all these things, I knew, as you can sometimes know things in dreams, that I no longer lived in this place, that I was only visiting, and I wandered about from room to room, looking at these things which were still so familiar to me, wondering what had become of them, and it seemed to me that they must miss us.

I didn't remember that dream for a long time. Many years later I found myself on a train traveling south from Prague to visit friends near Jindřichův Hradec. Wet snow had been falling all morning, but now a dull winter sun had broken through. Coal smoke hung like a mist over the towns with their smudged little houses. The train ran beside the river that curved against the hills and spread in great gravelly shoals between the fields, and everywhere I could see the remnants of a flood which only that past October had submerged all the things I was now looking at. I saw a sofa lying upside down on a sandbar and a white refrigerator like a boulder in the current. On the television antenna of a low abandoned building I glimpsed what looked like a pair of blue pants, stiff as a weathervane. And at that moment for some reason I remembered my dream — the dream I had had a year after we had moved out of our apartment on 63rd Road. I didn't think much of it at the time. I watched the country scrolling by. All along the way, beards of trash hung in the bushes and the trees like Spanish moss, except that here everything was at the same height — the high-water mark — everything below having been swept away by the current.

Strangely enough, just as dreams will sometimes color our memories, the view of the river that day and the dream it recalled together forced themselves on the past, so that afterward, whenever I thought of our old apartment, my recollections would always carry a residue of future times, and remembering our apartment I would immediately be forced, like a man stumbling down a series of steps, to recall wandering those same rooms in my dream, and from there to remember the winter morning I'd spent, years later, looking out the dirty windows of the train to Jindřichův Hradec at all the things, once caught in the current, the flood had left behind.

II

WHEN I THINK BACK ON OUR FIVE SEASONS AT THE LAKE,
I see my father reading in the big wicker chair that usually stood
in the corner under the lamp with the green shade but which he
would drag in front of the fire on chilly days. He was a great
reader, my father: at ease, engaged, capable of sitting for three
hours at a stretch without feeling the need to get up or move
about, indeed, almost immobile except for now and again a small
inward smile or a slight tilt of the head in anticipation of the
page's turning. Sometimes I'd see his arm swing like a crane to
the little table at his side. He'd pick up the glass with three
fingers, begin to bring it to his lips — all this without once looking up from the page — and stop. And the glass would just hang
there, sometimes for a minute or more, and I'd make bets with
myself about whether it would complete its journey by the time
he got to the bottom of the page, or be returned, untouched, to
the table.

My mother read too, though differently. For days or weeks
she would read nothing at all, or nothing but the newspaper,
then suddenly take a book off the shelf, pull a chair next to my
father's, and disappear. She read with an all-absorbing intensity,
her stockinged feet drawn up underneath her, that I understood
completely and yet still found slightly unnerving. Hunched over

the book — which she would hold at her stomach, forcing her to look straight down — she looked as though she were protecting the thing, or in pain. No smile, no cup of tea, no leg thrown easily over the other, this was less a dance than a battle of some kind, though what was being fought for, and by whom, I could hardly guess. Two days after it had begun — during which time my mother would often drag a chair out to the shore after breakfast, or retire to one of the hammocks my father had strung about the place, in which she would lie, straight-legged, smoking cigarette after cigarette, holding the book above her head — it would be over. I would find her lying in the hammock, staring up into the trees, the book tossed on the grass beside her.

I liked it there. I liked the rainy days when the three of us sat around the card table and played board games for hours on end, raising our voices over the dulling sound on the roof, and I liked finding things like the pencil-thin milk snake that crawled out of a crack in the foundation stone of the communal barn one day, but most of all, I think, I liked sitting on the dock with my mother on hot summer afternoons in July or August when a storm was rising out of the west and we knew it wouldn't miss us.

Such stillness. The sky above our heads remained perfectly clear, a deep, serene blue, but already the light would be changed, troubled, and with every deep rumble that seemed to move the wood beneath our chairs, I'd feel a thrill of anticipation, and sometimes my mother, who liked these storms as much as I did, would reach out her hand and squeeze my shoulder as if to say, "That was a good one — here we go."

It was the inevitability of the thing that we liked, I realize now: the hundred swallows flicking down to their reflections in the water; the mountain growing over us toward the sun, then swallowing it in a slow gulp, which always brought on a small, sad wind that felt good in my hair; and then the crash and rumble, extending, extending, longer than one would have thought possible, then subsiding into poised quiet. There was nothing to be done, nothing we could change, and there was a quiet joy in this.

Sometimes my father would come out on the sagging porch and tell us to come in, and we'd call back that we'd be right there and stay right where we were, transfixed, as the curtain rose higher and higher, and then what always looked and sounded like wind would turn the water on the other side of the lake mirror-green to pewter-gray, and in the next breath the squall line would be halfway across the water and my mother and I would be running for the cabin.

It was in our second season on the lake that my father shot the dog with Mr. Colby's gun and Mrs. Kessler fell in love with the man who lived in the cabin on the other side of the lake. He was much younger than she was, which was very important, and everyone talked about it those two weeks whenever they thought I couldn't hear, changing the subject to food or interrupting themselves to ask me whether I had seen the heron by the dam as soon as I came closer. She had made a spectacle of herself, which made me think of glasses even though I knew what it meant, and really it was a bit much, this carrying on in plain view. Everyone seemed angry about it, and though my parents and the Mostovskýs and some of the others didn't have much to say, I could always tell when people were talking about it by the way they would look slightly off to the side, shaking their heads, or the way their shoulders shrugged, as if they didn't care, or the way some would lean forward while others, giving their opinion, would lean back luxuriously in their Adirondack chairs.

I knew it was probably wrong and shameful for a married lady to fall in love with someone, and particularly someone younger, but the truth was that I liked Mrs. Kessler. She had come across me once while I was working on one of my many forts in the woods and kept my secret, and sometimes when Harold Mostovský and I spent the long, hot afternoons feeling around in the water with our toes, trying to walk the pasture walls that had disappeared when the lake was made, we would look up and see her sitting on the shore watching us, her arms around her legs, and when she saw we had seen her, she would give a hesitant little wave, raising her hand a bit, then a bit more, as though unsure of how high she should bring it, and we would go back to what we were doing. It never bothered us having her there, and then at some point we'd look up and she'd be gone.

Though I never saw it myself, I was told Mrs. Kessler lost her head so completely that at night she would walk down to the lake right after it got dark and get into the rowboat and row across to the other man's cabin while Mr. Kessler sat reading by the green lamp in their cabin. (I wonder what Kessler's reading, I heard Mr. Černý say. Must be good.) That she would sometimes stay for hours and hours, not caring what anyone thought, and that Mrs. Eugenia Bartlett had sworn she'd heard the creak of her oarlocks as she rowed back through the mist one morning just before dawn.

My mother, I remember, seemed almost lighthearted that second week in June, waking early, surprising me with special meals like apricot dumplings and *kašička* with drops of jam, asking my father about things in the newspaper. She threw out the stacks of magazines and junk that had collected under the sink and swept out the cobwebs and the bottle caps and the mouse droppings that looked like fat caraway seeds and the bits of mattress stuffing and lint from the previous winter's nests. One fresh morning after a night of rain she came home with the trunk of the DeSoto crammed with planting trays and seeds and bags of soil and fertilizer and sixteen hanging flowerpots and a paper bag with sixteen hooks to hang them on. In the back seat of the car were four carton bottoms filled with flowers. Except for the marigolds, I didn't know their names. Some were purple and white, like pinwheels, others a dark velvety red, still others the color of the sky just before it gets dark. They seemed to soak in the spotted light that came through the windows, trembling with life. She was going to garden, my mother said.

I saw my father looking at my mother as she first pointed out to us all the things she had bought, then started to drag one of the cartons out of the car. Here, let me get that, he said.

We carried the cartons down to the bit of shady, tangled grass by the water that served as our yard, placing them side by side so they made a long, lovely rectangle, then returned for the bags of soil and the tools. It was mid-morning. The air was warming quickly. A number of people had gathered out on the float in the middle of the lake, and we could hear them laughing. My father carried out the card table my mother said she wanted to work on, and for the next few hours, while my father drilled holes into the south wall of the cabin and screwed the hooks into them, my mother and I transplanted the flowers into the hanging pots, filled the seedflats with soil, and sprinkled the tiny seeds from the packets into furrows we made in the dirt with the eraser end of a pencil. When my father was finished he asked if there was anything else my mother wanted him to do, but she said no, that he had done a wonderful job with the hooks and that we could do the rest on our own, couldn't we, and I agreed.

My mother talked more that morning than I could remember her talking in a long time. She asked me about school and told me how happy she was that we had a cabin on a lake and how she hadn't liked it at first because it reminded her too much of home but that she had come to see things differently and now loved it as much, no, in some ways even more than the country-side she had known as a little girl. And she told me a little bit about the war and what the occupation had been like, and about a square called Karlovo náměstí in Prague with benches and flower beds and giant twisted oaks that had a house along it that had belonged to a man named Faust, who had supposedly been dragged to hell through a hole you could still see in the ceiling, and she told me how very well she still remembered that square along with a certain churchyard a few minutes away, and when a particular burst of laughter carried over the water, she looked at me and said, "People can be silly, can't they, complicating their lives for no reason, don't ever complicate your life, promise me that," and though I didn't know exactly what she meant, I said I wouldn't. Later, as we were planting the pinwheel flowers in the new pots, pressing down the soil with our fingers so the roots would take, she told me she had made some mistakes in her life but that it was never too late to understand things and that she understood things now and that she had never been happier than she was at that moment. She suggested we take a break for lunch, but later, when I found her in the hammock, smoking, she said she was a little tired, and it wasn't until the next day that we finished, and by that time some of the flowers in the cartons, which we had forgotten to water, had wilted badly.

I was reading in my room that evening after dinner when I heard my mother get up from the wicker chair and go into the kitchen. I heard the refrigerator door open and close, then the quick clink of glass against glass. I heard the water in the sink, then the creak of the wicker again. "What time is it?" she asked my father.

It took a second for my father to move his book to his left hand and, holding his place with a finger, push up the sleeve of his sweater. "Half past nine," he said.

"Almost time for him to go to bed," my mother said. There was no answer. A few minutes later she was up once more.

"You think she'll do it again?" she said from somewhere by the window.

"I think she might," my father said in his "I'm reading" voice.

"What could she be thinking?" said my mother.

"Pretty much what you'd expect, I imagine."

"I don't think it's just that."

"I never said it was."

"Time for bed," my mother called. I pretended I couldn't hear. "What's he doing in there?" said my mother, and walking over, she knocked on the wood plank door to my room. "Bedtime," she said. They were quiet for a few moments.

"She's a fool," said my mother. "I thought she had more sense, throwing everything away like this."

They were quiet for a long time.

"I don't know that you want to stand by the window like that," my father said.

"I'm not the one who has to worry about being seen. And him," she said, after a moment. "Him I can't understand."

"What would you have him do?"

"Something. Anything."

Again they were quiet. I heard a page turn.

"And for what?" she went on after a while. "Nothing."

"I don't imagine she sees it that way," said my father.

"You don't?"

"No."

"How does she see it, then?"

"Differently."

"So you're saying there's nothing wrong with him sitting there reading like an idiot while his wife . . ."

"I didn't say that."

"Christ, you're understanding."

"Am I?"

"You go to hell."

I heard my father get out of the wicker chair, then whisper something I couldn't make out: "I've never asked . . . little enough . . . to blame . . . fault." And then I heard my mother crying and my father saying, "All right, there, come now, everything's all right. It's just a date on the calendar. Nothing more."

The next morning my mother woke me while everything was still cool and fresh. She had made a big plate of *palačinky* so light and thin you could see the bruise of the jam through the sides of the crepes. She'd set out two deck chairs in the middle of the old garden plot, she said. We would eat breakfast outside, a special treat. She put the *palačinky* on a tray with two cups of sweetened tea, and together we walked up the steps away from the lake to the garden, where we sat under light blankets with the weeds and the thistles growing up all around us and ate with our fingers, draping the floppy crepes between our thumbs and pinkies so the preserves wouldn't come out and feeding them into our mouths. We laughed about stupid things and pretended to signal to a waiter who stood in the old strawberry patch and to be frustrated when we couldn't catch his eye.

"What do you think he's doing?" my mother said.

"He's not paying attention to us," I said. I waved my arms wildly, as if signaling a boat far offshore.

"Careful," my mother said.

I put my cup of tea on its saucer down on the ground, making a space between the long grasses. I waved my arms again. "Can I get some more jam," I called out. "And some hot chocolate, please."

My mother was looking at the overgrown strawberry patch as though a man actually stood there in the weeds. "What do you suppose he's thinking about?" she said, as if to herself.

I didn't know what to say.

"I think he's thinking about a girl," my mother said. She was looking at the strawberry patch. A small breeze moved the pieces of shade and sun on the ground, then returned them to where they had been. She laughed strangely. "I don't think we can get his attention."

"Why don't I throw something at him," I said, and leaning over, I picked up a short, thick piece of branch and sent it flying through the air above the strawberry patch. It fell in the weeds at the far end of the garden. "Missed," I said. I reached over for another stick. "This time I'll . . ."

"He's smoking," said my mother. "Look at the way he brings

it to his mouth. The way he stands with his elbows back on the bar."

I looked at her, wanting to follow her, to play on this new field she was making.

"I bet he gets in trouble," I said.

She nodded slowly, agreeing with something I hadn't said. "I don't think he's the kind of man who would care very much. I don't think he'll care at all." She looked around the dead garden, then shook her head and smiled, as if remembering an old joke. "So here we are. Nothing to do but call for the check."

That afternoon I remembered what my father had said the night before about the date and checked the slightly mildewed calendar that hung on the wall in the kitchen next to the refrigerator. Nobody had turned the month. May showed a picture of boys playing baseball. One, no older than myself, had just slid into home on his stomach with his cap falling over his eyes. A fat man was waving him safe. The page was curling in at the corners; a row of mold spots, like sloppy stitching, walked across the white frame. I turned to June. In the picture, a boy with ridiculously blue pants was sitting by the side of a pond, fishing. The mold had touched a corner of the sky. Flowering trees were overhead and you could see his red bobber on the black pond. A few feet away, a small brown dog was lapping at the water.

I went back to the living room and looked at the *New York Times,* open on the dining room table. The date was June 18.

My mother worked on her flowers all that afternoon, sitting at the wooden card table in the shade, a cup of coffee and a cigarette next to her, cupping big handfuls of black soil from the small mountain she'd spilled on the table next to her, packing the pots, then making a space for the root ball by pushing the dirt to the side with her fingers the way a potter shapes the sides of a vase. I went off to play for a while, then returned to find her sitting with her elbows on the table. She was holding the cigarette and the cup of coffee in her right hand as though just about to pick them up, and her head was tilted slightly to the side. She was looking at a spot on the grass a short distance away.

I didn't want to disturb her, so I sat down quietly on the wooden steps to wait until she started working again. Everything was still. Far across the water a group of kids I didn't know were jumping from the children's dock into the water. Their screams sounded strangely distant, as though I were hearing them from inside a closed room.

My father spoke from the open bedroom window. "Can I get you something?" His voice was very close, as if he were sitting next to her, but though I knew he was right there, I couldn't see him; the angle made the screen opaque as a wall.

"No," my mother said. She didn't look up.

"Something to eat? A cup of tea?" In the other room, the children screamed happily. I could see them run down the hill and onto the slightly lopsided dock, then spear into the water. They looked like little white sticks.

"No," my mother said again. And then, after a while: "Thank you."

It was not long afterward — three days, perhaps a week — that my father shot the dog. Harold Mostovský and I heard it first while we were exploring along the brook one quiet, cloudy morning — a furious, concentrated thrashing in the underbrush. There was no other sound, I remember — no growling or snarling. When we came closer we thought at first that what we were seeing was two dogs, then a shepherd with something around its neck. Only when it sank its teeth in its own tail and bayed in pain, then bit its own hind leg, did we realize something was wrong, and terrified of this thing trying to kill itself, we began to run.

I never thought to ask my father how he knew. Whether

someone had called him, or whether he'd been walking in the area, or whether he'd somehow simply sensed it, the way parents sometimes will. All I know for certain is that he and old Ashby, who lived in a shack a mile away and who always wore overalls and a sleeveless T-shirt and who hadn't yet begun drinking himself to death, were suddenly there and my father was yelling, "Whose? Where?" then running for the old white Colby house, which stood on a little rise a hundred yards away. As Harold and I ran up behind them, I heard my father ask, Do you know where he keeps the shells? then saw him tap the bottom right pane with his elbow and reach inside and open the door. A moment later he was walking out with the shotgun. He brought it up to his face, studying it quickly, then broke it and chambered a red shell he took from his pocket. "Stay here," he told us.

The shepherd was still there. It was trying to get at its stomach. It had bitten off its own tail; the stub ended in a small pink circle. It seemed to be trying to stand on its right shoulder. It had shit all over itself and the smell was terrible. My father walked right over to it, extended the gun, and shot it in the head. At the sound of the two-part crash of the gun, the dog flopped to the ground like a dropped rubber toy; I caught a glimpse of what had been its head — a grinning jaw of teeth, a mat of fur, something pink like a thumb — and then my father's body blocked the view and he was turning us gently around. "Go home," he said. "This is not for you. Go on." And then to Ashby: "Get the shovel. I would like to take care of this quickly."

And that was all, really. My father didn't talk about it much, except to ask if I was all right and to explain that the dog had gotten into some poison some idiot had left out and that the thing had had to be done. He seemed strangely happy that week, unburdened. It started to rain that same afternoon, and when the water began to spill over the sides of the leaf-clogged gutter in long wavering sheets that tore open to show the trees and the hill, then sewed themselves up again, he took off his shirt and shoes and walked hatless into the downpour and unclogged the pipe and dug at the mats of blackened leaves gathered against the back of the cabin with his hands and carried them against his soaking chest into the woods.

It rained for three days. Soon after it stopped, Mr. and Mrs. Kessler left the lake because Mrs. Kessler was in love with the man who lived in the cove and wouldn't listen to reason. I never saw them again. The man stayed on for a while — we could see him row out to the dock and swim by himself in the evenings just before dark — as though he didn't want to go or thought she might come back, but then he left too.

My mother kept gardening, and for a time the south side of the cabin burst into color: waterfalls of blossoms cascaded against the wood, and bouquets filled with air moved sluggishly in the afternoon heat, but by late August something had gone wrong and they began to die and my mother lost interest. My father made a halfhearted effort to keep them up but they died anyway, and one day he took the pots off the wall and dumped the soil out of them in a corner of the old garden, then came back down and unscrewed the hooks out of the cabin wall and got a small brush and painted the white insides of the holes with dark stain so they couldn't be seen. The sixteen pots of soil looked like cake molds, white with roots, and they lay there until my father broke them up with a spade and spread them out into the weeds.

12

THE SUMMER I WAS TWELVE YEARS OLD I TOOK MR. Hanuš fishing. He'd asked me if he could come with me the next time he came to visit, that he used to fish in the ponds of Moravia as a boy. He'd show me how it was really done, he said. I knew using the boat was out of the question of course, as was anything too elaborate in terms of equipment, so I rigged up two rods with bobbers and sinkers and dug a can of night crawlers out of the crumbly dirt by the garden, thinking this would please him and remind him of his childhood.

"Didn't trust me with the good stuff, eh?" he said as we walked slowly toward the dock. He stopped before the stone step that led down to the boards of the dock and moved one cane ahead of himself, looking for a point of stability. "I've got it," he said. He tilted to the left, like a toppling tree, then lurched back. "Give me just a second," he said. His shirtsleeve had caught on the handle of the cane, and I could see the white flesh of his arm shaking from the strain. The next moment he'd stepped down with an awkward lurch, steadied himself, and begun hobbling out over the boards.

"I'm guessing that's not coffee you have in that can," he said. He looked around. "Well . . . this is very nice." He began to lower himself down. "Here, a little help — there, that's perfect. We'll just put these right here and then we'll get down to business." A painted turtle poked its nose through the surface film, then disappeared. I could hear my parents and the others talking and laughing, but they seemed far away.

For a long time, Mr. Hanuš explained to me that afternoon, nothing happens. This was very important, this nothing. It made things the way they were. "For generations," he said, "everything stays the same, looks the same — nothing changes. There's the kitchen with the calendar, the same as always, and there's the red runner in the hall that's always bunching up by the bathroom door. You have to imagine it. It's June, let us say, and dusk. A man in his shirtsleeves is leaning out the kitchen window, smoking, his elbows on the sill, which is peeling. In the courtyard below, everything is still: the piles of wet sand and brick, the rabbit hutches stacked against the north wall, the bicycles under the overhang. In the garden the kohlrabi are pushing up into the dark. It's quiet: you can hear a sudden voice, the tinny bang of pots, a child crying. The year is 1923. It's been five years since this man — who is your grandfather, by the way — returned from the war, where he suffered more than some, and less than others.

"Now a boy, no more than three, comes into the room, climbs knee-first onto a chair. 'Did you wash your hands?' says a woman's voice. The man at the window doesn't turn around. He's half listening to the voices in the courtyard. His back feels good and strong under his shirt. He takes a last draw and stubs his cigarette on the outside wall below the sill.

"Years pass. Nothing has changed. The runner in the hall is maybe a bit thinner now. But there are the piles of sand and brick, the bicycles leaning against the shed. And there are the rabbit hutches, stacked like an apartment building against the bricks. Everything is wet. The air smells like steel, or brass. Far away, as if they were coming from another world, you can hear the tiny bells of a trolley.

"The same man is leaning out the window, watching the rain. '*Antonín*,' he calls without turning around, '*dones uhlí*,' and your father, who is twelve years old now, comes out of the room where he's been memorizing Latin verbs — or pretending to — takes the coal bucket, and disappears down the hallway.

"Year follows year. A thousand times this man, your grandfather, smoothes the heavy ripples of the runner with his foot. A thousand times Mrs. Vondráčková shuffles out to the rabbit hutches with a piece of stovewood. Wet flakes of snow are falling on the hills of sand and brick, they look like sugar on the cellar door, and then it's June again and the sun in the afternoons reaches halfway down the east wall and the air smells like fresh-turned dirt. On warm nights the windows are swung open to the courtyard. In the garden the knotty heads of the kohlrabi are cresting up through the soil again like rows of little green skulls. This is the world you know. You know it the way you know your room now.

"This is what I'm trying to say to you: For a long, long time, nothing happens. And then it does.

"In a place called Berchtesgaden, a tall Englishman with a white mustache named Chamberlain unfolds himself from a limousine. Arguments are made. Tea is sipped. Important men stab their fingers at the polished table. '*Sie müssen* . . . *Wir werden* . . . *Etwas Tee, mein Herr?*' In Bad Godesberg this Englishman smoothes his hair with his right hand and says, 'I take your point, Herr Ribbentrop. And yet, if I may . . . we feel that . . . in the matter of . . . Can I take that as your final position?' And it comes to pass."

Mr. Hanuš smiled. "Berchtesgaden. Bad Godesberg. Berlin. All those B's.

"But you look around. There's the sideboard that used to be your mother's. And your father's leather-bound editions, locked safely behind the glass. Nothing has happened. Young girls still spend the long afternoons lying in their back yards reading novels. The dance tunes of R. A. Dvorský still play on the radio. Nothing has changed.

"And suddenly they're there, like a thunderclap out of a March blizzard, the Mercedes limousines with their horsehair-stuffed seats moving down Národní Avenue past the statues and the frozen saints to the river. The city is quiet. No people, no trams. The tracks are still, the cobbles are marbled with snow like that cake your mother gets in that deli on Queens Boulevard. Gargoyles with long tongues stare from their niches under the pediment. You watch from inside your apartment, looking through cracks in the curtains, like everyone else. As they pass, far below, you can hear the snap and crack of banners.

"There's nothing to be done. Nothing at all. The motorcade passes over the Vltava. The walls of Hradčany Castle are barely visible; the archers' clefts are empty. In the woods of Petřín, which are also deserted, there is only the slicing sound of the snow, sweeping up through the orchards. The government, the newspaper says, has been dissolved. Bohemia and Moravia — the woods, the fields, the towns, the paths you knew, the ponds you swam in — are now called the Protektorat Böhmen und Mähren." Mr. Hanuš smiled: "'Etwas Tee, mein Herr?'

"And still, even now, inside of you, it doesn't feel as if anything has changed. Things go on. And they continue to do this until the moment something stops, and all those years of nothing tear like a curtain caught on a nail. Maybe you see someone struck on the street, or maybe it's a voice on the radio, a voice like you've never heard before, a voice like a beating. But whatever it is, suddenly you know that everything has changed. That nothing is the same."

People backed into heroism like crabs, my father once told me. Or tripped into it through clumsiness. They rushed into the fire, blindfolded by glory, and somehow survived to be paraded down the boulevard, or they wandered stupidly onto the surface of things, made it across by some combination of physics and fortune, then looked back and called it courage.

Generations of heroes, entire battalions of them, he said, were just ordinary people who had been overtaken by the course of events, who had done what they did with no more thought than a dog who bites when his tail is slammed in a door — people who, when their tails had been freed and their consciousness revived, felt like spectators of their own lives.

And yet — and this was the thing — every now and again, against all the rules of human behavior, it occurred: an act of heroism planned in advance, undertaken for the right reasons, and carried out with the full knowledge, one might even say tragic knowledge, of the risks involved. A thing as unbelievable as a rain of toads. It isn't possible, you think. You can't believe it. And yet there they are, bouncing on the pavement.

When that happens, he said, all you can do is marvel at it, and take off your hat.

I asked my father if he had ever been a hero. He said no, not even close to one, and because he was my father, I believed him.

13

BY THE TIME I WAS NINETEEN WE WERE LIVING IN
Bethlehem, Pennsylvania, in a depressing little community with
streets named after poets no one read: Lord Byron Drive. Shel-
ley Lane. Longfellow Circle. My mother and father barely spoke
now. The town was dying. The steel mills by the river stood
silent, blotting out the sky and the wooded hills behind them
— they seemed embarrassed somehow. My father taught jour-
nalism at the university, started a garden. Eventually, to his
own amusement, he took up jogging. He would run once
around Mark Twain Circle, then down Northampton Street past
the fringe of woods opposite the First Presbyterian Church,
turn right at the Electronics Warehouse, right again on the
broken dirt road that ran along the highway like something trying to call attention to itself, then start for home. It could be
a treacherous run: the construction sites for the new subdi-
visions bled mud onto the road whenever it rained — lollipop
swirls, slippery as oil, that scalloped into shells when they dried.
My father would run around or hopscotch through them
and appear on the back deck, soaked and red in the face, forty-
five minutes after he'd left. He would stay there for a while,
holding his knees and swaying slightly, then take a hand
shovel from a peg on the back wall of the house and slowly

start scraping the mud from the sides of his running shoes.

My mother, who could hear the click of the trowel behind her when my father replaced it on the peg, sat in the back bedroom with the small high windows and watched the soaps. "I want to see this," she'd say, in Czech, when I tried to get her to come out for a walk. "Janice is going to expose Rick's infidelity. What do you think is going to happen?" And she'd take a draw of her cigarette.

And I'd have that feeling, which I always had in those days, that she was angry with me for something, though I didn't know what it was. "C'mon, Mom," I'd say. "You have to come out sometime."

"Why don't you leave me alone," she'd say sweetly, not looking up.

"Because I want you to come out with me," I'd say.

"Out where? For a walk along Nezval Circle, maybe? Akhmatova Lane?"

"C'mon, Mom . . ."

"His wife doesn't know, you see. It's all very exciting."

And I'd stand there, wanting to leave, wanting to shut that door and walk out of that house, wanting to slap her like in the movies — "Snap out of it!" — but instead I did nothing. She'd wait for me all week, my father said. When I called to say I couldn't come till the next, she'd disappear into the bedroom, sometimes for days. "Don't listen to what she says," he'd say to me. "You're everything to her." And so I'd stand there those few seconds longer, ask one more time. I stood in that doorway for fourteen years. "You can't sit here all day," I'd say. "When was the last time you were outside?"

"If I needed your condescension, I'd ask for it," she'd say then, still not looking up from the set.

"I just want . . ."

"Or that long-suffering tone, for that matter. You want to play the martyr, do it with one of your girlfriends in the city."

"OK," I'd say, closing the door quietly behind me.

And I'd hear her laugh to herself. "OK," she'd say.

She was bleeding, of course, smoking her cigarette in a pool of blood as real in its way as any blood that ever flowed. And yes, I hated her, for her weakness and her pain, for the way she fed on it like a glutton, for her unwillingness to be done, ever. I hated her because she and her grief were such a perfectly matched pair, because I had grown and she no longer wanted anything but to be left alone, because life had cheated her, exquisitely, and she could neither forgive nor forget.

At some point I didn't know who she was anymore. At times I could still glimpse — through an inadvertent laugh, a moment of stillness — the person I'd once known, who had once known me, but it was like seeing someone's face from a passing car, or looking up during intermission at a play to see someone — someone familiar — looking at you through a hole in the curtain. And for this I hated her too.

It became my little burden to bear, this awkward sack of hatred and love. There are worse.

The winter after I left for college, I had a dream. In the dream my mother and I were on a boat in the middle of a blue ocean tacked tight to the horizon. Everything was still: the boat, its reflection, the pale hot circle of the sun.

My mother had decided to go for a swim. Far off, she was calling for help, her arms flailing in the air. I was there instantly. She grabbed onto my shoulders and neck as if I were a board flung into the water, crazy with fear. I tried to drag her back to the boat, but I couldn't do it — her terror had given her outrageous strength. She fought and twisted as though shot through by some giant current. Holding her across her chest and under her arm, as I had learned to do in lifesaving class, choking and strangling, I somehow dragged her to the surface, only to be pulled under again and again.

84

It was then that I realized she was swimming down, deliberately trying to drown us both. I could feel her pulling into the dark, reaching for my face, my throat, and I began to fight, striking down with my fists, desperate to separate myself from this thing which only moments before I'd been determined to save, and woke myself with such a spasmodic wrench of my body that I knocked my glasses off the reading table by my dormitory bed.

I never told my father about the dream. He had his own dreams, I felt sure. And so did she. The next weekend, I took the bus from the city and walked home through the winter cornfields at dusk, the red and green Holiday Inn sign growing smaller behind me, lifting my feet so as not to trip over the frozen stubble. My mother was in the kitchen, making *bábovka*. She hugged me hello, and I felt her small back, how frail she'd grown.

And I remember knowing that the dream was true and yet realizing, in some half-formed way, that men rarely had the courage or the cruelty of their dreams and that this was good because life was lived among many kinds of things, all of them pushing for space, for air, all of them equally true: a wilderness of love and despair, laughter and rage, heroism and pain, while dreams, dreams were a haunted parkland — a stately oak, a bench, a fountain gushing blood.

14

I ASKED HER ONLY ONCE. IT WAS ON ONE OF THOSE UN-naturally warm, yellow October days that feel lost somehow, as though a day in June had floated loose and found itself in a world of frostbitten tomato plants and half-bare poplars. We were sitting on the back deck of the house in Bethlehem, which had a view of the rectangle of lawn and the row of pines intended to block out the neighbor's house. A short distance away was the stump of the maple my father had cut down during the summer. I looked at the pines. They had caught some kind of blight and seemed to be rusting from the needles in, like discarded Christmas trees.

"You should give them a feeding of Miracid," my mother said.

"Why bother?" I remembered my father saying once, when my mother had insisted I douse a pine in the front yard that had browned at terrible speed, as though it were burning. He'd chuckled. "Look at it. It doesn't want to be here."

"A good feeding can't do any harm," my mother had said.

"You might as well feed a shoe."

"Still."

My father smiled and waved his hand. "Water away," he'd said.

"Can't do any harm," my mother was saying now. "You should give them a feeding when it cools off a little."

I said I'd do that, and then asked her who he had been, this man she had loved all the years I was growing up. I told her I'd known about him since I was a child, and that I thought, now that I was grown, she might finally tell me the story. I didn't blame her or resent her in any way, I said. Far from it. I was curious. What kind of man had he been? How had they met? What had happened to him? Had she met him before she met my father?

I knew it had happened during the war, I said, speaking quickly now. Sometime in 1942. Had he been in the Resistance? Had he died in the purges after Heydrich was killed? Could she tell me anything at all?

My mother took a dry, wafer-like cookie off the plate between us and took a small bite.

"I don't really want to talk about that right now," she said.

We sat in silence. I couldn't think of anything to say.

"Your father's a good man," she said. And then, after a while: "I'm sorry."

My mother was looking out over the yard — the poplars, the shadows on the lawn, the rusting pines. She was biting her upper lip, which made her chin stick out a bit, as if she were deciding something.

"You really should give them a good feeding," she said at last. "It can't hurt."

15

WHEN I WAS TWENTY I STAYED FOR A TIME IN A *CHATA* by a pond, seven kilometers from the town of Bystřice nad Pernštejnem, with my father's childhood friend Mirek. I'd fallen in love with a girl who was vacationing with her friends a few cabins down from ours. She was older than I was. We would spend every night around a campfire we built for ourselves along the shore, and always, often toward morning, end up making frantic love, still dressed in our smoky sweaters, our pants around our ankles, in the cold, dew-soaked grass. In the afternoons she would go on long sleepy walks in the woods with her friends, and I would swim across the pond with Mirek.

We always swam the long way, from the muddy little beach in the grass to the mill whose watermarked roof, furred with jigsaw pieces of moss, rose above the embankment on the far side. It would take us half an hour, sometimes more, and Mirek, whose right leg had withered to a stick half a century earlier when his father had refused to have a doctor set the toes his son had broken, would roll about in the dark water like a happy walrus, one moment paddling with his arm extended straight ahead as though lying on a sofa, the next raising his white belly like a hill into the air.

It was on one of these long swims across the pond that he told me about the afternoon when my father and his old friend Pavel

Štěpánov had looked into the execution yard. They were not yet twenty years old, he said, turning on his back and paddling along with small, flipper-like strokes while raising his head partly out of the water. About my age. At that time, he said, the people living in houses with windows facing the courtyard of Kounicovy koleje, a nondescript cluster of three-story dormitories that the Gestapo had turned into a prison, had been instructed to board them up. Not that it made any sense, Mirek said. Everyone knew what was happening there. The volleys usually began at ten in the morning and, except for a pause between one and two, continued until four. Every day except Sunday, shortly before ten, heavy trucks would bump up to the gates and disappear behind them. In the afternoon the gates would open again, usually around four-thirty, and they would leave.

Pavel Štěpánov, Mirek said, had discovered a crack in one of the boards over the upper bedroom window. By inserting a bread knife into the narrow part of the bolt and twisting gently, he could widen the crack to a centimeter or so. It was a still, hot summer day; the air in the half-boarded house was stifling. No one was at home. It was just after two. Štěpánov reached under the fringed shade of a bedside lamp and turned on the light. On the other side of the boards they could hear someone yelling orders. And though he didn't want to, Mirek said, my father put his eye to the crack, and saw what he saw.

"It changed him," he said. "It wasn't a sudden thing. Of course I can't tell you for sure that it was that day and not some other one, but I think it was. It turned something inside him. He has this smile, you know the one I mean, almost sweet, but closed, like this" — and he raised a closed fist above the water — "that only appeared afterward. The funny thing is that when I think of your father now, I see that smile. As if that was who he was supposed to be. It's the same with Štěpánek," he added. "That irritating laugh of his."

"I never saw what happened there myself," Mirek continued. "I remember the German *hausfrauen* walking past our gate during breakfast. They would walk down Tolstého Street to the corner, then up toward the dormitories. We couldn't see what they saw, but from our kitchen window we could see them standing against the post-and-wire fence they had there, holding up their children to see."

We swam quietly for a while. Mirek was looking up at the sky. "How far are we?"

"Maybe halfway," I said. I looked down into the water between my arms. "How deep do you think it is here?"

"Can you touch the bottom?"

"No."

"Then it's deep."

We swam on. "What did he see?" I said.

But Mirek couldn't tell me. "More than he should," he said.

His own father, he told me, whose prison cell had overlooked the courtyard at Kounicovy koleje for almost a year, until he was shipped off to Dachau, said the things one heard were the worst of all. He'd learned to insert pills of toilet paper into his ears, then wet them to make them expand. Others would crawl under their mattresses, supposedly, or wrap their bedsheets around their heads to keep from hearing. An unstable man named Žáček, a butcher, had somehow managed to rupture his own eardrums with a smuggled pencil.

It was all very organized, Mirek's father said. The holding area was separated by a barbed-wire fence from the execution yard itself, which was right where the trucks came in. The children were almost always taken first. Sometimes, just before they were led away, the parents would try to press themselves against them, or whisper something to them, as though giving them a message to deliver. Surprisingly often they would yell at them — Stop crying! Listen to me! — as if their words through some last miracle of habit or authority could make that place something other than what it was.

Sometimes the mother would lose consciousness, Mirek's father told him. More often she would begin to scream as soon as the first child was taken. The father might try to do something then, run at a guard, perhaps, or try to kick him, which only meant that he wouldn't have to watch. Mostly, though, the parents would just stand there, like sleepwalkers waiting in line at a bank. Some would make odd, spastic little gestures — reaching up as if to touch their right cheek, for example, or frowning quickly, or suddenly fingering a button. The men watching them from the windows would often unconsciously do the same.

It was the strangest thing, Mirek's father said, to see the same gesture duplicated, as if in a mirror, fifty meters away; it reminded him of that elementary school contraption that copied on a second sheet of paper — through the use of a kind of movable armature attached to a pencil — whatever was drawn on the first. Often, he said, you could tell what was happening in the courtyard simply by looking at the person watching. When the watcher's face turned away slightly and his head began to shake, for example, you knew it was almost over, because people about to be killed often developed an odd, Parkinson's-like tremor, looking off to the side and shaking their heads as if denying what their senses told them.

We lay on the grass bank under the mill for a long time that afternoon, moving east to stay ahead of the shade. I remember Mirek leaning up on one elbow, twirling and untwirling a blade of grass around his finger, his belly resting comfortably on the ground, his bad leg thin and ridged as a ham bone. I remember realizing, dimly, how much I loved this man — his round, happy face and his strong, soft shoulders and the thicket of white hair covering his chest. During the war, when my father and the others had intercepted the arms that dropped like dandelion seeds into the Vysočina forests — cutting them loose from the parachutes, then rushing them through the dark on makeshift stretchers — he had been the one waiting in the wagon, the one who covered the crates with firewood or manure, then drove them out to the safe houses alone, the horse snuffing wetly in the morning air.

At the far eastern corner of the pond, at a small beach, I could see tiny children leaping off a dock, their screams sounding strangely close over the still water. Just to the right I could see the space in the reeds where we had had our fire the night before: there were the blackened stones, like flecks of pepper, and there was the stunted willow, like a child's drawing, whose roots had scratched my back.

"We should go," Mirek said, sitting up on the bank. "I have a date tonight."

"It's going to be cold," I said, looking at the water.

Mirek stood, a bit unsteadily as always, and started toward the water. "Courage, boy," he said. He slapped his belly, and the sound carried across the water like a single clap. "Courage and fat."

I watched him wade in up to his knees, throwing water on his arms and chest, then plunge in. But I hesitated. The sky was darkening. The children were gone. On the spillway a carp fisherman had set up his stool. I watched him finish rigging his line, cast out past the trees to the darkening sky, then settle himself carefully on the stretched fabric.

Later that night I waited on the dark path under the trees, carrying a small sack of sausages and *rohlíky*, tin cups and tea. The wind moved, making the lights of the cabins wink on and off. And suddenly I felt terribly lonely, as apart as I ever had in this world. The air was cool, but every now and then I could smell the hot smell of the fields. A woman's laugh came from one of the cabins. She was enjoying herself. She wouldn't come. I waited in the dark under the trees for a long time, leaning against a huge old chestnut with smooth, skin-like bark, thinking every few moments that I saw her flying along the bank or down the road to meet me, then threw the sausages and the *rohlíky* and the cups into the water one after the other and went home.

16

ON MARCH 17, 1984, MY MOTHER APPARENTLY DECIDED
to walk to the Westgate Mall in a freezing rain wearing a summer
dress with a raincoat over it. It had been raining for a long
time. She tried to cut through a cornfield behind the subdivi-
sion on Whitman Drive but found herself lifting clods of clayey
mud with each step, and retreated to the road. She walked to
Hochstetler Lane (the town fathers having run out of literary
lights), then along the gravel shoulder past the gas station and
the little shopping area with the H&R Block to the stretch of
sidewalk over the highway and then another mile or so past the
Sears Automotive Center to the vast parking lot of the mall.

Inside the mall, made to look like the street of a small town,
she sat down on one of the shiny green benches set up under the
eave of the Bavarian Haus. Music was playing. A group of se-
niors on an excursion from the retirement home came and sat
down on the bench next to her to wait for the bus to Allentown.
Every few minutes the music stopped and after a few seconds a
woman's voice came over the loudspeaker: J. C. Penney was having its annual electronics sale. For that day only, everything
would be marked down 20 to 50 percent. Then the music would
come on again.

It was raining hard. The rivulets of water rushing down the
glass made everything seem oddly submerged. A tall boy in leder-

hosen with a ravaged face offered her some flavored cheeses on a wooden tray. The cubes were impaled on toothpicks. My mother said something about the bits of colored cellophane on their tips, but didn't take any. She was very polite.

From where she sat, she could see the imitation street lamp to the left of the Century 21 real estate office and a sign with white letters saying MAIN STREET. On the ceiling, high above the steel rafters, someone had painted a summer sky, though you could barely see it. I don't know if she noticed it.

A frail old man in a pink windbreaker sat down next to her on the bench. "Goin' to Allentown?" he asked. My mother looked at him. She seemed to be thinking about it. "I don't think so," she said.

A poster taped to the brick wall showed a snarling tiger on a small stool, a clown with a huge white mouth shooting a tiny bow and arrow, and a powerful man with long blond hair holding a whip. He was yelling something, but he looked as if he were crying.

My mother stood up.

"Shprecken Zee Dutch?" said the old man.

My mother took off her raincoat, folded it neatly, and placed it on the bench. "Have a nice day," she said, then walked out into the rain, across the parking lot and out to the turnoff ramp from the highway where she stepped directly in front of the 4:38 bus to Allentown.

And I can see her saying it: "Have a nice day." That sardonic half-smile. We hadn't spoken in seven years. She left no phone message, no note. No taped cassette on the dining room table. Just a casserole dish half filled with ashes and a few feathery bits of letter paper. I poked around in the ashes with the eraser end of a pencil. Along the edge of a blackened piece of blue *Luftpost* letter paper I made out two words: "I still." And that was all.

PRAGUE

Intermezzo

MY MOTHER ERASED HERSELF SO THOROUGHLY THAT for a long time after she died, I couldn't find her anywhere. Two years later my father died, and not long afterward I resigned my job and moved to Prague. I was thirty-seven years old. I hadn't forked any lightning, wasn't really expecting to. Maybe I was looking for them, I don't know — men do all sorts of foolish things. Or maybe I was hoping to discover how our particular story, of which I knew so little, really, fit the larger one. Face to face with that larger, known puzzle — of the past, of Prague, of war — I would see the empty space that was us, recognize its shape. And I would understand.

I found stories enough, but not ours exactly; empty spaces we should have fit, but didn't. Everywhere I went, things seemed to speak of her, to hint of her, yet revealed nothing; they were like a stranger passing in the street who whispers your name, then denies having said anything at all. Held up to life, metaphors melt like snow.

That first summer I moved to Czechoslovakia I stayed for a while in an old inn, a wood and plaster building located at the base of a grassy dam that rose like a mountain just meters from the back windows and gave the light a permanently hooded, storm-like cast. The building had once been a mill house; the brook that had been stoppered up long ago still trickled past the parking lot. At night, lying in bed, I could hear it through the open windows after the drunks had gone home. At my back, basking in the moonlight, was the reservoir, stretching for kilometers through the mustard fields. No one seemed troubled by the fact that a continent of water hung above their beds, that carp slurped at the air five meters above the kitchen chimney.

I stayed four days. I was the American eating trout by himself every evening in the small wooden dining room with the dirty tablecloths and the outraged-looking boar's head which appeared to have simply rammed itself through the wall and stuck fast above the lintel. The one just comfortable enough in the language to be uncomfortable in his own skin, surrounded by quiet families who grew noticeably quieter every time he entered the room, who pretended to be busy wiping their children's faces whenever he glanced up from his plate, who watched the waitress approach his table as though she were a matador entering the ring. Not quite knowing what to do with myself (I had no one to talk to, and reading would have seemed rude), I would pretend to be fascinated by the room itself — looking this way and that with the curious, benign expression of a parrot on a branch — eat quickly, and leave.

One day I passed by a small, weedy pond that was being emptied. Four young men in heavy boots were plunging about in the mud, grabbing the huge silver carp that everywhere flopped and slithered in the dwindling water and throwing them into the bed of a truck that had been backed to the water's edge. It was a beautiful day, fresh and hot, and the men, who were strong and quite brown from the sun, were enjoying themselves enormously, shouting and laughing as they splashed after the carp that tried to get away, grunting every time they turned and spun a heavy fish over the rail. The carp slapped around for a time, then died, buried under their fellows. I watched the men work, turning from the hips like discus throwers, their heads thrown back with effort every time they released a fish into the air, then went on my way.

That evening I recognized them as I ate dinner at a local inn. They had washed and changed their clothes. Their hair was combed. They seemed so dull and sullen, sitting over their glasses of beer, that for a moment I wondered if I was mistaken. And then one of them turned toward the bar and I saw a carp scale, like a giant silver fingernail, stuck to the back of his sun-tanned neck.

I don't know what I had expected. Some of the people I spoke to — a humped-up woman with a hairy mole under her eye whom I met at a wooden bus stop, a small badger of a man hurrying along a fence — remembered my mother. They seemed touched to hear she was dead — they remembered her when she was like this, playing right over there — but no more than they were by the fact that her son had come all the way from America to find the family house. They'd heard that she'd gotten mixed up in something during the war, that she'd escaped, immigrated to New York. The Resistance? Another man? They hadn't heard. I was invited inside, plied with cups of thick Turkish coffee and *jahodový táč*, taken into the back room and shown the bust of President Masaryk hidden behind the curtain. They had had him there through everything, they assured me. I learned nothing I hadn't known.

I collected facts, as I always had, like a child hoping to build an oak from bits of bark. I traveled to the few towns I recalled my mother mentioning, visited the houses where the partisans had met, hunted down the places where they had died. I pored through documents and letters, talked to those who had survived. The majority of those involved in the Resistance had been executed immediately or deported to camps right after the

Heydrich assassination in 1942. Most of this second group had died there, some at Mauthausen, others at Terezin, still others at Auschwitz. Which told me nothing. Many had died.

One hot June day that summer I took a bus to see a certain town in Moravia I had read about whose citizens had been particularly active in the Resistance and had suffered for it. I'd heard my mother mention it. The air in the bus was stifling — most of the windows seemed glued shut — and when I discovered that I'd gotten off one town too early, rather than get back in, I pretended that that had been my destination all along. But this wasn't Malá Losenice, the driver explained, trying to save me from my mistake. No, no, this was exactly where I wanted to go, I assured him, and finally, with an irritated wave of his hand, he dismissed me. A young woman with a heavy bag of groceries started to climb into the bus. Conscious of being watched, I headed up a tilting dirt road lined with squalid houses as though I knew precisely where I was going. The smell of the fields, of sun and drying hay and stables, came in hot waves.

I asked directions. Malá Losenice was eight kilometers by the main road, I was told, five by the red-marked trail that led through the woods. I would have to watch carefully for the turnoff for the blue trail.

The path left the town quickly and meandered up through mustard fields and young wheat, still and unmoving in the heat, then turned into the forest. A hunter's stand of cut pines stood against the trees, a small pile of rusted cans at its base.

I got lost. There was no blue trail, nor any other for that matter, and when I retraced my steps after an hour or so, I didn't recognize any of the places I came to. To make matters worse, I hadn't brought enough water, and there didn't seem to be any streams in these woods. I walked on and on, sitting down to rest every now and then, then nervously jumping up to walk another mile. It was absurd, all of it. What had I been thinking? I was going home . . . as soon as I could figure out which direction home might be.

Walking down a long, sloping dirt road through the fields, I found myself behind an old woman dressed in black, making her slow way toward the forest. Setting her stick ahead of her, then moving up to it, she reminded me of a fragile spider testing unfamiliar ground.

When I was still some distance behind her I cleared my throat so as not to startle her. She had paused by a wooden fence to catch her breath, one hand on the top slat, the other on her cane. Hearing me, she transferred both hands to her stick, which she had planted in the dirt, and pivoted slowly in my direction.

"*Dobrý den*," I said, greeting her. She didn't respond. She was very old, her face and neck under her kerchief fissured like bark. As I passed, I could see her mouth working as if searching for a bone with her tongue. When I asked her for directions back to the town I had started from, she raised a trembling claw and pointed in the direction I'd been going.

And suddenly — perhaps it was the heat — I had the absurd desire to ask her if by any chance she remembered a couple, a young man and a woman with very black hair, from the early years of the war. It wasn't completely mad. She was certainly old enough. I'd grown up hearing about the forests of Moravia, had seen the look on my mother's face when she spoke of them. Maybe this woman had seen them one July evening as she was coming back from the well. Or glimpsed them through her kitchen window one morning just as her husband called to her from the pantry to ask if she'd said apricots or cherries. I wanted to ask her — this one woman out of a hundred thousand, living in a place that most likely had nothing to do with them at all — if she remembered . . . something. To take a wild stab at chance, at the miracle of coincidence.

I didn't. Her hands, veined and speckled, grasped each other over the flat head of her walking stick. I continued on. When I turned around at the edge of the pines I could see her, half a kilometer back, making her way down the road toward the trees like the shadow of a small, dark cloud.

I moved to the apartment on Italská Street in Prague when I was thirty-seven. I still go back and forth as I can. I've learned that human beings are like the Silly Putty I used to play with as a child, that pressed to a piece of brick, we take the imprint of this world, then carry it like a sealed letter marked God and God alone to our deaths. I've learned that nothing in this world resists us like ourselves. And I think, if this is true, how then can we hope to know someone else?

I

IN MID-AUGUST OF THAT FIRST SUMMER I FOUND MY-
self walking up a steep, badly cobbled road in central Moravia
that tilted to the left like a sloping hill. The village I was passing
through, called Polnická, seemed deserted. No one moved in the
dilapidated blue and cream-colored houses crowding the road
from either side until an old man in slippers suddenly appeared,
carrying a basket of apricots through a gate. Apparently recog-
nizing that I was not from those parts, he invited me to his wine
cellar for a glass of wine.

He led me through a neglected garden to a half-sized door
with a wig of roses hanging over its skull-cracking sill. Through
this door, which opened into a low, rounded hill, we entered a
damp stairwell, tight as a burrow. The stairs descended a full
five meters to a tiny earthen room. Two old men were already
there, huddled in heavy, mouse-eaten coats, sitting on wooden
benches. Three small barrels lay on a scaffolding made of sticks.
A row of small glasses stood on a dirt shelf. A few roots, some
cut flat, others still growing hopefully, protruded from the wall.
This, my guide explained, was the wine cellar, and here the three
of them could sit, sub rosa so to speak, safe from the great
flapping ear of the Party, which sat listening like the old Victrola
dog to every sound they made.

One had eyebrows like white brushes that drooped over his eyes; another, whose teeth seemed one size too big for his mouth, was dressed, under his bear-like coat, in a brown jacket, his shirt buttoned tight against his wattled neck; my host, who regularly refilled my glass from a snout-like hose attached to one of the barrels, had hands as seamed as paws.

I listened to them talk. Every now and then I thought I could hear, high above us, someone knocking on the little door at the top of the stairs. No one else seemed to hear it.

I asked them about the war, which they remembered well. Eventually there was a quarrel over whether it had rained on a certain day during the war when someone they had known had shot himself. My host was sure it had. The professor — for that was what I thought of him as being — was sure it hadn't. The man had shot himself in the head, my host said, and collapsed face-down in the mud. He'd left his glasses on the rear-view mirror of his car, then walked up to the cemetery in the rain and shot himself. The professor called my host an idiot. "It was a day as blue as that house," he said, pointing to a small, mildewed painting hanging from a root. Looking at me, he tapped the age-spotted skin over his temple. "Senility," he said. "Everything's blurring together for him." He pointed at the ceiling half a meter above our heads. "It's raining now, you see, so he thinks it was raining then. If it was snowing, he'd be saying he killed himself in a snowdrift."

My host told him to go to hell. They argued.

"Goddamn it, I should know," yelled my host at some point. "Vladislav Popelka was the graveskeeper, and my sister went to school with his daughter."

"I remember her," interrupted the one with the eyebrows, who had been quiet all this time. "Her brother had a *hospoda* in Nedvědice. I used to see him at the station sometimes after the war."

"What was it called?" asked my host.

"U kolejí," said the other, taking his glass.

"I remember that," said my host.

"They had the most wonderful little game hens in nut sauce."

They were all silent for a while. Again I could hear the knocking on the door at the top of the stairs.

"It's that son-in-law of yours," said the professor.

"I think it's General Secretary Gorbachev, come to ask me what to do about the economy," said my host.

"I could be wrong," said the professor.

They were silent again.

"What time is it?" asked the one with the eyebrows. He'd promised to take his wife to see the new American film playing in Žd'ár, a love story of some kind. That actor was in it, he said, you know. Which one? they asked. The blond one, he said. With the mole on his cheek. "Redford," said the professor. "Robert Redford." "That's him," said the one with the eyebrows. "The wife had a dream about him the other night. Said he knocked on our kitchen window while I was taking a nap after dinner and asked her to come out to the barn with him. She was just taking her apron off to go outside when I woke her to ask where she'd put the keys to the shed. She wouldn't talk to me the rest of the day."

"So take her tomorrow," said the professor irritably.

"To hell with Robert Redford," said my host.

He had to go, the other said, standing into a kind of crouch. It had been a pleasure to meet me, he said, though I had hardly said a word the entire time, and with that they beckoned me up the narrow, clayey stairs to the half-sized door at the top, through which I emerged into a warm, sunny drizzle.

2

ON A WET APRIL DAY IN 1999, IN A TRAM ALONG THE
Vltava River, I asked a frail man in a Homburg hat for directions.
He wore glasses and was dressed in a dark suit of some heavy
material. It had worn to a dull shine at the elbows, and I noticed
that he had rubbed shoe polish into the thinning spots to hide
them. He had a fine white mustache, and he asked me where I
was from and ended up telling me about his father who had
been a Latin teacher in a local high school and a collector of
birds' nests.

Every spring in those years during the war, he said, his father,
whose displeasure could provoke even the dullest students into
prodigious feats of memory, and who could seem so severe behind his small rimless glasses, what with his creased cheeks and
his thin brown hair combed straight back, would wander in the
woods around Prague listening for bird calls. He knew them all
— *skřivánky* and *pěnkavky* and *rákosníky*. Having located a nest,
he would wait patiently for the chicks to hatch and then to leave,
returning week after week until the nest was empty. He would
mark the spot on a map, with a symbol like a footnote, then describe the position in more detail in a small leather notebook he
carried with him, triangulating his position with the local land-
marks: a scarred oak, a steeple, a stone road marker like a tiny

gravestone. Only after the birds had abandoned it, the man assured me, turned half around on the tram's uncomfortable plastic seat, would his father add the nest to his collection. When he finally harvested a nest, the mood would be festive; his father would be in good spirits all day. Sometimes, especially when there were trees to climb, he would take his son with him, handing him the thin-bladed, collapsible saw, instructing him where to cut.

Collecting birds' nests was his father's passion, the man in the Homburg hat told me, and every fall and winter through the early years of the war, whenever his father had spare time, he would work on his displays at a small desk in a corner of the living room — mounting each nest on the appropriate branch of the appropriate tree or bush or reed — all the while regaling his family with amusing stories of how he had come to secure this particular treasure, what he had said to this or that acquaintance who had happened by just as he was scrambling up a tree like a schoolboy, how he had lifted his hat to Madame So-and-So with one hand while holding on to a branch with the other.

Sometimes, when an egg didn't hatch, his father would blow it out through a pinhole and place it in the nest to add realism to the display. Everyone, he maintained, needed a *koníček,* a hobby, especially after a certain age, and his was certainly no more absurd than many others. He himself, said the man in the Homburg hat, had started collecting stamps soon after he had turned forty. He found that it gave his life a kind of order that nothing else could supply. There was a real pleasure, he said, on receiving a bundle of stamps from some acquaintance from overseas, in sitting down under a good lamp on a rainy evening to study and sort and perhaps affix them in their proper places.

I told him I had some stamps my parents had collected over the years for some reason, and that I recalled my mother saying that some of them were from places like Siam and Ceylon, countries that, as he knew, no longer existed under their former names. I had no idea if they were valuable, but if he was interested I would send them to him. He said he would be very grateful, and I handed him a pencil and a store receipt I found in one of my pockets and he placed the receipt against the window and wrote down his address for me. "Four more stops," he said.

So he had inherited his father's collection? I asked, in part to fill in the sudden silence.

He shook his head. The collection had been destroyed when his father was arrested.

I was sorry, I said.

The old man waved it away. "The Gestapo came for him in July of 1942," he said matter-of-factly. "I was thirteen years old. My father's collection must have had close to a hundred nests in it by then. It was really quite something. They were all over our apartment — in the parlor, in the dining room, in the hallway, so many that at times it was as if you were walking through an enchanted wood, a wood in which walls had miraculously begun to appear among the branches, while at other times it seemed as if the walls themselves had come alive and sprouted through the plaster. A wondrous home to grow up in."

After breaking his father's nose with the butt end of a rifle, he said, the soldiers had made his father tear the nests out of the walls and step on them. The three of them — he and his mother and father — had just sat down to breakfast when they heard cars screech to a halt in front of the apartment. He remembered his father slowly folding the morning paper in half and laying it alongside his plate, then looking at his mother — not at her face but her chin and hair and throat, tracing the frame — and then they were there.

He remembered them going through the apartment. He remembered them standing about in the hall in their boots shouting *Los, los, schneller!* — Step out, faster, faster! — and his father bringing the branches into the living room like armfuls of stovewood while the blood poured from his nose and throwing them in a pile on the rug. There were big white pieces of plaster, like puzzle pieces, hanging off the ends.

"Why was he arrested?" I asked.

The tram had come to a stop. People streamed out into the wet spring air, others pushed in.

"Three more," he said.

They had learned later, he said, that one of his father's students had mentioned his father's name under torture. He shrugged. "Who knows what people will say under those circumstances? My father had given him a four — what to you Americans would be a D. Perhaps my father's name floated into his head by accident, as in a dream."

At the time, said the man in the Homburg hat, he and his mother hadn't known anything about this. They had no idea what was happening. It was all a terrible mistake. It was only much later, after the war, that they had learned that two of the parachutists sent to assassinate Reinhard Heydrich had hidden themselves for a time near one of his father's favorite collecting places, a stretch of scrubby woods near an abandoned quarry twenty minutes from Prague, and that this coincidence, coupled with the young man's mentioning of his teacher's name in a delirium of pain, had been enough.

"What happened to your father?" I asked.

"They tortured him for three days, then cut off his head. They did that sometimes." He paused. "A curious thing. When I was fifteen or sixteen — an unfortunate age under the best of circumstances — I became quite obsessed, morbidly so, you might say, with the details of my father's death. I thought about it all the time, until one day, on an outing near Klánovice, I offered a villager fifty crowns if he would let me kill a chicken. I can still see him — a big, thick-nosed man in blue overalls. He looked at me strangely — he must have thought I was crazy — then went into the hen house and came out carrying a chicken and a short hatchet. I took the chicken by the neck — it was squawking terribly — and walked over to a kind of chopping block that stood in the middle of the yard. I was a city boy. I had no idea what to do. I put the chicken on the block, but everything kept blurring because I was crying and I couldn't take off my glasses to wipe my eyes. I was worried I'd cut off my fingers on top of everything else, so I held its body down as best I could with my right foot and stretched out its neck like a rubber band and chopped off its head. I had been afraid it might run around, but it didn't do anything. I lay the head and neck — a floppy, boneless thing — next to the body, paid the money, and left." He shook his head. "What idiots we are," he said.

"It didn't help?" I said.

"Not a bit. I still thought about it, just as I had before. I thought for a time that I was losing my mind. And then at some point, for no particular reason, I stopped thinking about it."

It had all been a very long time ago, he said. These days he passed the building in which his father had been interrogated at least three times a week. It was still there, a huge, blocky structure with bars in the windows, just down from the main train station. A statue of a barefoot prisoner, representing all those who had been interrogated there during the war, had been erected above the sidewalk on the southeast corner. He was an old man now. He never thought of it. The only thing that still troubled him at all was that the last memory he should have of his father was of him in his rest-day clothes, barefoot like the statue, trying not to cry out as he stamped on the branches strewn over the living room floor. More than a few of his father's species, he explained, had nested in thorns.

I said something about how horrible this must have been for him, and how tragic a mistake.

He glanced out the window. "The next is mine," he said. "Yours is the one after that."

There had been no mistake, he said. Shortly after the war, in 1945, a man had knocked on their door and told them everything.

His father, Oldřich Růžička, had been a valuable member of the Resistance, he told them. He had relayed information from a man named Jindra. He had hidden two of the parachutists who had been dropped into the country by the RAF in an old cellar in the middle of a raspberry field, then kept them supplied with medicine and food and information for nearly two weeks until they could be moved to safety.

The man had read to them from a small book as he sat on their sofa. "On November 7, 1941" — here the old man looked at his open palm as though a notebook were lying in it — "Oldřich Růžička carried crystals for a radio transmitter from a house in Žyžkov to an apartment on Poděbradova. On December 12 he relayed a message to someone code-named Jiřinka at the Olšany Cemetery. And so on."

Curiously enough, the old man said, rather than give them comfort, this knowledge had taken away the one source of comfort he and his mother had had left. There were no certainties now, only questions. It was as though the man they had known had really been someone else. Next to every smile, every anecdote, there was now an asterisk, and though his father's face and voice and hands remained as vivid to them as if he had just stepped out of the room to get something from the kitchen, they could no longer be sure exactly who it was that had left.

They had learned to live with it as best they could. In time, the man said, his mind had simply grown around this unwanted information, this other, alternate father, the way a tree will grow around an iron spike, incorporating it, enfolding it, until at times it seemed to him he could almost remember his father hinting at his other self, speaking in code, winking as he lifted his coat off the hook below the *skřivánek*'s nest in the hall and went out for the afternoon.

But it was a lie, and he knew it. An uncertainty was still an uncertainty. A spike, though buried, was still a spike. And it still bothered him, particularly now, in his later years, when he realized it would outlive him. What troubled him most, he said, though he recognized that there was something wonderfully absurd about it, was that he would never know whether his father's interest in birds' nests had been real — that is, whether it had come first and then been used by him as a convenient cover when the war began — or whether he had adopted it when the need arose. Whether all those nights — the man's entire childhood, it seemed — that his father had sat at his work desk in the corner of the living room, tucking in strands of straw and tufts of lint with a needle and telling them about his adventures, had been genuine or only part of a long story he told — and lived — to protect them.

There were other options of course, said the man in the Homburg hat. Perhaps his father's interest in birds had started out false and grown real with time. His father's leather notebook, in which he had kept all his notes, had somehow, almost miraculously, survived — hidden in plain view on the bookshelf. More than once, he said, he had looked at it, with its location diagrams and crude pictures and descriptions of birds' nests, and wondered how much of it was in code. He shrugged. Neither he nor his mother, in the years before she died, had been able to recall with any degree of accuracy when his father had started his hobby. It was not something he was likely to find out in this life. Perhaps the next.

It made for a very strange feeling, he said, to look at his father's fountain-pen drawings, still so familiar to him with their arrows and circles and tight, angular handwriting, and to not know whom they had been intended for. Here and there, he said, one could find, in the thicket of Latin genus and species names, *Lanius collurio* or *Emberiza calandra*, a date and a time, (*23. dubna 1942, 15:14*), and next to it, carefully noted, the height of the nest from the ground in centimeters and the number of eggs that had hatched. Only recently, he said, had he noticed that there was always only one or two, and never more than three. He had no idea what this meant, if indeed it meant anything. "Here, let me show you," he said, and leaning down, he opened the battered briefcase resting against his leg.

"You have it here?" I asked stupidly.

"Ah, here it is," he said, taking a small, cracked-leather notebook strapped with rubber bands out of his briefcase. "Let me . . ."

But the tram was already slowing. He glanced up. "I'm afraid we won't have time," he said. He dropped the notebook back inside the briefcase and snapped it shut. It had been very nice talking to me, he said, and if I could remember to send him those stamps when I returned home to America, he'd be very grateful. And grasping his briefcase, he walked out into the wind.

I got off the tram at the next stop.

All that fall I carried the receipt with his name and address on it safely tucked in my wallet until, on a crowded train, a week before I was to leave Prague for a few months, someone stole it from my inside breast pocket. When I tried to find the name I remembered, I got nowhere, and when I located a street whose name sounded much like the one I remembered him writing down, no one there could tell me anything of a frail-looking man with a white mustache who collected stamps.

For years I thought of him, still waiting for the stamps from Ceylon and Siam to arrive from overseas. And then I stopped.

3

ON A COLD NIGHT LATE IN 1988, I MET A MAN IN A *hospoda* in the village of Třebíč. The room was full of round tables covered with dirty white tablecloths and when the waitress came over with the beers which she carried three to a hand, she made a mark on a red cardboard coaster with a short black pencil. When I told the men at the table next to mine what had brought me there, they took me to a back table where an old man with bloodshot eyes sat sullenly in front of a mug of beer. His name was Ota Rybář.

Ask him about the parachutists, they said. But the man seemed too far gone. *"Musíme ho naolejovat"* — We have to oil him — someone said. "Another beer," someone yelled. "You can all go to the devil," the old man said.

He'd been a young man, he said eventually, the night he saw them come down — not even forty. Back then he could still pee in less than half an hour.

Of course he did, he remembered it very well, every bit of it. He raised his heavy stein of beer, then put it down again. "America?" he said.

"Co si pamatuješ, Oto?" — What do you remember? — said a bear-like man at the table next to ours, who was leaning forward over his beer as though protecting it. A small, whiskered dog

with a face like a ferret was lying against his leg. Whenever I looked at it, it turned its head, as though ashamed of its predicament.

"Everything," said Ota Rybář.

I looked at the dog again. It looked away.

"Every-fucking-thing," said Ota Rybář.

"It was cold as hell that winter," Ota Rybář said. "Our village, Nehvízdy, is in the fields, and the wind blows like a bastard. Snow was everywhere.

"There was no wind that night. I was lying in bed next to my wife, who didn't snore yet then, and when I heard the plane I didn't think about it until I heard it come back around again. It sounded lower this time, and the dogs began to bark. That made me curious, and before I knew what I was doing I was pulling on my boots in the hall. I managed to get the ladder from the barn without making any noise and I set it against the roof and climbed up behind the chimney. I tried to be quiet because my youngest was sleeping right there, no more than a meter under my feet. And then I saw it, a shape coming down out of the sky. It was swinging back and forth like this, like a child in a playground. I lost sight of it behind the chimney, then found it again. I could see it plainly enough against the stars. It came down somewhere not far away.

"Well, I knew right away who it was, of course: we had heard rumors of parachutists — our boys, trained in England and dropped into the Protectorate — and I'll tell you right now, I nearly crapped myself. We'd managed to sit out the war all right until then. Keep our noses clean. What if someone saw me up there on my roof at three in the morning? I thought. How could I explain the snow scuffed off behind the chimney? Everyone would think I'd been signaling them. My legs began to shake so badly I had to wait a few minutes before I could make it back down the ladder. I took it and put it away and went back in the house and got into bed next to my wife and tried to sleep but I couldn't because I knew I would have to go out into the fields in the morning.

"I tossed and turned the rest of the night. I couldn't see any way out of it. I worked on the roads then, but a few weeks earlier I'd taken a second job as a gamekeeper, working for some rich factory owners who'd rented a hunting lodge a few kilometers away. Every morning I would go around with a big rucksack full of forage for the game. If I didn't go out that morning, people might get suspicious. Better to act as though everything was the same as always, and simply go about my business.

"So after breakfast the next morning I went out to the barn, loaded up, and set off. It was a beautiful morning but cold as shit. I didn't say anything to anyone about what I'd seen, of course. I was no fool. It was simple mathematics. Every person who knew something doubled your chances of being shot. And not just because they might blurt out something by accident. Any idiot could be an informer: some bastard who had never liked you, or thought you'd slept with his wife, or wanted to buy your field . . . I just put on my pack and went out.

"I found their tracks halfway across the field, about two hundred meters from a group of trees like a small island. It was quite a shock; I'd pretty much talked myself into believing I'd imagined the whole thing. I can't tell you what a strange sight they made, those two sets of tracks suddenly leading off across the snow. Any fool could see them. The snow had been disturbed and piled up in a kind of heap, and when I kicked at it, a rope tangled around my boot. I took off my pack and pretended to drop some forage in case anyone was watching from the village, then followed the tracks across the field toward the trees. Why? I don't know why. I think that somewhere in the back of my mind I just wanted to see them.

"Behind the woods the ground dropped away into an old, unused quarry. It was a pretty wild place, thick with briars and scrubby trees and in the summer there was a pond at the bottom and a cave where my boys used to piss around when they were kids, playing at bandits and whatnot. It's still there. And that's where I found them, at the bottom of the quarry: two men hardly older than my oldest, maybe twenty or twenty-two, pretending to study a map. They were ordinarily dressed, in old coats and boots. They had seen me. One of them, who was tall and slope-shouldered, had his right hand in his coat pocket. The other, a slim, dark-haired fellow, simply looked up from the map and nodded.

"I knew that I couldn't walk away, so I made my way down the hill toward them, slipping a bit in the snow. They watched me the whole way. How goes it, boys? I said as I came closer.

"They were doing a survey, the taller one began. There was talk about mining the quarry again.

"I nodded, but I could see right away that the other one knew I didn't believe it. I saw him look slowly up along the rim of the quarry to see if there was anyone else there. I knew I had to say something, and quickly, or they would just shoot me right there. I know who you are, boys, I blurted out. I found your parachutes in the snow. I covered them up for you.

"The tall one started to say something but the other one stopped him with his hand. I got the sense that he was some kind of superior. He didn't say anything. He just looked at me. What's in the pack? he said. Forage, I said, I can show you. He shook his head. You do this every morning? he asked me. Four times a week, I said. How long had I been doing it, he wanted to know. I told him. I'd needed a second job, I said. I had a big family. Did anyone else know about them? he wanted to know. I said I didn't think so.

"All this time he never took his eyes off me for a moment. All right, he said, and nodded at the hill behind me. You better be on your way before someone notices you're late.

"I can help you boys, I said. I swear to God, I'd had no idea I was going to say that. It just came out.

"You have a family, he said.

"I said it again: I can help you, I said. And that time I meant it."

"I learned later that they'd been trying to figure out where they were. It turned out that they'd been dropped at least twenty kilometers off course, the taller one told me. The pilot had miscalculated in the dark and brought them too close to Prague. They had a transmitter with them, which they protected like the goddamned Holy Grail. Over the next week I brought them blankets and bandages — it was bitter cold that whole time, and the taller one had hurt his foot coming down — and a small bottle of slivovitz and even a wedge of Christmas cake which I told my wife I'd eaten while everyone else was sleeping, which she bitched me out about. They asked me about the police in the village and a lot of other things — whether there were any troops moving about and such — and the quiet one gave me an automatic pistol in case something happened. I'd never held a pistol in my hand before. I carried it in my rucksack, and every morning when I came home from the fields I'd hide it in the barn in an old can under a handful of nails where no one could find it.

"Nothing happened for a few days. One morning I was making my way down the hill to see them, holding on to these ratty little birches that grew out of the rocks, when I noticed someone crouched against the cliff. I couldn't make out who it was — it was snowing hard — but I was sure he'd seen me, so I couldn't go back. I said to myself that as the gamekeeper I had the right to know who was about, so when I got closer I shouted, and he came out into the open. It was Baumann, the butcher. What the hell are you doing out here in all this? I said. I could hear my own heart in my chest.

"He'd been skating, Baumann said. Ten meters below us, the pond was frozen solid as a brick. The wind had blown most of the snow off.

"Where are your skates, then? I said, and because he was

afraid he got angry and said who the hell was I to be wandering about the country asking him questions and that he'd only meant that he'd come out to look at the pond and check the ice to see if he could bring his kids there, but as he was talking I saw him glance over my shoulder toward the cave the boys were staying in, and I knew he knew.

"I took the chance. So you know about them too? I said.

"He admitted he did, and we discovered that both of us had been bringing them food and information for days. Being careful men, they hadn't told either of us about the other one.

"After that I saw Baumann every day in the village, and our secret was something there between us. I didn't like it one bit. I'd known him since I was a kid. I'd never liked him — thought he had the makings of a real son of a bitch. My nerves were shot all to hell. I couldn't sleep.

"The parachutists stayed for a little less than two weeks. I heard later they moved on to a safe house in Šestajovice, and from there to Prague. But you know the rest. I had no idea they were Anthropoid — we'd never even heard of it then — or what they'd been sent to do. I wouldn't have believed it if I had. Who could have believed such a thing back then?"

"I remember the day it happened," interrupted the bear-like man at the other table. "We had the curtains closed to keep out the sun, and my old man came home early and closed the door and called my mother and said that there had been an attack on Heydrich's car up in Líbeň. 'God help those boys,' he said. I remember it because it was the first time I'd ever heard my old man mention God — my mother was the religious one in our family. And I remember my mother just pulled a chair out from under the dinner table and sat down on it sideways. 'God help us all,' she said."

"They were good boys," said Ota Rybář. Another beer had appeared in front of him and he took a long drink, then wiped the foam off his upper lip with his sleeve. "Funny — there are times even now when I find it hard to believe they're gone," he said. "I grew quite fond of them. After they'd left I wondered sometimes what became of them, but it wasn't until after the eighteenth that the pictures came out and we knew they'd all been killed in that church.

"Of course that's when things got really bad. Until then I'd been more or less all right. After the assassination, when the purges started, I was sure they'd come for me sooner or later. And after the thing in the church, it was worse. For a long time I waited for the knock on the door, but it never came, and then one day I realized that the only one who really knew my name, or that I'd had anything to do with them, was Baumann. As I said, I'd never liked him, what with that chickenshit mustache of his and his fat finger always on the scale. My wife claimed he was Jewish, but he wasn't, since he was still there in '42 when all the others had been taken. I can tell you this: it didn't make me like him any better to know that my life was in his hands. I actually thought of killing him. I could shoot him with the pistol, I thought, and no one would ever know. And who could blame me, really? He was the only link to us. By shooting him I'd be saving my family. It never occurred to me that he might be thinking the same thing."

Ota Rybář stopped. He seemed to have lost the thread of his story. He took a long drink of his beer. "Christ that's an ugly dog," he said.

"So what happened?" someone asked.

"How do you mean?"

"I mean what happened?"

"You want to know what happened?" said Ota Rybář. "I'll tell you what happened." He had been drinking for a while now. When he turned his head, it wobbled like a child's toy in need of tightening. "I'll tell you what happened," he said again. "When they came for him, the bastard kept his mouth shut and they never came for me. He was killed later, and I heard his whole family died at Mauthausen. The funny thing is that after I'd seen his name in the paper, even though I was sorry for it, I was able to breathe again for the first time in months."

He was silent. "That's it?" someone said after a while.

At that moment there was a loud crash at the bar — someone had knocked over a bottle — and a man laughed and the dog with the ferret's face stood up and then lay down again.

"What the hell was that?" said Ota Rybář.

And that was the end of the evening.

4

JUST OVER THREE YEARS AGO I FOUND MYSELF SITTING
on a bench near the white statue of Eliška Krásnohorská in
Karlovo náměstí, the square my mother had talked about the day
we planted flowers together at our cabin on the lake almost forty
years earlier. It was a still, sullen day in June, overcast and dull.
A warm wind was blowing from the east. Three kids were riding
their skateboards over a ramp they had set up on the sidewalk
under a tree with branches so huge they appeared deformed,
like thick, twisted ropes; the largest of these, a child-thick tentacle running straight out from the main trunk as though hoping to
strike out on its own, had very nearly sunk to the ground of its
own weight, and been propped up on a short steel crutch.

I had long before given up hope of learning anything conclu-
sive, if in fact I had ever hoped for that. In any case, there had
been nothing to see; the door was closed. A war had come. My
mother had loved someone who had died. She'd married my father. On a bench across from me, two old women leaned toward
each other holding their pocketbooks on their laps with both
hands. Behind them, on the avenue, a tram slowed to a stop.
The bell rang, the doors closed, the tram left. A store behind the
stop was selling out its stock of shoes. The one next to it sold
electronics.

The wind brought the slightly sickening smell of the flowers in their beds, then a gust of fumes, then the sudden coolness of plaster. It had happened right here; the entire square, I'd been told, had been cordoned off. The partisans had been hidden in the church whose cross I could almost see from where I sat. On a June morning like this one, all seven of them had died there. It told me nothing. There was no entrance; the past was closed for inventory.

The trolley bell rang again. In one of my father's stories, a hunter shooting at a bird in a dark wood was surprised to hear the arrow strike something with a dull, metallic clang. Going to investigate, he parted the branches of a thick pine to reveal an entire town, abandoned a century ago to the plague. His arrow, missing the bird, had hit the village bell tower.

One of the skateboarders drumrolled onto the wooden ramp, spun and missed, ran three quick steps.

I was watching another trolley move past the storefronts when a small white dog trotted up and began to sniff my leg. I could see his owner, a blocky old man in a suit, like a hydrant dressed for church, hurrying up the walk. *"Bud' hodnej, Karlíčku. Nezlob"* — Be good, Karlíček — he said to the dog in a tone full of good-humored sympathy for Karlíček's winsome ways and not intended to be taken to heart. When Karlíček started to sniff my crotch I gently pushed him away, and Pavel Čertovský and I began to talk. So I was from America. He had been to America once, to visit his brother in Chicago. It had been very hot there. Most young people these days didn't care about history, he said, when I explained to him, as best I could, why I'd come to Prague in the first place — it was all gadgetry and computers now. Why, just the other day he had read in the newspaper that 42 percent of students entering the gymnasium thought Charter 77 was a rock-and-roll group. "Come here, Karlíček," he called out irritably, as though the dog were somehow responsible.

And then he told me, yet again, all the things I already knew: That there had been seven of them. That they had been trained in England by the RAF. That they had parachuted back into the

Protectorate to assassinate Reichsprotektor Reinhard Heydrich, who I no doubt knew had been Hitler's personal favorite and likely successor as well as the architect of the Final Solution. That thirteen days after Heydrich died, in the early morning of June 18, the group, hidden in the crypt of the Church of Sts. Cyril and Metoděj on Řesslova Street, had found themselves surrounded by two full divisions of Wehrmacht and three hundred SS — betrayed by one of their own, a man named Čurda. That even though the situation was utterly hopeless — they were outnumbered three hundred to one — they had fought bravely, desperately, three from the rectory, the other four from the crypt itself. That the three in the rectory had been killed almost immediately but that the others had held on for hours even after the fire hoses had been pushed in through the little window on Řesslova Street and the water in the crypt had begun to rise, until they came down to their last four bullets, which they had been saving for themselves.

He remembered the morning they died, Pavel Čertovský said. He waved his hand to indicate the half-kilometer-long square we were sitting in, or perhaps the entire city. "The whole square, from there, to there, all the way down to Večná Street, was cordoned off, a four-hundred-meter radius in all directions from the church. They had guards watching the sewers letting out into the Vltava . . . they thought of everything. Still, the boys held out longer than anyone would have thought."

"You saw all this?" I asked.

"My parents lived right over there," said Pavel Čertovský. My father and I watched the whole thing from the kitchen window. My mother just cried the whole time. There wasn't much to see, to be honest, but you could hear the gunshots — *pock, pock-pock* — and I remember the fire truck coming up a side street and the puff of smoke when they dynamited the rectory. People guessed right away what it was about but of course there was nothing to be done — God himself couldn't have saved those boys that morning." Pavel Čertovský shook his head. "I prefer dogs to people," he said. And he scratched the dog, who had laid his head on his owner's lap, on the top of his nose, and the dog looked up at his face with an expression of adoration and sorrow that reminded me of fifteenth-century paintings of Christ looking up from the cross to a merciful heaven.

"After that it all went to hell, basically," Čertovský went on. "The day after they killed Kubiš and Gabčík and the rest, we heard they'd gotten one of the main figures of the Resistance in Prague, a woman named Moravcová. She was able to get to some poison; her husband and son had it much harder." He paused. "But you probably already know all of this," he said.

"Some," I said. "Tell me, has this place changed much since then?"

"The trees are bigger, of course," said Pavel Čertovský. "And a few of the buildings are different." He paused, as though gathering something. "It seemed happier somehow. You have to understand," he said quickly. "I was twelve years old; everything seemed possible. Huge things were happening, every day something new was happening, but it all seemed to be occurring somewhere else, to someone else, not me. I can't explain it. I can't defend it. It was as if things had no gravity. Terrible things happened — you saw them happen — but then they'd just float away." He shook his head. "Youth. In old age you go around creaking like an old garbage truck loaded down with shit, if you'll pardon me.

"But listen to me running on — here, let me tell you something you may actually find interesting. If you go back to the church," he said, indicating the direction of the church with his head, "go to the back room of the museum where they have that wall of photographs and look at the fourth from the right, three rows down. It shows the crowd gathered around Gabčík's body that morning after they'd dragged it out into the street. If you look closely in the bottom right corner, between the legs of the man with the camera taking a picture of Gabčík's face, you'll see a foot with a white sock and a brown sandal." He patted my knee conspiratorially. "That's me," he said, "and right next to . . . *Karlíčku, přestaň!*" — Stop that! — he called to the dog, who had wandered over to the huge supported branch of the oak and was peeing on the crutch. The dog lowered his leg. "What was I saying?"

But he was an old man, and had forgotten. "Funny," he said. "I can't remember four seconds back — I've already forgotten your name, I'm afraid — but I can see every detail from half a century ago. Every absurdity. I remember that our dog had to go that morning — dogs have no appreciation for history — and my father decided to take him out. This was still during the siege of the church, but well before we knew what it was really about. My father and I went out through the cellar to the back, then walked away from the square to the churchyard of St. Katherine's on Viničná Street, just up from where the hospital is now, and the dog promptly did his business. I remember that as we were leaving he stopped to drink from a bucket someone had left on the walk, and I saw a couple on a bench to the right of the big wooden doors there; they were both quite young — beautiful young people, really — and she was holding him and he was shaking like a child and it wasn't until that very moment that I had a sense of how bad the thing happening four blocks away really was."

But he had to be going, he said, and we said our goodbyes and he and Karlíček walked off together past the skateboarders who stood about sullenly, holding their boards under their arms until they had passed.

A gray day. The wind, a warm breath, moved the leaves, lifted the dirty curls of one of the skateboarders out of his eyes, slid a paper bag a short distance along the walk. And sitting there I could suddenly feel them — the facts, the dates, the stories, the couple on the bench in the churchyard — gathering like iron filings around an invisible magnet, suggesting a shape.

5

THEY HAD BEEN HERE, ALL OF THEM, AND NOW THEY were gone. What could match the wonder of that? They'd leaned against a sun-warmed wall on a particular afternoon in June, scratched their noses with the backs of their wrists, pulled an oversoft apricot in half with their fingers. And now they were gone. I'd come to love two of them: their voices, should I some-how hear them again in this world, would be more familiar to me than my own. But others had known them. I never had, really.

Someone once said that at the end of every life is a full stop, and death could care less if the piece is a fragment. It is up to us, the living, to supply a shape where none exists, to rescue from the flood even those we never knew. Like beggars, we must patch the universe as best we can.

1942

A Novel

I IMAGINE THEY DIDN'T SPEAK MUCH THAT FIRST HOUR
or so as they made their way deeper into the forest, up dank
sloping paths where rainwater had left shores of pine needles
like sea wrack in the dirt, past piles of logs spotted white where
their branches had been lopped close to the trunk, then off the
trails entirely. Damp, sweet gloom, resiny and wet, then a shot of
strong sun, as from a different world, then shadow and sun,
shadow and sun. A Gypsy wagon, its wood swollen fat with water, stood in the middle of a dense patch of woods, barred in by
ten-year-old pines. Covered in needles, its canvas gouged by
branches, it seemed to have been dropped from the sky. They
passed through an old abandoned orchard, then made their way
along the edge of a marshy field that might have had a lake at its
center, its reeds loud with birds.

His name was Tomáš Bém, the surname just one step removed
from the umlaut and the German "Böhm," and he came from
Vyškov, a village twenty kilometers north of Brno. He was twenty-
two years old that summer, a man of average height, not particularly handsome. There was something concentrated about
him, as if the energy of a larger man, and the bitterness of an
older one, had been forced to fit that slimmer frame. The day

they met — a hot, still day in late July of 1941 — he took the early train from Brno to Žd'ár nad Sázavou, then a bus that bounced interminably over bad roads as women fanned themselves with whatever papers they happened to have handy and men sat sweating stolidly into their collars. When the bus stopped at a small wrought-iron bridge near a country market he got out, shouldered his rucksack, swung the tin cup that hung from a leather thong around his neck over his shoulder, and began to walk. As he made his way up the long sloping road he could feel it, tapping lightly on his back. Ten minutes later he was in the forest.

He walked steadily for three hours along vast, empty fields, through the shade of pine forests mossed and tufted with thick, soft grass, stopping only to eat his lunch on a pile of fresh-cut pines that someone had stacked by the road. Sap bled from the cuts. He watched two women, only their upper bodies visible above the shimmering wheat, cross the field that began just on the other side of the pines. There had to be a path there. Or a road. One of them suddenly skipped ahead, her hands flying up like a girl's. Perhaps she had jumped over a washout in the road. The road angled down the slope of a hill. He watched them until they disappeared, sinking into the grain.

Two yellow butterflies, drifted in from the edge of the field where hundreds like them fluttered in the weeds, settled on the end of a log and walked in small, tight circles. *Žlut'ásci*. His kid sister Majka had once caught ten of them in a jar because he'd told her she couldn't, then forgotten them in the sun.

Shouldering his rucksack, he jumped off the logs and walked a short distance back the way he had come to where a deep seam of overgreen grass marked a stream trickling through the forest loam. Ten meters off the path was a stone basin. A metal cup hung on a hook. He drank, then poured the second cup slowly over his head. Behind him he could hear the wagon go by — the clop of steel on dirt and stone, the quick creak of wood. He let it pass without turning around.

He'd memorized the directions to the house. A man from the factory had come up to him as he walked to the train after his shift, told him the directions and how to announce himself, then veered off up the hill. They would be expecting him, he'd said. He was to put nothing on paper — ever — unless expressly told to do so. The leader's name was Ladislav Kindl.

He appeared at the back door of the house just after dark with a rucksack on his back and the tin cup hanging from his neck half full of raspberries. The others were already there, sitting awkwardly around the living room, bits of fern stuck in the straps of their sandals. Kindl, whose house it was, introduced him. He nodded hello, then took a chair off to the side and listened. My mother, who was twenty-one that summer, sat next to Kindl's wife on the sofa. She had come alone. My father, who was not yet my father but just a man she had come to care for, was sick in Brno.

It was the way he listened maybe, as though attending to every word being said, but from somewhere else. Or the way he would look at someone, straight on, until he had seen what he wanted. There was a kind of mild, innocent ruthlessness about it, though he himself seemed neither mild nor innocent nor particularly ruthless. He sat leaning forward on the uncomfortable chair Kindl and his wife kept in the pantry for getting preserves down from the shelves, strangely immovable, like a man looking out of a statue, and yet when he moved he moved with a smooth youthful abruptness, a complete lack of adjustment or preparation, that was somehow disconcerting. It was as if he were on fire inside, had been on fire for years, but with no way of getting at the flames, had simply learned to live with it. She looked at him, at his hands folded over each other, at his short black hair, his mouth. There was something slightly misshapen about the face, she decided. Something about him irritated her, she couldn't quite say what.

. . .

By the time they left the house that night the moon was up and a warm wind was moving the wheat. The others had already gone: some toward Vrchovice, others toward Havlíčkův Brod, three weaving down the road to the car they'd left at the inn, their arms around one another's shoulders, singing.

There had been a great deal to discuss. Radio contact between the government in exile and Prague had been reestablished, Kindl had informed them. President Beneš himself had communicated his gratitude from London. The expansion of existing cells of resistance in Bohemia and Moravia was now of paramount importance. London had instructed them to acquire a copy of the poem "Enthusiasm," by Svatopluk Čech, in the World Library edition. It would be used to set up a secure code. Teams of parachutists trained by the RAF were to be dropped into the Protectorate. Every effort would have to be made to help them. They would have to be provided with the addresses of safe houses and the code names of partisans. They would need identity cards, police declaration forms, work papers, ration books. And so on.

Kindl walked out to the back fence and stood there for a while, smoking a cigarette in the dark. Nothing. No light at all. He could barely make out the silhouettes of the houses across the road. It was odd to think of the entire Protectorate — ten thousand homes, towns, cities — slipping into darkness every night, disappearing. Three years of blackouts. He looked again at the blocky shapes across the road. He didn't like them — it was easier to see out of a dark house. Still, it was late. He waited. The wind moved. There would be mushrooms tomorrow. Christ, it was a beautiful night.

He leaned over a bit to see around the edge of the house. Before the war he could see the electric street lamp by the inn, two hundred meters away. Moths would be flying in and out of the light. He started another cigarette, then stubbed it out on the wood. He didn't like that moon. Or the windows he knew were there.

He had oiled the hinges two days earlier, so when he lifted the latch from its bed and pushed open the low wooden gate it swung soundlessly until it thumped back against the fence. They came out of the pantry then, walking quickly: Svíčka, the girl, and three steps behind her, moving as easily as if he were going out for a game of tennis, the new man, Bém. There was something he didn't like about him — he couldn't say what exactly. That green shawl she'd worn around her neck that evening — or not a shawl, more like a big *šátek* of some sort — had looked old-fashioned, like something her grandmother might have given her. Strange how good it had looked with her hair.

A warm night. From the shadow of the house he watched the three of them slip through the gate, then hurry across the open ground, their number doubled by the moon. Svíčka was a good man — rational, methodical. Rumor had it that his wife knew nothing whatsoever about his activities, that he'd thought it best to hide them from her, the way another man would an affair. The forest was right there, narrow at one end, then widening out. It looked like a strip of black fabric torn from the sky and the field. Kindl breathed in a chestful of air, then slowly let it out.

The door opened quietly behind him. "Come in the house," he heard her say from the dark.

"I'll be right in."

He had heard a rumor that Bém was going to England. He wondered how he would go. From Gdynia, probably, to one of the French ports. He would have gone too, once.

"It's late. I'm tired."

"So go to bed if you're tired."

They were there now. He could barely make them out against the wheat. Svíčka was still in the lead. The girl was holding her shoulder bag to her side to keep it from swinging. He'd seen her looking at the new man. It was too bad, really. He'd liked the other one better. He hoped it wouldn't cause any difficulties.

The wheat was a low, pale wall. He watched them come up to it, then disappear, one by one.

AS THEY CROSSED THE OPEN GROUND AND STARTED UP the path toward the wheat field, my mother could hear nothing: Svíčka's steps, her own breathing, the slight chuff of her bag against her clothes. Nothing else. It was as though he had simply disappeared. And yet she knew he was there. She felt shaky, overdrawn, but absolutely alert. The moon, the scratch of the crickets — she noticed everything. Svíčka's legs looked like a wishbone. She wanted to laugh.

As they came up to the edge of the field it reached out to meet them — a sigh of sun-warmed grain in their faces — and then they were in, plunging arms forward like divers into that close, pale world. The moon was everywhere. It scored the double of every stalk, every seed-filled head on her legs, her arms, her shifting bag. A million soft little hands scratched and tugged and brushed her face — but why couldn't she hear him? Two meters ahead of her, his hands up and his head turned slightly to the side, Svíčka shifted to another row. She knew what he was doing, looking for spaces, trying to walk as much as possible between the grain. It wouldn't work. She had walked a thousand fields before this one. She shifted with him, listening. Nothing. She resisted the temptation to turn around, concentrated on following. Why had he decided to leave with them? They would have been better off without him.

And suddenly the edge of the field and then the shadow of

the trees and they were out. Not far off, along the edge of the field, stood a hunter's stand of cut pine, like a chair on stilts. She turned around now just as he stepped out of the grain, behind her. She couldn't see his face but she could see the shape of him — his hair, his shoulders, the rucksack with its belts and straps. He walked past her and squatted down with his back against a tree, the rucksack still on his back. When the match flared she saw his face: the nose, the black hair, the impatient mouth.

He paused, holding the cigarette down by the ground, then, as if remembering, brought it up to his mouth in a big arc. She had thought he was smiling.

He was holding something out to them with his left hand.

"Go ahead," she heard him say. "Take two."

"Where did you get these?" Svíčka said.

"Don't ask," he said.

Her eyes were adjusting to the darkness now. Here and there in the forest behind them she could see spears of light cutting down through the pines, and farther off, where the trees opened, a well-lit space, like a small room between the trees, and then another, and another. The air moved, bringing the dank, loamy smell of roots, and right after it the hot, strong smell of horse and pig and oats. There would be mushrooms tomorrow. Even now they were prodding up through the loam and the black needles, their fat brown heads capped with bits of turf like the soft felt hats of cardinals.

They talked about which way to go. Vrchovice was too close, they agreed. Best to put some distance between themselves and the house. The logging roads and the trails were clearly marked, Svíčka said, and they had at least four hours of darkness left. He smiled. "It's eighteen kilometers. If we walk hard and skip the picnic we can make it to Žd'ár by dawn."

He turned to the other one. "Are you familiar with this area?"

"No."

"Then I suggest you take the train from Mělkovice. It is only two kilometers from Žd'ár, and there is a train for Brno at five-oh-five." He turned to my mother. "Ivana, you and I can leave from Žd'ár. I have a train to Prague at six, and there's another for Brno at six-forty-five. Does that sound all right?"

She said she thought it was a good idea.

"Then we're agreed."

Bém stood. A single gesture: abrupt, unhurried. There had been no adjustment of weight, no release of breath, no scrape of leather against bark. He was suddenly just standing. And my mother, sitting with her back against a huge, rough-barked pine, saw him turn to adjust a strap by his neck, and something about the way he turned at that moment opened a door inside her. It was as though she were seeing something she'd known and forgotten, something she'd loved a hundred years ago. It made no sense.

"What time do you have to be at the factory?" she heard Svíčka asking.

"I don't," the other said.

"I'm sorry?"

"I don't have to be at the factory."

"I don't think I follow you."

"I'm not returning to Brno."

"Is that right? Does Kindl know about this?"

"He knows."

Svíčka paused. "I'm sorry. I'll need to know what happened. You understand why I have to ask."

"I do. What always happens. We were interfering, slowing the work."

"Someone informed on you in other words."

"One of the lathes had been put out of commission. Some good citizen wanted to make the quota."

"Forgive me — why didn't the Gestapo arrest you then?" said Svíčka.

"I was out sick."

"They didn't come to your home?"

"They came. I wasn't there."

"Why didn't they wait until all the saboteurs were present at the factory the next day. Or the day after. They're not usually given to such errors."

"I don't know. I've asked myself that question."

"Did you find an answer?"

"No."

"And that satisfies you?"

"No. It doesn't."

Taking off his glasses, Svíčka breathed gently on the lenses, then rubbed them with a handkerchief. "This complicates things."

"Does it?"

For just a moment, a tiny moon appeared in one of the lenses, then disappeared. "I'm afraid it does, yes. We have to assume they're after you."

"They're after all of us."

"There's a difference," said Svíčka quietly.

Bém took a long drag of his cigarette, then turned it into the dirt with his heel. "You're right," he said. "I should go." He looked at my mother, sitting with her arms around her knees in the dark. "Goodbye," he said, "I'm sorry we . . ." He nodded, then turned to go.

It was Svíčka who stopped him. "Wait," he said — and that word was the pivot on which everything turned. Everything. Or maybe not. Maybe she came to see it as the thing that only made visible what had been coming their way forever, calmly measuring its steps even as they played and grew, fought and lost, separated now by fifty kilometers, now by five, even as my father and I waited patiently in the wings, as the theater began to darken . . . Maybe that one word simply served to flush the situation into the open so it could breathe and leap before being run into the ground like a crippled stag.

"Wait," Svíčka said, and the other stopped and turned in a

white stripe of light that cut him shoulder to thigh like a bando-lier. It was night, Svíčka said. A weekday. They could cover the first eighteen kilometers together, then separate at the turnoff for Mělkovice.

They would be safer alone, the other said.

"Nonsense," Svíčka said. "Everyone would be safer alone — don't you agree?" he asked my mother. Besides, it was well after midnight, he said. No one but the devil would be out in the forest that late.

As they set off along the perimeter of the field, my mother turned around. In the woods behind them the changing angle of the moon had erased entire rooms and expanded others into great misshapen halls filled with one-legged tables and elfin chairs, richly upholstered with moss.

The logging road was long and straight, like a road in a dream, and they walked hard for the first hour, passing crossroads where logs as thick as men had been piled head-high in the ditch. Eventually a stream joined them. They could hear it burbling to itself in the dark, running through the grassy tunnels that cut under the road, then back. When it passed beneath them a third time Svíčka said they had to watch for the trail, and when they found the thumb-sized marker on the pine, its white frame barely visible in the shadows, Bém stepped up to it and lit a match, cupping the flare in his hands, and she saw the blue.

He looked up the mossy little track, veined with roots, that meandered off into the dark. "You say this will save us time?"

"Kindl said it was considerably shorter," said Svíčka.

"It is," my mother said.

Bém turned toward my mother. "You know these woods?"

My mother nodded. She had picked mushrooms here with her father when she was a child. The blue would stay small for two or three kilometers, she said, hardly more than a game trail, then widen. They would have to be careful — there were branching trails in the open woods, and one section led along the edge of an open field — but it would take six or seven kilometers off the distance by road.

They should stop and think, Svíčka argued. It would be slow going. They would have to stop at every marker. And six kilometers wasn't much. If they stayed on the logging road, they could make up the time without the risk of getting lost.

"You think we should take the trail?" Bém asked, looking at my mother.

"I do."

"Then lead on," he said, stepping aside.

And she did. Here and there, between the trees, or on a long slope spotted and cut with light, she could see her father in his black boots, walking with the slight stoop of the mushroom hunter, his hands behind his back like a schoolmaster listening to sums, or prodding beneath the grass with his stick. The pond called Vápenice appeared to the right, a scattering of stars between the pines. Listen, her father said. It was March, dusk, spits of crusty snow still holding on in the shade. Far off, a riot of croaking, ecstatic and desperate. You can hear the pond before you see it, he said. It passed now on the right, a small black circle, its surface half covered with pine needles.

And then the ferns, reaching for their legs, another marker, another match. Blue. He nodded to her, indicated with his hand. They went on. A long downward slope through stands of thick oaks, a different dark, and then the birches like scratches or matchsticks and finally the vast, low, shore-like edge of the fields, mustard and barley, open to the sky. What was he thinking? Was he looking at her? The way he moved — the long smooth stride, the pull of his hips . . . that hair looked like it had been cut with a pair of garden shears. She led them quickly along the field, then across a narrow wooded peninsula filled with boulders, and suddenly they were back in the cool, dark smell of the pines, and the wooden sign nailed to the tree at the crossroads said Mělkovice, four kilometers; Žd'ár nad Sázavou, seven. She looked for the name of the town they had come from, to see how far they had come, but it wasn't there.

He was looking down the road, distracted. What could she have been thinking? This was ridiculous. She was going home, to Brno.

"Can you give me a light?" Svíčka said. Bém lit another match. Svíčka looked at his watch. It was almost three-thirty. Bém swung the rucksack off his back and took out a tin canteen of water.

"So tell us, what did you do before all this?" Svíčka asked. "Before the war, I mean."

"I was a fitter." He offered my mother the canteen of water.

"Good work?"

"I didn't mind it. Not what I would have chosen."

"What would you have chosen?" my mother asked.

It seemed almost like a smile. "Something different," he said after a moment.

"Can I ask you something?" Svíčka said.

"You can ask."

Svíčka took the canteen from my mother, took a sip of water, then handed it back to Bém. "When they came to look for you, what happened to your family?"

"I have no idea."

"I'm sorry," Svíčka said.

"Thank you."

"Perhaps. . . ?"

"Perhaps."

Svíčka shook his head, then shrugged into his rucksack. "And so now you're going abroad," he said. "Well, *audentes fortuna iuvat*, as the saying goes — fortune belongs to the daring."

Bém looked at him for a moment.

"We'll see," he said.

• • •

They came to the turnoff just after four. The air above the fields had begun to change, tracing over the edges of things, darkening the horizon of woods. Mělkovice was just down the road. Bém could take the early train, Svíčka said; he would go on from Žd'ár. Since men were mostly the ones leaving early for the factories, my mother would wait in the forest for an hour so as to avoid drawing attention to herself, then follow. She still had the sack for the mushrooms? Good. She should pick some. Svíčka took out his watch and opened it, holding it close to his face. He nodded at Bém. It was time.

A quick good luck and he was gone, walking fast, his slim form disappearing against the trees before he had reached the curve. Nothing. There had been nothing. My mother and Svíčka walked on together toward Žd'ár. She would be all right? She had everything she needed? She barely heard him. He said goodbye and left.

When she couldn't see him anymore she took the net bag out of her pocket and unfolded the handles and smoothed the creases out of the mesh against her leg, mechanically running her hand over and over the wrinkled mesh, then turned and started back into the forest. She could feel something trembling inside her. She felt soft somehow, hollow . . . For a moment she thought about my father — his face, his hands on her . . .

It was still dark when she came to the turnoff. There was no one there. The moon was down, the forest strangely silent. She stepped over the choked little ditch and walked into the woods, picking her way between the stumps and the broken branches that blocked her way. She had an hour, maybe more. An easy walk. She knew the station well: the low wall across the tracks, the pruned trees along the road, that *hospoda* where she and her father had seen the dwarf sitting on the bench. Some mushrooms would go well tonight. My God, what a fool she was. There was one! Even in the gloom she could see the fat pale stem. She rocked it gently out of the humus and put it in her bag.

She could almost see. The sky overhead, blue-black, was beginning to fill up with light. What had she been thinking? There had been no sign, no understanding. Another! Funny how you could see them so well against the soil. And so arrogant, in his way. And here she was, stumbling about the woods. She could actually feel her heart. She stopped, smiled to herself, then spun and smashed the half-full bag against the trunk of a tree. As she turned to go, a small, hard branch clawed deep into her calf. She pulled up her dress. She could see the gouge welling up with blood. She held her hand to her leg for a moment, then wiped it on the moss. It was time to go.

My mother picked up the net bag of smashed mushrooms. The woods were graying quickly now, the mist sweeping through the trees in long tatters like steam over a pot of water about to boil. She was tired. She had misunderstood. Anyone could misunderstand. There was nothing to think about.

He was standing at the turnoff by the grassy V where the roads split, his rucksack by his feet like a dog.

She walked right up to him. She could see him breathing. He shook his head slightly. "I couldn't . . . ," he began, and it was as though she'd known that voice forever.

"I know," she said.

"I couldn't seem to leave you," he said, then added quickly, as if he'd surprised himself, "I'm sorry, I shouldn't . . ."

"I know," she said.

They didn't touch. They stood there looking at each other for a moment, trying to understand that they were both here, that this was happening, and then he bent and picked up the rucksack and slipped it over his shoulder. "Which way?" he said quietly. And she turned without a moment's hesitation, without a single thought for the world she'd known or the woman she'd been, and led him into the forest.

ON ONE LEVEL, THEY KNEW WHAT THEY WERE DOING:
losing themselves in the forest, in a mazework of paths leading
off from roads already knee-high in grass, passing through the
gates of gamekeepers' wooden fences and around the edges of
abandoned fields and small black ponds where butterflies slept
in the sun slanting through the trees. It had been done before,
after all, though with mixed results.

Ten months later, when she saw him step out of the trolley
on Náměstí Míru so much thinner than she remembered him,
when she saw the new, rimless glasses and the newspaper under
his arm and the briefcase in his hand and watched him make his
way through the crowd holding his hat to his head as though that
would help with the rain, not seeing her standing there in front
of him as fixed and still as the cobbles under her feet because it
simply wasn't possible that it should be him, that she should be
seeing that face, that mouth; when they wandered that one flying hour out to the vineyards and then down to the square,
where they sat helplessly on a bench in the drizzle before he got
on another trolley and left without having told her how he came
to be back in the country or what he was doing in Prague or
where he would be; when she ran into him yet again later that
June, as though fortune would have it no other way, and they

145

spent that oppressive dying day and the night that followed as in a fevered dream wandering from Vinohrady to the cemetery, from the cemetery to Líbeň, from Líbeň to the Vltava where they saw the yellow carp floating in the foam among the boards and the garbage . . . when those days came, and all the days after, *these* were the days she remembered.

She remembered waking from a drugged sleep that first afternoon to find him looking at her. The sun had moved on. Next to her, a shirt hung over three curved sticks pushed into the ground, a shade for her face. It lifted quickly, as though someone were peeking beneath, then fell.

"Thank you," she said.

He nodded. "You're welcome. I felt somehow responsible."

"Did they teach you that in the Scouts?"

An almost-smile, a flash of that crooked tooth. "I don't remember the Scouts being much help in situations like this."

"And have there been many . . . situations like this?"

"No," he said. "There haven't."

"That's good to know."

"Four or five at the very most."

"I'm glad."

They looked at each other for what seemed like a long time.

"Can you tell me what's happening here?" she said at last.

He shook his head. "No." Reaching over, he caught a strand of her hair on the back of his fingers and moved it off her forehead. "All I know is that I can't leave right now."

A high breeze was playing with the light on the grass. My mother could hear the stream. There was an afternoon slant to the light.

"I should get dressed," she said.

"No," he said. "Never."

He watched her dress, raising her hips, slipping her skirt up over her knees. Reaching around, she brought the ends of her hair in front of her face and began looking through it. "What will Mother think?" she said.

"Let me do that," he said, and moving against her, he began to pick the bits of grass and leaves out of her hair. She could still feel him, the sweet shock of him, pushing inside her. She could feel his hands moving through the heavy mass of her hair, combing out the strands. Her scalp was still slightly damp along the hairline. She could feel it cooling.

"How long do you think we have?" she said.

"A few days."

"Just pull on it — you don't have to be so gentle."

"I thought I *was* pulling at it."

"And then you have to go."

"I do. Sorry — there's a knot here."

"For how long?"

His fingers paused for a moment, though they might have just been working out a tangle. "I don't know. A year. Maybe less."

"Just pull on it," she said.

"You won't have any hair left."

"I'll live with it."

"All right."

"I need to tell you something," she said. "Not for you. For myself."

"Tell me, then."

"I've been seeing someone. For about a year now. In Brno."

"I expected there would be someone."

"That doesn't bother you?"

"It doesn't surprise me."

"It doesn't bother you either?"

"No." And then: "A little."

She turned around to look at him.

"Done," he said, gently brushing off the collar of her blouse. "Mother will never suspect a thing."

"It doesn't matter anymore. Any of it. Do you believe that?"

"I do," he said. He reached for her hand, began rolling the knuckles with his thumb. "Tell me the truth — can you do this?"

"Can you stay?"

He nodded. "For a while."

"Then I can do anything," she said.

"It's dangerous," he said.

"I know that," my mother said, and then, feeling his hand: "How did you get this?"

And he told her about the wine glass he'd stepped on while wading along the shore of a carp pond as a boy: how he'd felt a kind of tender, caving crack, as if he'd stepped on a thin-walled shell, and how he'd reached down to feel what he couldn't see and understood the moment the blood plumed up out of his hand, and listening to him she felt an absurd rush of anger toward the nameless drunk who had thrown his glass into the pond and at the same time a small thrill at owning this thing, this knowledge.

They walked all that afternoon, slightly giddy from making love, their arms around each other's waist despite the heat. She could feel his hipbone under her hand, the slip and clench of the muscle, the wetness of his shirt. And though it might have been more comfortable for them to walk apart, they didn't separate for a long time, struck alike by the comfort of their stride, the sudden pleasure of fronting the world together, neither one realizing that they were a contagion upon this world, that as they stood at the crossroads or came upon the woman with the basket on her arm standing at the edge of the forest cutting away the bad parts of a mushroom with a small knife, it was already a part of them, turning whenever they turned, touching whatever they touched. They knew nothing. They walked down long forest roads between grassy ditches filled with tannin-brown water, listening to the frogs shriek and leap from the narrow banks as the sunlight tilted toward evening, and for the rest of her life my mother would remember passing a lonely little pond and glimpsing a man, as in a dream, neatly dressed in a suit and tie, sitting on a chair he'd set up by the shore as though expecting a waiter to bring him a glass of wine. But by then the scene would have a different cast — the future had tainted the memory, the absurd had taken the tiny step toward nightmare — and the thing they had laughed at now laughed at them.

She spent years trying to keep the memory of their days together free of irony, blowing off the fine dust of death. She failed. History and time were too much, even for her. How could she erase the fact that even as she walked next to him that first afternoon listening to the straps of his rucksack tap gently against the leather, the gods were already slapping their thighs and heaving with mirth, having glimpsed how perfectly the thing would work: how it would turn, slowly at first, then with gathering speed, whipping around to strike down precisely the most selfless, the most brave — better still, striking those who, like care workers during the plague years, had by their own decency chosen themselves. Bém would become known. His contacts, however accidental, would be traced. And it would be their love that made it possible.

By the time they came out of the fields into the village of Dobrá Voda, the shadow of the churchyard wall had reached across the road. A bird was calling from the oak as they passed under its branches. They crossed a small stone bridge and started toward the town. On a side road a boy with a flapping shirttail slapped at a hoop with a stick and ran after it, while another, behind him, tried to balance on his bicycle while standing still. *"Tak pojd' už!"* — Come on, already! — the one with the hoop called out behind him without turning around.

She knew there would be no store here, that if there were one it would be closed, that if it weren't closed it would be empty. But a store was not what they were seeking necessarily. A woman with a pitchfork would do. Or a man hitting a cow on the rump with a stick, or a fisherman on a folding stool.

They passed the churchyard, the steeple, the charnel house with its wrought-iron cross and skull rising over the red, split-tile wall, then a black pond, already still with evening. The town seemed strangely empty. A bell began to ring.

When the man in the wagon came around the turn Bém let go of my mother's hand and stepped into the road and the man twitched the reins and the horse shook its head and stopped. She watched him as he talked to the old man with the brambly eyebrows who sat leaning forward, elbows on his knees, the reins loose in his brown, thick-fingered hands. So this was how he was with the world! She felt an odd sense of ownership, as though his manner, his way, were also hers now. Something she had on her side. No idle conversation, no explanations or apologies, no observations about the weather. He simply wished the man a good evening and asked him whether he knew where they might buy some food.

The other did not seem to mind the directness at all. What did they need? A small dog, lying by his feet, stood and stretched its back like a cat. "Lehni," he said. The dog lay down.

Whatever anyone could spare for a fair price: some bread, a few eggs, a bit of sugar or fat. It didn't really matter.

The man nodded. The neck, the heavy shoulders — there was a stillness about him, she thought. The stillness of an anvil, or a shovel leaning against a wall in the dark.

If the lady didn't mind riding in the wagon, he said, looking straight ahead between the reins as though talking about someone else, he would see what they could do. There wasn't much. And he waited, not turning around, till he had felt them climb into the empty bed of the wagon, then moved his right hand and the horse began to walk.

A half loaf of bread, two dozen apricots, a small jar of milk. Half a kilo of fatty pork cuts and a few spoonfuls of lard. She would remember it for forty years.

. . .

150

As they rode up the grassy path toward the plain, plaster-sided farmhouse, a tall angular woman with a dark purple stain on her face and ear which looked from a distance like an odd loop of hair came out of the barn, wiping her hands on a cloth. They had nothing left, she said. They had nothing left — he knew that. Just quotas they couldn't fill. They were being bled like pigs.

"*Jirko, bud' ticho*," said the old man. Be quiet.

Not that she would begrudge the Wehrmacht anything. She knew how much they needed her eggs. *Kraft durch Arbeit* — strength through work. Others' work.

They were standing on the dirt now, the dog sniffing at their legs. Across the road, a woman in a light-colored housedress was calling someone named Marie to dinner. A breath of cooler air, as from somewhere underground, passed through the yard and was gone. They were sorry to have troubled them, my mother said. They knew how things were these days.

The old man, as though his task were done, had begun un-hitching the wagon.

"You're from these parts," the woman said, looking at my mother.

"Račín," my mother said.

"I have a sister in Malá Losenice," the woman said.

She looked at Bém. "Are you from the highlands as well?"

"No." Funny how he could do that, my mother thought, and have it be neither cold nor abrupt nor anything but what it was. An answer.

The old woman looked at him the way a woman of a certain age wiping her hands on a rag and wearing a baggy, meal-colored blouse and a pair of cracked rubber boots will look at a man. Not giving a damn for his black hair or his mouth or anything else visible to the eyes. And saw that he didn't either. He simply looked back. Polite enough. When he saw Jožka begin to push the wagon into the barn, he lay his pack in the grass and walked over to help. And Jožka, who did not like help, particularly from people he didn't know, moved over without a word and let him. She looked back at the girl. Here was another one. God help the mother whose daughter she was — there'd be a soul to go with that face, a reckless kind of soul. She could see the way she looked at him. Keeping nothing in reserve. Though he was not unmoved, no, not at all. The way he'd stood next to her. The way he'd touched her arm when he went to help Jožka with the wagon. No, there was a chance here. And a fine couple they would make, no denying that.

"Well, come into the house, then," she said to my mother.

When they came back out into the yard, the dark had begun. A warm summer night. The pear trees by the wall were a solid mass now, stretching nearly to the house. The two men were just crossing over from the stable. Jožka had something wrapped in a rag. *Zbytky ze zabíjačky,* he said gruffly. Trimmings from last week's butchering. She knew better than to argue.

"You're sure?" Bém said to them as he took the rag.

The old man grunted and wiped his nose. "Nothing from nothing."

"They've lent us a blanket," my mother said, indicating her bag. "And a pot."

He looked at them. "Thank you," he said, then squatted down and put the bundle in his rucksack. A small light blinked just above the weeds. Another against the stable door. And another. Standing up, he reached into a pocket and pulled out some money.

"*To si můžete nechat*" — You can keep that — the woman said before he could speak. "What would we do with it?"

"Buy yourself something," my mother said.

"Nothing to buy."

"Then just . . ."

"I don't have time to stand here debating with you. Really."

"You're sure?"

"When I want a new fur, I'll look you up."

"Thank you."

"You'll be all right?" the old man said.

They would be fine, they said.

The road had begun to emerge, pale against the dark. They walked under the cherry trees that lined the road, then back through the village, where small wavery lights showed through the windows. A woman's voice was calling someone, a child answered, then the thin clank of a pail. On one of the benches by the pond a couple sat still as stone, locked into one shape.

They didn't say anything now. She felt his fingers as they walked. His hand felt cool, dry. She explored the knuckle of his thumb with hers, felt the scar, then the square, smooth nail.

By the time they came to the churchyard, the wall with the archers' clefts was just a paleness narrowing into the dark. She could hear their footsteps scraping on the dirt of the road. She looked up: the steeple and the skull had disappeared, leaving only their starless shapes behind.

NIGHT, NIGHT. THE OTHERNESS OF IT! LIKE A DOOR TO a room we've never entered, hidden behind our childhood dresser. Like another world, living inside the one we know. The wind in the grass sounds different here. The wind in the wheat reminds you of something. The bone-whiteness of the fields reminds you of something. No dream can match this dreaming. And now the moon, raising itself above the fields.

The night my mother and Tomáš Bém walked into the forest from the town of Dobrá Voda the sky was clear and huge and hot, the moon just two days short of full. It rose, slightly misshapen, as they walked between the fields, so that by the time they entered the shadow of the forest, diving under a wave of air smelling of moldering loam, mushrooms, and sap, the way was already shot through with bits of light. They stood for a moment, letting their eyes adjust to the dark, learning to read the shapes of things, then went on, stepping carefully over the deadfalls, ducking the black branches that swept down from the ceiling.

They came to a vast pool of light which they thought at first was a meadow. An emptied pond stretched before them, a hollow socket, barren and sad. A stream ran through the hardened mud. They walked around the perimeter, backing away whenever the ground started to pull at their feet, then followed the stream back into the dark until they came to a place of thick knotted grass and put down their things. You could almost see. To the right, between the trees, a small rise like a long, soft shelf. A low mossy stump. A fallen pine, level enough for sitting on.

"Here?" she said.

"All right," he said. They hadn't said anything for a long time. She liked hearing the sound of his voice. It made him familiar again.

He kissed her. "Welcome home," he said, then walked into the shadow by the stump and lay the rucksack on top of it and began taking out their food.

The stream was right there, she thought, listening. She began to feel over the surface of the ground with her hands, tossing aside thumbnail-sized pine cones and broken sticks, clearing a space.

"Hungry?" she heard him say.

"Tired."

"Come have some of this." She could see him holding out the jar, blue in the moonlight. She walked over and sat next to him on the fallen pine. The milk was cool and smooth.

"You didn't get much sleep last night," he said.

"Neither did you, I think."

"True enough." She could almost see his smile. He poured a little water from a canteen into the empty jar, then spilled it out on the grass. "Maybe we should just give up on it altogether," he said.

"Sleeping?"

"What do you think?"

"Maybe we should."

They slept that night, lying naked on the clothes she had spread on the grass like a rag quilt while he took the meat and put it in the empty milk jar and placed the jar in a sidewater below the bar where it bobbed quietly in the dark, herded in by rocks. They slept, her head on his arm, half covered by the blanket, the wet rag and his rucksack and her bag hanging off the broken branches of a pine as from a giant coat rack, not hearing the stream chuckling to itself, or the sudden call of a bird from somewhere by the dry lake, not feeling the long, fine file of ants, like a thread dragged endlessly across his calf, or the fat-bodied moth that settled on her hair like a child's barrette, or the mosquito that lit lightly on his eyebrow and danced along that line until it found its place and grew quickly dark with blood. They slept, not seeing or hearing any of these things, and woke together, as lovers will, his arm around her and her breasts pressed flat against his ribs, to find the gullies in their blanket and the clothes on which they had lain and the soft little crevasses where skin touched skin filled with pine needles, as though they had slept for a week, or a month; and sat up and shook out their things and then my mother, leaning over, picked the tiny brown spears one by one out of the hair on his chest.

How was it possible, she thought, that a place they'd known only a few hours, eight of them while they'd slept, could grow so familiar? How could the grassy rise and the food stump and the way down to the stream and the pine by the bed-place so quickly begin to feel like a home: a home without walls or roof, windows or door, but a home nonetheless?

The fire was small and almost smokeless. He built it between two flat-topped stones. She watched him push the bigger one down into the dirt to make it level with the other, then try out the empty pot between them to see how it sat, then move the rocks again. Getting it right. When the dollop of lard began to hiss and sizzle he broke the eggs into the pot one after the other until they were done, laying the shells next to him on the grass, then pushed them back and forth with a pocketknife, reaching into the pot to get the knife blade flat, then rolled down his sleeves and took the pot off the fire and set it on a stone he'd brought over from the stream, covering the pot with the rag to keep out the pine needles. Reaching for the jar, he began impaling the squares of fatty meat he had cut on a stick he had stripped of bark, threading them over the raised parts, lining them up like so many fat beads on a string.

My mother watched, surprised by his competence, by the quick, thoughtless economy of his movements. A turn of the wrist, a small adjustment, the fingers reaching to nudge or to shift or to tap into place, this man knew his way around the world of things, and they leapt to him like filings to a magnet, eagerly, helplessly. There was something lovely and ruthless about it, something she hadn't seen before. Or maybe she had sensed it from the beginning, had known it would be like that all along.

When only a hand's width of space remained on both sides, he placed each end of the stick in the crotch of a branch he had pushed into the dirt on either side of the fire, and they ate the eggs, taking turns with the pot and the knife, sucking them carefully off the blade.

When they were done he reached over to a pile of short sticks he had prepared — each about the thickness of a man's finger — and began to place them carefully one by one on the flames. The meat spit and dribbled. He turned the skewer. She watched him raise the branch a bit to turn it past a knot, then settle it back in place. The greeny-white wood between the pieces had begun to turn black. He reached for the bread, cut another slice.

"Would you like some more bread?" he said.

He handed her a slice and she watched him tear off a small piece and pause, as though forgetting for a moment what he had meant to do with it, then remember and wipe the bottom of the pot. Something in the stillness of his mouth. Something in the deliberateness with which he turned the skewer, his sudden distance from what his hands were doing. She knew what it was.

"Almost done," he said. He wiped his fingers on the rag.

"Should we talk about it at all, you think?" she said.

He looked at her, and there was such utter regard in that look, and such a lake of rage beneath it, that she understood, perhaps for the first time, the quality of his love.

"I don't know how to talk about it," he said.

"You don't know when you're coming back," she said. Not if — if was not possible.

"No."

"And I won't be able to see you."

"No." He smiled. "Is it crazy for us to talk like this?"

"I don't think so. Does it feel crazy to you?"

"That's what's so crazy about it."

"I know."

He moved the stick a half-turn over the flames. "It's just that I didn't expect you. Everything was set before."

"Would it be any different if we hadn't met?"

"Everything would be different."

"But you say you have to go anyway?"

"I do."

"And you can't tell me where you're going?"

"No."

She glanced at the scaly twig she held in her hand. "Then how will I find you again? After."

"I'll find you."

"But . . ."

"I'll find you."

"It took you a while the first time," she said, not smiling.

"I'll do better this time," he said.

The meat began to smoke. He picked up the ends of the skewer with two sticks and laid it on the stone next to him, then broke up the fire, spreading the ashes. They could break camp while it cooled. My mother stood and picked up the blanket that lay knotted on the ground. Exposed beneath it, an orange and black beetle, like a miniature shield, began to stumble over the deadfalls of flattened grass, running from the sudden light.

ON JUNE 5, 1942, TOMÁŠ BÉM LEFT THE SAFE HOUSE IN which he had been hiding for nearly a week and crossed the city of Prague from the Dejvice district to Nové Město, wearing a lightweight suit, a hat, a coat over his arm, and an ampoule of strychnine around his neck. Soldiers were everywhere. A warm, still summer day. Crossing the Vltava, the air moving through the open window of the trolley, he smelled the water and the wet earth smell from the Petřín orchards.

It was just before noon. Eighty-three had been executed in Prague the day before, 106 the day before that. They were everywhere: a knot of four — boots, caps, riding crops — striding quickly along the south side of Národní Avenue, men and women stepping out of their way. A convoy of four cars, then another. Sentries on nearly every corner.

Three or four times a day, while Bém lay in the dark in the crawl space behind the sofa, old man Moravec would sit down heavily and read the paper aloud, interrupting himself at some point to call out to his wife in the kitchen, "Are you all right in there? Do you need anything?" and while Madame Moravcová called back that she was fine, that she would be right in, the old man would tap twice on the sliding panel — so close they could have touched hands — and then read on. SS Obergruppenführer

Karl Hermann Frank had declared that the attackers would be found, he read. They and all those who had helped them, along with their families, would be shot. The Wehrmacht would comb them out like lice.

Well, that certainly was welcome news, Madame Moravcová would call from the kitchen or the pantry. And then, to her son, Ota: "*Pro kristapána, obleč se už.* For Christ's sake, get dressed already. "*Kolikrát to musím opakovat?*" How often do I have to repeat it? And did the newspaper happen to say when the authorities thought this might happen? No mention of that, my dear, her husband would reply, the pages rustling. It seemed they had the bicycle and some other things the attackers had left behind on display in Václavské náměstí, where the populace could see them. There was a reward of ten million reichsmarks for anyone who could identify the owners of these things. A bicycle, said Madame Moravcová. It didn't sound like much to her, unfortunately.

And lying in the dark, unable to see them, Bém could hear their words, spoken for the benefit of the walls, the door, the keyhole, as well as himself, all the more clearly — feel the thing, so very near hysteria, moving just behind the screen. It was too much. These were brave people. But even the brave could be broken in time. Forced by fear, the crack was growing, branching; at any moment the laugh might go on too long, the gesture fly loose, the record skip.

But it didn't. They held on. On the fifth day, Madame Moravcová, while walking down the white gravel path from her mother's grave in the vast Olšany Cemetery, met a very nice, scholarly-looking gentleman who commiserated with her about the times but maintained, while tipping his hat or exchanging a few words with passersby, that even now, with all the pain being visited upon the country, nature provided perspective and comfort. He himself, despite everything, still found solace in the changing of the seasons, he said, though he was more than prepared to admit that this was so because he had been raised that way — that our adult havens were invariably shaped in child-hood. Didn't she agree? His wife, for example, as befitted her upbringing, had returned to the church.

And where did his wife worship? Madame Moravcová asked. At the Church of Sts. Cyril and Metoděj on Řesslova Street, the man told her. She must know the place — a fine building. An ornament. It seemed that it gave his wife some sense of security, the man said. Perhaps it was the company she found there. One of the priests, she said, a Dr. Petřek, was particularly kind. And they chatted a bit more about the church, and the species of sparrow that he said was given to nesting in the thick ivy of some of the higher monuments, and then he lifted his hat and wished her a good day and they went their separate ways.

Just before noon the next day, Bém walked out of the house and down the hill to the tram stop. No one seemed to see him, though he himself knew he would never know if someone had. There was a soldier at the bottom of the hill, two more at the tram stop by the park. A small group of people — three business-men with briefcases, an older woman with a net bag, a girl of seventeen — waited silently off to the side, not looking at the others, not looking at anything . . . Behind them, a large red poster plastered to the telephone pole listed the names of those executed the day before.

He joined them, the coat draped over his right arm. There would be no need to fumble for the pocket; just squeeze the trig-ger through the fabric. His forehead and temples were sweating under the hatband but he resisted taking off his hat. No unnec-essary gestures. Nothing to attract attention. He could hear the crickets, sounding the heat. When the tram came at last and the doors opened, the group shuffled back. One of the men looked down at his briefcase; the other, as though thinking about some-thing suddenly, or testing for a sore tooth, slowly ran two fingers along his jaw just below the ear. When the soldiers had climbed in, the group followed them.

Three stops later the soldiers got off the tram, and Bém took off his hat. The coolness of the air coming through the windows felt good in his hair. He could smell the orchards and the river. Thousands had been arrested, Moravec had told him. Round-the-clock interrogations were being conducted in the five-story building down from the central train station. He looked out the window. The city, though emptier, seemed faster somehow — electrified, spasming. Even the ordinary seemed strange. Two boys, dropping something into the Vltava, leaned out over the rail, their right legs bent into identical L's behind them. A man and a woman, trying to get past each other on the sidewalk, feinted left, then right, like football players on the pitch. The bell sounded. He didn't like this idea of the church, of all of them together in one place. Everywhere he looked, the red posters of the dead — mothers, fathers, entire families grouped by surname — on storefront windows, on walls, on light posts. The tram passed into the shade of the buildings. A white sign with a long number on it passed by too quickly for him to read it.

At Karlovo náměstí he stepped off the tram. It made no sense. Better to separate, stay still, then get out of Prague. Across the street, three soldiers were walking south along the storefronts. He turned into the square, toward the white statue of Eliška Krásnohorská. He could see the bench where they had sat. He wondered where she was now. If she was safe. The air in the shade smelled of flowers and stone.

He sat down on the bench, folding the coat next to him. He'd walked off the tram and almost directly into her. A city of a million people.

The church was only a few hundred meters away; he could afford a few minutes. They had sat right here, both of them stunned by the force of it, the suddenness of it, trying to speak but unable to say anything that didn't seem false the minute it was spoken. Banalities. Little gestures and politenesses. As though they had become different people in those few months, traveled too far from themselves, and the only way back was over a long, narrow bridge of clichés. As though they were afraid of frightening something. He remembered the rain, asking if she was all right, if she could take the time. Of course. Yes, he'd had to get glasses. No, he didn't need them exactly. A nuisance — he didn't like them.

She asked if he'd been well, whether he'd been in Prague for long. He could see the rain running down her hood, gathering at the edge, then dripping down. She herself had left Brno soon after . . . Anyway, it had seemed best. He'd nodded, looking at the oak behind her, at the branch hanging down like a huge, drooping tentacle. A relative had helped set her up, she said, found her work at the Language Institute in Líbeň. She'd missed him, she said.

There was the branch. A slight breeze, moving the heat. She had sat right there, to his left. Looking at it now, he felt a sharp pang of love for it. As though it remembered them, held them in suspension. Above all this horror. Absurd. In a few years you could sit in the crook of that branch and read a book, she had said. He could tell her nothing. They had said nothing. Before he could stop her, she told him she was staying at 7 Italská Street with her aunt and uncle who — "Stop," he'd said. "Please. I can't know . . . ," and seeing the sudden understanding in her face, the quick brimming of the eyes, he looked away at the puddles on the walk, the fountain, busy in the rain, the tram just coming to a stop in front of the stores across the way.

"How long before this is over?" she had asked. "Can you at least tell me that?"

"I have to go," he'd said.

"I see," she'd said. And then: "Will I see you again?"

"Of course," he'd said, and even smiled.

"But . . ."

"I have to go," he said. A quick kiss, her wet hair in his fingers, another, more desperate "I love you," he said, "I swear to God I do" — and he was on the tram in two leaps, escaping something, feeling like something hollowed out and about to cave in. Strange — it had been right there; he could see the stop. For that matter, he'd probably seen the church that day, never realizing that he'd be coming back to it after it was all over. How very hard it had been. A quick wave and she'd been gone behind the rain and he'd sat down on the seat and begun the hard work of kicking himself back into vigilance like a drunk berating himself into paying attention. One misstep and it was gone, all of it. All the planning. All the lives on which it was built. One error, one moment of inattention or softness, one accidental turn, and the whole thing would go. And it couldn't go.

A stocky man leading a dog with a pointy nose was coming up the path, the two of them passing through the dark, leafy shade and into the sun. Even now, dogs had to be walked. A beautiful summer day — there was no denying it. The way the light played against the stone. He watched the man and the dog make their way around a flower bed. When they reached the shade of the tentacle branch, he got up to go.

SHE UNDERSTOOD. AND SHE DIDN'T. SHE UNDERSTOOD
why he sat next to her that afternoon like a clenched fist, why
they couldn't speak, why she kept noticing things — the oak, a
white cloud of rain behind a passing tram, the black steeple of a
church — as if she were falling down a well and these were roots
to grab on to. She understood why he'd walked away from her so
quickly, walking through the puddles like a man striding away
from an avalanche, an avalanche he'd been waiting for his entire
life. The tram windows had been steamed over, blurred by rain.
He'd leaped on board, disappeared.

She understood. And she didn't. She didn't understand at all.
She didn't understand how a face, a voice, a certain kind of half-
smile could leave such a vacuum in her, how his absence could
work on her like a chemical need, like opium withheld. She
missed the physical fact of him, the lean, compact weight of
him, his mouth on hers, his hair, the feeling of him in her hand.
She missed talking to him, about everything really, the occupation and cheese, fascist Spain and the fashion in hats. She liked
the way he listened to her, the way he would lie on his side,
watching her as she talked. She liked his calm and the suddenness just beneath it; the pain in him and the pure unblinking
dangerousness that pain had given birth to. She liked the quick

smile that seemed to surprise even him. And now he was gone and she moved through the days diminished, transparent somehow, less like a ghost than like the last living, breathing soul in a world of ghosts. She understood how absurd this was, how self-indulgent. It couldn't be helped. Holding him again mattered. Nothing else.

She clung to every bit of news now; her moods turned on a word. "This young man of yours," her uncle had called out from the living room one night as she and her aunt wrapped the last of the dough around the canned apricots and lowered them into the big white pot steaming up the kitchen windows, "he'll be back, I'm sure — if he loves you as you say, he'll be back," and because she was so miserable even this well-meant platitude had given her comfort and tilted the evening that followed — the dinner, the hour or so spent reading afterward — toward something like hope. Maybe it was all that simple. He loved her. He'd be back.

And then she saw him step off the tram and they sat on a bench in the rain and he was standing up to leave. And she felt his mouth and touched his face and for just one moment she glimpsed the fear and the determination inside him, side by side like orphans in a doorway, and understood that it could never be that simple. And he was gone.

Winter. It was as if the year would never die. She stood on lines, went to work, translated documents that meant nothing to her with two older men who seemed capable of moving nothing other than their right hands, and even those minutely, for hours at a time. The one window looked out on the stones of the building opposite. She listened to the pens' scratch, to the windy shushing of rain, the sudden scattering of sleet.

At times she could almost imagine it, see it: the leather straps, the cords, the notched wheels . . . The country was being torn, slowly, irreversibly — and worse, learning to live with it.

There was no food. The lists of the dead grew longer. Outrage folded outrage, building a soil of known things — of habit — from which anything might grow. Every afternoon now, crossing over the tracks on Vinohradská Street, she saw the trains, their windows nailed over with boards.

They were everywhere now. Russia was the answer, her uncle said that winter. He could see it starting already. The bastards would break their teeth on Russia. When the declaration of war on America was announced that December, he could hardly contain his glee. The idiots. They'd bitten off too much. The factories of Chicago would bury them.

He clung to it all that winter, even after things began to turn again. The Russian soul. The factories of Chicago. The Macháčeks, who lived in the next building, had been deported. A childhood friend he'd known since the day he'd hit him with a toy bucket in a sandlot forty-six years ago was taken into the courtyard he walked through every morning on the way to work and shot. They'd pay, he said. And all the quislings and collaborators with them. They'd taken too much. They'd choke like dogs. A year, maybe two, before the bone found the throat.

But the next morning, seeing their visored caps, their coats, their wet boots through the tram window, she knew that in some way it didn't matter. Entire worlds could pass in a year or two. The factories of Chicago were far from here.

IN ANOTHER TIME, THERE MIGHT HAVE BEEN SOME HUMOR in it. How perfect, after all, to hide the living among the dead; no one would think to look for them there. Just as no one would think to search for the dead among the living.

It was so simple, Bém thought: to escape death, all you had to do was die. The priest moved the cement slab, the cold breathed out, and down the stairs you went, carrying your long skier's underwear, your sweaters, your hat, your woolen socks, your blankets — all the necessary provisions for the grave. Or the crypt, at any rate. And there were your comrades, like skiers in hell: Opálka and Valčík, in hats and bulky sweaters, squatting by a small stove; Gabčík rising on his elbow from a mattress laid out in one of the deep niches in the wall; Kubiš pacing under the one small window. The other three were upstairs in the rectory, standing guard.

He'd made it! By God, they'd known he'd make it. They had been here four days. It was cold as hell. Gabčík had hurt his eye in the attack but had managed to bicycle away with one hand. There was a plan, they said. They would be taken out in coffins — in a few weeks, maybe less — then driven out of Prague in a funeral car. The priests had it all figured out. They would stay in a storeroom in Kladno, then be moved to the forests in Moravia.

Petřek, the priest, had arranged for a gamekeeper's cabin. They could hide there for months if necessary. But how had he gotten here? What news was there?

"What news could there be?" said Kubiš. And it was true: he had no news to give them.

He had to get dressed, they said. Quickly. Once the cold got into his bones . . .

A supply line had been established. The teacher, Růžička, came once a day with supplies and food.

But how had he made it? They had heard of the curfew, of ten thousand arrested, of interrogations, executions — the entire city under siege.

They had thought of turning themselves in, Valčík said. To stop it.

He had thought they were done talking about that, said Opálka.

But they were the ones the bastards were looking for, Valčík said. It was all because of them that this was happening.

They were done talking about it, said Opálka. The message from London —

But this wasn't London, interrupted Kubiš, who had paused in his caged pacing to light a cigarette.

They were done talking about it, said Opálka. It would accomplish nothing.

It would accomplish something if it stopped it, said Valčík quietly.

They turned to him, the last man in, the last to see how things were. What did he think?

Nothing would stop it, he told them.

He would come to know it well: the low, dank, vaulted ceiling, the corner with the buckets, the sealed-off stairs on the north end, the bottom of the cement slab . . . He memorized it. The water stains, the gouged wall, the heap of crumbling mortar beneath it. The two bricks missing from the floor between the cooking area and the stairs, like broken teeth.

It was the hollow emptiness of the place that was most striking: no table, no chairs. Just columns, stairs, bricks, cold. This place had never been meant for the living. And though there were at least four of them there all the time, they made no impression on it. They knew they were trespassing, and the place seemed to know it too.

The sleeping wall: sixteen black niches like a giant's honeycomb dug into the stone, coffin wide and coffin deep. The four on the left had been sealed off for some reason, as if with wax, making the illusion complete. They slept in the others. There was nowhere else. None of them thought to ask the priests what they had done with the coffins, or where they now stored their dead.

The middle hole on the top row, slightly larger owing to the curvature of the ceiling, had been given to Gabčík, who was still recovering; during the day he would sit in a low crouch near the entrance or lean up on an elbow, smoking. The others were worse. And because it was bad they made jokes about roses and buttonholes as they slid into place feet-first, the damp cement pushed so close to their faces by the thin mattresses the priests had managed to find for them that at times it felt as though the whole church — no, all of Prague — were poised above their chests. At one time or another, each of them, waking during the night, had smashed his head into that sudden, unfamiliar ceiling; every night, it seemed, they were awakened by someone cursing. There seemed to be no getting used to it.

He could see the problem immediately: these were not men accustomed to being still. Trained to move — chosen precisely because they could move when others could not, because their minds would not stop them — they could be patient enough when patience was required for some kind of action. This was different. This was just waiting to escape. There was nothing to do, nothing to plan. All they could do was think about what was happening in the outside world, what their actions had caused, and, unable to smother these thoughts with tasks, unable to keep themselves from turning inward, they began, by slow degrees, to grow human. To become afraid. It made for a particular kind of hell, he thought, a hell crafted to their natures: a perpetuity of fear and regret, stasis and rage, the rage of paralytics forced to watch their families being attacked.

They moved about, tried to sleep. They paced back and forth, looking up at the crease where the ceiling met the wall. They spent some time throwing bits of mortar into a can for points, then grew bored. They waited silently for their shift in the rectory. Two hours before the attack, Kubiš had been almost lighthearted. Coming out of the Moravecs' apartment building that morning, the sten gun carefully packed inside the ubiquitous brown leather suitcase, he had joked with the Moravecs' boy, Ota, who had been up half the night worrying about his Latin exams. "Why the face?" he'd said, tousling his hair. "Look here — it's simple. You either pass or you fail. If you pass, you're a scholar; if you fail, I'll find you a job digging ditches," and the boy had smiled and looked relieved. There was no humor now. There was nothing to set it against. And day by day, memories were coming back, occupying the vacuum.

She would come to him constantly while he was still on the outside: the thought of her, of her strength . . . for him. No one had ever aligned themselves with him the way she had. Immediately. Unquestioningly. No one. He remembered watching her once, sitting in the shade by the side of a pond, lost inside herself, and when she had looked up there had been no shift, no translation. Everything was open to him. Everything. He'd never known such courage. He wanted to live inside her — he damn near had — but inside her voice too, inside her thoughts, her dreams. It was obsession, he told himself, but it didn't feel like obsession. There was nothing weakening about it, nothing unclean. It felt like air, like sanity itself.

But all that was before. Before this place. Air was not wanted here, nor too much sanity, either. What had been strengthening before was something else now. A diluting thing. The look on her face underneath him — the bitten lip, the strand of hair, the yearning for the precipice, and then the long, sweet fall — the feel of her against him at night, the meals shared — all these had to be put away now, ruthlessly. They could only hurt him here. And yet, five, six times a day, inadvertently, helplessly, he'd catch himself whispering her name, the very sound of it, Ivana, Ivana, like a talisman, like hope, like a holy relic to a failed apostate.

He thought of odd things, small things. For the better part of two days he tried to place the scent he'd caught when the priests had moved the slab and the cold air smelling of stone and urine had rushed up into his face. He smelled it now and again in the days that followed, more faintly each time, and having little else to do, he spent some time vainly trying to put a name to this ghost until the moment someone's spoon scraped against the side of the pot and he had it: the courtyard of the building he had grown up in. He remembered it now. He and Miloš Mostovský had spent days digging a network of tunnels through a small mountain of wet sand. They hardly spoke. By late morning the sun would move across the courtyard, but in the shade the sand felt cold, and every day an old man who was building a low brick wall along the communal garden would scoop wet cement from a small wheelbarrow with a trowel and slap and scrape it between the bricks. The smell of wet cement — it was as though that smell had simply disappeared from the earth in all the intervening years, till now. As though it had been kept here for him, preserved like a jar of cherries or pickled mushrooms until the day he discovered it again.

He remembered the courtyard perfectly: the way the air felt, the smell of soil and garbage. Every now and then his eye would catch a movement in the rabbit hutches against the wall. Amazing to think that these same hands had dug through the sand those mornings until the sand loosened and he felt, with that strange shock of the living touching the living, fingers grasping his, reaching from the other side. That he was that same person. That the years should have brought him here.

During the days he managed to keep the thinking away, filling in the hours with the work of staying warm or making stew (they skinned the rabbits the schoolteacher brought them by hanging them from a spike that protruded from the wall, tying their legs with shoelaces) or rereading the newspapers, which told him nothing. At night his dreams, as though taking their revenge, rushed back, crowding each other in their eagerness to reclaim the territory from which they'd been expelled. And always she would be there, somewhere, waiting for him to find her.

He was back in Manchester, in the soldiers' barracks, packing for the mission, and suddenly knew the plane had left without him. He was in a seaport at night — he recognized it as Gdynia. He was on the ship he was to take to France — the engines had already started — but he had to find the stairs to the crypt. They were covered with a slab. In the dream he realized quite clearly that he wasn't supposed to know about the crypt yet, that he had not yet been dropped into the Protectorate, that he had not even been to England, but it didn't matter. He rushed down the ship's narrow hallways and stairs, looking for the door. Everyone he met seemed eager to help.

Now he was in the plane, sitting on the wooden board in the dark. The door was open. Strangely, there was no wind. Outside, a shoreless blackness. His father was sitting next to him. He looked at his father and realized that his father was terrified for him, that he didn't want him to jump but knew he couldn't stop him. And in the dream he reached out and patted his father's stubbled cheek reassuringly. "I'll be fine," he said, and his father said, "But it's dark out there. How will you know which way is up?" "The ground is always down," he replied, and his father seemed comforted by this and said, "Don't worry, I'll tell your mother."

Every night the dreams bled into each other, leaving him exhausted. He was back in school, worrying about an exam. He was opening a suitcase filled with grass. He was standing by a frozen lake with Kubiš. It was snowing. Someone was coming toward them and he put his hand on the gun in his pocket, but now it wasn't Kubiš behind him anymore, it was her, and the man coming toward them was saying, "Just some trimmings from last week's butchering." He could feel her there behind him. It was dark. They were in the forest now but something was wrong — there were cobbles under his feet instead of pine needles. Far ahead, a tiny white light kept appearing and disappearing behind the trees. He wondered what it could be. When he realized he was looking at a candle flame high in an apartment window, he stopped. "What's wrong?" he heard her say. "I don't know," he said, "there's been some mistake," and taking the tin cup that dangled around his neck he swung it over his shoulder and woke feeling her presence so intensely that for one mad instant he almost reached behind him to see if she was there in the space between himself and the stone, as if, before reason destroyed the illusion, his faith could make it real.

He thought about his parents now, his sister . . . spent hours remembering their apartment on Michalovská ulice: the hallway with its worn red runner, the kitchen, the window overlooking the courtyard. More and more it seemed impossible not to; the pictures came back to him in quick, uninvited flashes as he slid into his niche or out of it, as he laced his boots or cut the eye out of a potato: his mother standing by the kitchen table, complaining about the price of meat; his father's voice yelling at him to get the coal from the cellar; his sister's face when he did or said something that hurt her — the way her eyes filled and she sucked in her lower lip before coming after him. At times these stabs of memory brought with them a pain that was distinctly physical — a seizing-up sensation in the chest, a sharp tightening of the throat, as if he might actually suffocate — and in those moments he would move quickly, desperately, bending down to tie a boot that didn't need tying, or wrenching himself abruptly to the left or right if he was lying down, as if freeing himself from something closing in around him.

More often though the memories were so distant they seemed someone else's, and in his mind he would wander through his old apartment as dispassionately as if he were giving himself a tour of his own home, and even when he heard himself saying *This is the room where your sister used to live,* or *There is where your mother used to beat the rugs once a year in the spring,* even when the voice in his head informed him that he would not see them again, it seemed as if these were things he had known for a very long time, and had grown accustomed to. *They were gone.* Yes, he knew that. Certain things simply were what they were. There was nothing to be done.

And yet, though he felt a sense of relief in being able to face these facts, he noticed that his memories at these times had a certain vague quality about them, as if drawn by an artist who, while adept at sketching the general outline of things with quick, nervous strokes — the torso, the bend of the legs, the perspective of the room — left out the specifics. His mind leaped from thing to thing, touching here, erasing there, darkening, reinforcing, then leaping elsewhere before the picture took on life. He could think of the evenings at the beginning of the war, for example, when the four of them would sit around the dining room table listening to the BBC on the radio his father had positioned on top of the cupboard for the best reception (*and here's the kitchen table where you would sit listening to the BBC . . .*), and everything would be fine until he remembered his father's socks as he stood on the chair to reach the dial, or the way he would bend his head, listening, his finger raised to mark the burning sound of static while the radio lit up slowly, like an oven, waiting for the opening phrase of Beethoven's Fifth Symphony — *ta-ta-ta-taaah* — which always marked the beginning of the BBC's broadcast into occupied Czechoslovakia — and suddenly something would catch in his heart like a long thorn and he'd know, really know, that they were gone.

This is how things were now.

ON THE FOURTH NIGHT IT RAINED. THEY HAD SEEN AL-
most no one: once a hunched figure with a basket over its arm;
another time a couple on a distant hillside, the man asleep, the
woman sitting over him, her arms around her knees; the third a
fisherman sitting back against a tree by a reedy pond, his arms
crossed, staring at his rod in its holder. Nearby, his black bicycle
leaned against a pine. He didn't see them.

Where the forest had been cut, letting in the light, they
picked raspberries, raspberries so ripe they trembled like water
on the end of a branch and dropped at a breath, two or three to a
handful, big as the joint of a man's thumb. The raspberry bram-
bles were close and hot and still and afterward they washed the
bloody stains and the itching yellow hairs off their arms and ate
what they had not already eaten in the shade. They picked
mushrooms which they fried up in lard and ate with bread and
tore handfuls of yellow chamomile buds for tea, and they swam
in ponds so lonely and lost they seemed never to have seen another human being but to have been waiting there for centuries
under the midday sun, untouched. They slept in the morning, or
at noon, and woke in the middle of the night and made love and
then lay next to each other and talked, sometimes for hours,
then walked gingerly over the pine needles to the muddy shore
of a warm, shallow lake. Wading in, they could feel their feet

pushing into the yielding bottom, smell the faint green smell of decay, and standing where the water was nearly up to their chests, they would hold each other like a statue of lovers half drowned by the tide.

On the third day she had walked out of the forest into the town of Nedvědice and sent a telegram to her parents, knowing my father would go to them eventually to see if they knew where she was: Do not worry *stop* Am well and safe *stop* I'm sorry *stop*, then scratched out the last two words and passed the paper under the little barred window to the telegraph operator, a thin, sad man in a black vest who pushed her change back to her coin by coin with the tip of his finger, collected her change and walked back.

It had felt odd to be alone again. She had refused to take the gun, and he had not tried to convince her. She would be back before noon. The walk in had taken a little over two hours. The trail had led out to a grassy path that wound around a muddy pond, then meandered up through terraces of uncropped grass and wildflowers and overgrown wooden fences. She came to a gate sagging on its hinges and lifted it up off the grass and swung it open and passed through into a rising field of wheat that shook and moved like the mane of a horse whenever the wind went over it. At times the trail was swallowed up in the wheat and she had to guess her way by what seemed like a gap between the rows. A small flock of birds burst out from under her feet as though shot into the air. Pushing up to the crest of the hill, sweating now, she startled something, a fox perhaps, that moved off through the grain like a fish under water, disturbing the surface.

From the crest of the hill she could see the lane, the thinning edge of the field marked by dun-colored weeds and spotted with poppies — a scattering of drops, arterial red — and stopped to catch her breath. The sheer beauty of it was so insistent, so undeniable, that she couldn't help but marvel at it: the white storybook clouds in the hot sky, the smear of lupines along the ditch, the long, stately row of lindens that marked the road's progress. In the far distance, a cluster of red-tiled roofs, an ornate steeple. The landscape lay before her: half asleep, enchanted, shameless.

Walking down that long, straight road, silent except for the wind in the high trees and the tired insects in the hedgerows whenever it died, she noticed with a kind of wonder how strange to herself she'd grown. She was the same person, holding the same conversations inside her head — wondering how much farther it was to the turnoff, or whether she should stay on the road or cut through the pastures — except that now it was as though she were talking to him as well, as though a third person had entered the room that only she and herself had shared. She wanted to talk to him, think aloud with him. His entrance had displaced something essential, she knew, then realized with a kind of voluptuous sorrow that she had been waiting for this displacement all of her life, that things would never again be quite the same and that she didn't care and wouldn't miss them.

The post office was a small stone building not far from the central square. She opened the heavy doors and passed into the cool, dim interior. The man behind the window bars looked like a man trapped in a canary cage; he slid the telegraph form over to her with long, parrot-like fingers.

She didn't hesitate. She remembered his face, the walks they had taken, the long afternoons in the Špilberk gardens. He seemed a long time ago. A good man. A decent man. A courageous man, even. She wrote out the message. It would come as a shock to him. It couldn't be helped. She wasn't sorry. She'd never been less sorry in her life. She collected her change from the worn wood and walked out into the heat and found the other one, two hours later, sitting with his back against the pine tree where she had left him, waiting for her.

That night it rained. There had been no sign. Or perhaps they had missed it. They were asleep under a low-branched pine, their heads almost touching the rough trunk, streaked with candied sap. A long, hollow rumble, a silent flash. And then the rain.

They woke into a deeper dark, already full of the sound of water and small breaking branches. A sudden gust. Another. They sat huddled together. For a minute the million needles over their heads distracted the rain; then the branches started to drip. "The forester's shack," she said, yelling over the sound of the rain. Did he remember? "An hour," he said. "Maybe more." "I can find it," my mother said.

And this was the thing she remembered most: the two of them, already streaming with water, stuffing their clothes into his rucksack by feel in the vain hope of keeping them dry and setting out naked into the storm with only the shoes on their feet, her idiotic shoulder bag running water from a corner as if it had grown a faucet there, searching for a one-room woodsman's shack in a continent of rain and darkness. And him slipping in the mud as he helped her up a small slope, standing there spattered and streaked and strong like some lean nocturnal animal, shaking the rain off like a dog just emerged from the water. They plunged on through fields white with rain, down slick hillsides of flattened grass, through dribbling, hissing, mumbling woods where they had to hold their arms in front of their faces to protect their eyes, and they held each other's soaking hands and yelled over the noise of the rain and he made fun of her direction-finding, saying he was sure he'd seen the spires of Hradčany by the light of the last bolt, that Prague was surely just ahead. Or Warsaw, maybe.

And of course she found it, a one-room shack like a hole in the wall of the forest, tucked deep in the cove of a meadow that looked just like every other meadow for days in either direction. Mossy black boards, a small porch with a crude table. A wooden bench against the wall. A cup, hooked on a wire, bobbed and dipped in the wind.

"There's a lock on the door," she heard him call, and went up and joined him. He felt around the hinge with his fingers, then pushed the door and felt it again. When the metal had loosened from the wall, he used one of the screws to pry the others out of the sodden wood, and suddenly they were in. They felt around in the musty dark, a pantomime of the blind, and then a match scratched and he was tipping the glass of a dirty lantern and lowering the smoking wick. Wooden shelves, two windows, a narrow musty cot with mouse-speckled sheets and a thin brown blanket. A squat black stove with a pot on top of it and a rusty file for opening the stove door and picking up the pot and probably stirring whatever was in it. He closed the heavy wooden door against the wind.

She would remember it all, that flyspecked cabin and everything in it: the rag they used to dry themselves and the man's blue shirt with the hole just above the left breast that she wore and the name on the can of nails they emptied out and set on the floor under the drip coming through the roof. She would remember the can's deep red, and that there were three wooden shelves to the left of the stove, and that just in front of the metal bed there were two hollow-sounding floorboards that hid the pantry: a chest-high hole in the earth with a basket on a string for lowering things down and taking them back. And she would remember the key she discovered outside, above the windowsill, and the taste of the walnuts they found in a bowl on the third shelf and ate with the raspberries they picked in the rain, and how he looked sleeping next to her, and how the rain coming off the porch at first light looked very much like a curtain that tore open every now and then to reveal the forest, then sewed itself up again. All this and more.

They stayed, assuming that no one would come into those dark and dripping woods. They were right. He found a flat brass box with some tools and a few tin boxes of screws and moved the hinge up into harder wood. They made love whenever the moment found them; almost any task could suddenly take a detour of an hour or more and did, often. "Can I borrow your spoon?" she'd say, walking her fingers under the bowl on his lap as they sat cross-legged in the morning with the watershadows moving up the walls, and he'd look at her with that half-smile, so very confident, so beautiful, so *hers*, and say "Be my guest," trying not to move as she helped herself for a minute, then two, smiling at him — "And some cream, please, sir?" — and by the time they got back the tea would be cold and he'd take it out on the porch and toss it in the long grass and walk out after it as naked as the day and then talk her out as well and she'd run laughing, still sticky and warm with him into the sodden field and hold him as the wind raked the world around them. When they weren't making love they'd busy themselves by gathering what they could into meals and by sitting next to each other on the porch with their backs against the wall and their feet drawn up, watching the pine branches dip and wave and the wind comb the tall grasses, talking. She told him things: about her village and her parents and her summers with her mother on the Bečva River and the dog she had lost when she was eight. And she told him about the man she had met in Brno the year before and what he was like and that they had talked about getting married once.

Days of small rituals. Three times a day they would move aside the floorboards and pull out the basket with the shrinking bit of cheese and the quarter loaf of bread she had bought in town with the last of their money, then lower it back down and cover the hole with the boards like a secret. Twice a day they would walk out into the rain to collect whatever half-dry wood they could find, snapping the small branches from inside the prickly hearts of pines, searching under overhangs for pine cones. One day they came across a door lying flat on the grass in a meadow, then a broken window, and realized they'd come across an old shack that had fallen years ago. Some of the wood that was off the ground looked burnable. They picked up the window and pretended to look through it to see what the weather was like outside and propped up the door because it looked so strange standing in the middle of that meadow like a memory of something, then dragged it back through the soaking woods to their shack, where he broke it up with an ax he'd found leaning against the wall by the stove. The helve was loose but someone had driven a nail through the top to keep the ax head from sliding off, and they started a small pile of boards and sticks to the left of the door and every night they made a fire in the stove and the wood cracked and spit and before she fell asleep she would look at the orange light coming through the crack around the stove door, like a thin, crude circle in the dark.

It was on the fifth day, as they sat on the floor of the porch sipping tea they had made from chamomile buds and strained through a piece of burlap, that she told him about the morning she had walked with her father to bury her brother. Her brother, she said, had lived only a few hours in this world, like a moth, and been buried in a coffin the size of a loaf of bread. She'd never known him, and perhaps it was for this reason that she remembered that morning not for its grief but for its warmth.

A magical morning. On the way to the cemetery her father had held her hand and told her a wonderful story about a *trpaslík,* an elf, who knew of a door in a hillside — a door no larger than a hammer, he said, with a wig of grass hanging over its sill — which led to another world, the world below the pond.

The people who lived there, her father told her, spent their days looking up like astronomers, watching the signs of the upper world, mourning what they had lost. A fisherman's red bobber touching the sky, a dog's pink tongue lapping at the horizon, children clothed in silver bubbles, like frogs' eggs, which would unpeel and follow them as they kicked to the surface . . . These were the things they lived for, and in the long winters they would sit in the icy dark by their watery green candles and spin fantastic tales from the bits of misunderstood things they had seen.

But the *trpaslík,* her father said, who knew the upper world for what it was, in all its beauty and corruption, felt sorry for them. Not realizing that they loved their sadness, that the truth would be as poison to them, he resolved to tell them what he knew. One day, taking an especially deep breath — for *trpaslíks* could hold their breath for almost an hour, her father said — he opened the secret door and walked down the long narrow stairs until the clay began to get soft under his feet and he saw, far ahead, the dim circle, rimmed with roots, that marked the entrance to the pond.

He found them, as always, swaying like water weeds in a gentle current, looking up at their watery sky with tears in their eyes. He would save them, he thought. And he began to speak, but as he did, a look of even greater sadness came over their faces, a sadness different from the one he knew, and they bent as if in pain and tried to stop up their ears with their soft green hands and when they found they couldn't block out the sound of his voice telling them the truth they wrapped those hands around his throat and held him until he stopped speaking. And the *trpaslík* woke, her father said, and in his heart was a pain and a love he'd never known, and he looked up at the sky toward a watery light he didn't understand and thought if he could only look at it forever he would never want for anything more.

She didn't know why she loved that story so much, she said, looking out over the soaking meadow, or what it was about the memory of that morning that meant so much to her, but she had wanted to tell him about it. She wanted to tell him everything, she said, even the things she didn't know.

And Tomáš Bém, who did not yet carry an ampoule of fast-acting strychnine around his neck, sat on the floor of the porch with his feet out of the rain and nodded. "Tell me, then," he said. "Tell me everything."

And he fixed some things and told her what he cc
life and memorized what he could of hers and when th
stopped and their time was up they put the nails back i
and made the bed and locked the door behind them
placed the key on the sill and left. And yes, my mothe
around at the edge of the meadow and looked back, a
more after they had parted at the turnoff to Mělkovic
agreed to meet at the same place a year later at dawn if
had ended and he had not yet come for her, and on the
each month after that. Not quite the year-and-a-day of tl
tales, but close enough.

And he turned at the bend of the road as she knew he
the rucksack on his back, and stood there for a moment, l
at her across all that space, then raised his right hand as tl
taking a pledge, and was gone.

HE DIDN'T TALK ABOUT IT WITH THE OTHERS, NOT BE-
cause he didn't know or trust them, but because he knew —
from their silences, from the absurd ways they tried to keep
themselves busy, from their small hard flashes of anger — that
they were all fighting the same enemy, an enemy they were
uniquely unsuited to fighting, an enemy that grew stronger by
the day. When they talked, they talked about other things: the
stove, the cold, whether the schoolteacher was coming too often. They talked about whether it would be possible for them to
leave the church for a few hours at a time to break the monotony
and get some hard information about what was happening outside. They talked, in bits and pieces, about the places they'd
known in Poland and France (Gabčík had joined up with the
Czecho-Slovak Legions in Agde, Kubiš in Sidi Bel Abbes; both
had been in the fighting along the Marne), about the Egyptian
ships that had taken most of them to England after France had
fallen, about the men they remembered from Manchester and
Ringway.

He liked them all, if not equally, recognized the value of their
hardness, their stubbornness, admired their capacity for pain,
but of all of them he liked Gabčík best. Trained as a metal-
worker and a machinist, he seemed an unheroic character at

first glance; with his sloping forehead and his pointy features and his small, almost womanly lips he reminded Bém of the wooden, swivel-headed puppets parents liked but children never played with, the ones whose cone noses always fell off before the day was done. And yet there was something about the man: his eyes, maybe, which seemed almost sleepy but weren't, or the unselfconscious way he would lie on his side propped up on an elbow, smoking. Unlike the others, who seemed to be pacing even when they were still, Gabčík alone seemed willing to wait, to lie on his elbow and smoke, watching the others in that slow way of his, until something came up that required movement. He and Kubiš made a good team; the one shorter, quicker, more volatile, the other tall and slow and quiet, his eyes always one step from a small, sad smile, his big body storing energy like a cat in the sun.

Strangely, instead of irritating Kubiš, Gabčík's silence provided an outlet for jokes and insults, which helped calm him to a degree. "Look at him," Kubiš would complain to no one in particular, "just lying there by his bowl," and Gabčík, ignoring him, would move the cigarette over to his left hand and slowly reach over to the pot and dip a ladle in the soup without rising from his elbow. "You have no idea what it was like living with him in that goddamned cellar in Poděbrady," Kubiš continued. "He ate everything. At night he'd creep out and graze on berries in the moonlight. You're going to get us both killed, you fool, I'd tell him. I'm hungry, he'd say."

Gabčík put the ladle back in the pot, stirred once, then moved the cigarette back to his right hand.

"He didn't stop eating for three days," said Kubiš. "When we ran out of food I started getting nervous. I thought I'd have to shoot him, like in that Jack London story."

"What Jack London story?" said Gabčík.

"The one where he shoots the dog."

Transferring the cigarette again, Gabčík reached over the pot, moved the ladle this way and that, as though clearing a space, then delicately dipped some soup and brought it to his mouth. Replacing the ladle, he moved the cigarette back to his right hand and took a long, thoughtful drag. "Don't think I know that one," he said.

And Bém, watching from the side, appreciating their gesture, as the others did, thought again that if it came to it, Gabčík would be the one he'd want next to him. More than Opálka, their commanding officer; more than blond, stoic Valčík, who looked like a spellbound shepherd when he slept; more than any of them. Two days earlier, in the middle of the morning, a sudden shouting from the street followed by three quick shots had sent a surge of fear and adrenaline through them all. It had had nothing to do with them, they learned eventually, but in the first ten seconds they had all reacted in their own way: he himself had stayed precisely where he was, behind the column next to which he had been standing; Opálka, gun drawn, had run to his predetermined position by the sleeping wall; Kubiš, as though some catch had been released inside him, had sprung to the wall under the small high window that looked out on the bricks of the building opposite. Gabčík, seemingly without haste, had taken three long strides to the central column midway between the stairs and the west wall, put his back against the stone, and stopped, his gun pointed at the ground and his head bowed as though listening to someone explaining something important. On his homely, wooden-puppet face was the same expression he'd had while stirring the soup: calm, inward, attentive but removed. It was only later, after everything had passed, after the trembling in their leg muscles had stopped and the taste had gone from their mouths, that Bém realized that Gabčík had moved instinctively to the one place in the crypt with a clear view of both possible entrances, the covered stairwell and the high window.

On June 8, shortly after the bells had rung noon, Opálka left the church for three hours. He returned visibly shaken. The reprisals were getting worse: hundreds dead, thousands more arrested or tortured, the Resistance under siege all through the Protectorate. Rumor had it that on hearing of Heydrich's death, the Führer had demanded the immediate execution of ten thousand Czechs, chosen at random, and had only been dissuaded by Karl Hermann Frank's argument that a reprisal of such magnitude and visibility would hurt morale among Czech factory workers and lower output from the munitions plants.

The new way was no less bloody, Opálka said. The net was tight: intellectuals, writers, former government officials, sympathizers, anyone suspected of harboring pro-Resistance sentiments, all were being arrested. Some had escaped. Others were apparently hoping to somehow slip through. Many, especially those with children, seemed frozen in place, unsure of where to run. The reward for any information leading to their arrest, Opálka said, had been raised to twenty million reichsmarks.

At times he wondered if it seemed as unreal to the rest of them. If they too found it hard to believe that just over their heads, not ten meters away, a hot June day had begun and that men waiting for the tram on the corner of Řesslova were taking off their hats to wipe their foreheads, or that two hours from now, schoolgirls lying out in their gardens listening to the big-band sound of Karel Vlach on the radio would be moving their towels into the shade. How amazing that life should continue on as it did, that the trams should come and go and people should shop for food and fall in love and complain of indigestion. It seemed absurd, like cooking a meal in the kitchen while a fire raged in the living room. And yet for most, that was how it was. Children who had been born when the tanks pulled into Prague were almost four years old. Time had done its work; the fire in the living room, though roaring now, was nothing new.

It was getting harder not to think about her — to guess where she was or what she was doing. He tried not to remember her walk or her smile, the way she would look at him sometimes. He tried not to remember her spontaneity, the sudden glimpses she gave him of the child she'd once been. He tried not to think that she was out there, a five-minute tram ride away. It didn't work. It made no sense to exclude her. How much easier the whole thing would be, he admitted to himself now, if he could only talk with her for an hour — one hour — absorb a bit of her strength.

They were to be taken out of the church on the nineteenth, Opálka had told them. Bém tried not to think about that either, about the eleven days still ahead of them, about the coffins they would have to lie down in with their guns at their sides, listening to every noise coming in from the outside world, and yet there was nothing else to do but think about the coffins, the days still ahead, that date interminably crawling down to them like a glacier in the sun.

That his life could end on the nineteenth, or any day before that, he simply did not consider. Over the past two years he'd grown as used to the idea of dying as any man could — he'd tried to think about it clearly and rationally, but the thought of not hearing her voice again was not possible. He would not permit it. He would survive. He knew this. He would find her again. He would make it to the other side through sheer force of will.

The others, he felt, believed much the same thing. A new kind of strength was taking over now that they had a fixed date toward which to aim. They would survive this frozen crapper and the goddamned sleeping holes, and they would survive this war, and Gabčík would marry Líba Fafek, who had been with them at the hit, and Opálka would return to his family, and Valčík would work on his motorcycle until the Second Coming of Christ, and someday when the war was over they would get together and bore everyone around them silly recalling the stove and the cans and the goddamned window and the missing bricks, arguing over how many columns there had been between the beds and the wall or whether Petřek, the priest who looked like an aging goat, had actually had a goatee or not.

At times it all seemed possible. The day would come. They would get in the coffins. The plan would work. At other times they would suddenly remember what they had done, and the enormity of it would flood over them as if for the first time and they would see it as if from the outside — as if someone else had been responsible, not them — and they would know that it could never be that easy.

They had done the unthinkable, and in their own hearts they did not quite believe it. It had seemed strangely unreal to him even on the morning of May 27. He'd woken early, instantly conscious, and quickly gone to the living room and removed the gun from the hole under the sofa cushion. The ammunition was where he'd left it. The family he was staying with was still asleep. He'd told them the night before as they were eating dinner not to worry if he didn't come home the following night, that he might be staying over with a friend in Židenice for a while.

"For how long?" the father had asked, tearing off a piece of bread.

It was hard to say.

Was he taking everything?

It seemed best, he said.

"I'll get up and make you something for breakfast," the mother said.

He shook his head, pierced yet again by their courage, by the plain-faced little girl across the table with her straw-blond hair and her raw, bitten nails, by the plastic yellow tablecloth with its smiling, semicircle burn mark. He'd be leaving very early, he said.

The father broke off another piece of bread. "You'll be careful, yes?"

"Of course," he said.

"You take care of yourself, Tomáš," the mother said.

"I will," he said.

Sitting at the kitchen table, he loaded the gun, put the rest of the ammunition in his pocket, then forced himself to eat a piece of bread and drink a half cup of coffee. He hadn't noticed the vase, the jasmine cuttings. It didn't seem possible that this was it — that after five months of waiting and planning, the day had come. Leaning over, he moved aside the heavy blue curtains. The sky was lightening. It would be a beautiful day. Four hours. He could picture the turn in Líbeň, the tram stop, the row of stores. The spot by the wall where he would stand — 110 meters from the turn, 40 to the nearest side street. He stood up, feeling the pressure of the gun under his left arm. All right. He slipped the money under the vase, swept the bread crumbs into his cup and saucer, and brought the dishes to the sink. He'd never prayed in his life. It seemed ridiculous to begin now. On a whim he clipped off a cluster of jasmine with his fingernail and slipped it in the buttonhole of his lapel.

By the time he walked out of the building to catch the tram to Vysočany where he was to meet the others it was morning. A pale, buttery light was already spreading from the east. There were few cars. The trip was uneventful, the tram nearly empty. Three and a half hours. The sudden rise of nausea, to be expected. He looked out the window. Wet pavements. Street sweepers. Here and there a uniform. The suit they'd gotten him was too hot. Three and a half hours. It didn't seem real. It occurred to him that it might never seem real, and that it didn't matter if it did or not.

He could see them now, again, standing by the corner of that little park that smelled like smoke, Gabčík carrying the battered suitcase with the sten gun and Líba Fafek making jokes about the bonnet she was to wear to signal to them whether Heydrich's car had an escort or not, tilting it down, then back, like a girl preparing to pose for her portrait. They were just a group of friends: university students perhaps, now that the universities were closed, or musicians after a long night. The tall one carried a suitcase stuffed with grass for his rabbits, which were legal to raise in the Protectorate. Prague was full of back-alley hutches and suitcases of grass; entire fields were being moved this way and that.

Opálka went over the plan one last time. Everyone knew his station. Heydrich's schedule had been confirmed the previous afternoon by a watchmaker named Novotný who had been called in to fix an antique clock and had seen a document left open on the desk. The Reichsprotektor was being summoned to Berlin that afternoon. He would depart his castle at Panenske Břežany between nine-thirty and ten. His car would take the usual route. Since it was a beautiful day, he would demand that the Mercedes be open to the weather.

Bém knew it by heart. They all did. Líba Fafek was still playing with the hat. Kubiš, who along with Gabčík had been chosen to carry out the assassination, stood off to the side, nodding his head as though listening to fast music. Líba Fafek was to turn onto the road in front of Heydrich's car. Valčík would be stationed above the curve; he would signal Heydrich's approach with a pocket mirror. At the turn in Líbeň, Líba would step on the brakes, forcing the Heydrich car to slow. Kubiš and Gabčík would be waiting by the side of the road. Kubiš would kill both Heydrich and his driver with the sten gun; should anything go wrong, Gabčík would back him up with a grenade. The others would be stationed above and below the turn to distract any police. After the hit, Gabčík and Kubiš would make their escape on bicycles. Was everybody clear on their destinations after the hit? Opálka asked.

A wave of sweetness came to Bém from the flowering lindens growing in the park. For a moment or two he thought he would be sick. A schoolboy with a boxer on a leash was walking the dog around an empty fountain. And suddenly it was as if he were outside the group, as though he were the boy with the dog, seeing them standing there at the corner — the man with the suitcase, the woman with the hat — feeling the tug of the leash in his hand. And then it passed and he knew he would be all right.

Gabčík had put his big arm around Líba Fafek, who wasn't smiling anymore. She had taken off the hat and was holding it over her stomach.

They had a little over ninety minutes to be at their positions, Opálka said. No more waiting. He looked at Kubiš and Gabčík. The bicycles were waiting for them in the schoolteacher's garage as arranged, he said. They were women's bicycles, but since bicycles were in short supply, no one would notice.

Valčík abruptly leaned over and vomited into the bushes. "It's fine," he said.

"You're all right?" Opálka said.

Valčík took a white handkerchief out of his pocket and neatly wiped his mouth. "I'll be fine," he said.

"You're sure? If not, I have to know now."

"Quite sure."

Kubiš shook his head. "Women's bicycles," he said. "As a kid I wouldn't have been caught dead."

Gabčík, next to him, smiled that small, sad smile of his.

"I'm sorry," said Opálka.

"When this is over, I'm going to put in a complaint with London," said Kubiš.

"I understand."

"Yes, well." Kubiš looked around at the group. "Maybe we should go, don't you think?" He turned to Gabčík. "Wouldn't want to keep the goddamned rabbits waiting."

They shook hands all around, feeling awkward, then turned to go. Gabčík kissed Líba quickly and picked up his suitcase.

"I just wanted to say that it's been a pleasure," said Opálka suddenly, but though Valčík nodded and wished him luck, the others were already walking away, and didn't hear him.

And then it was just him and Opálka. A trolley went by. He could feel the fear now, like a physical thing, like a train in his body, one valley over. It was time. The boy with the dog had disappeared. He hadn't noticed him go.

THAT SAME AFTERNOON, LESS THAN SIX HOURS AFTER she saw him turn and disappear around the bend of the road to Mělkovice, my mother stood waiting outside the Škoda factory in Adamov.

A darkening day. The women with the bowls of vitamin pills were already in place inside the steel-and-barbed-wire gates, waiting for the night shift. She heard the whistle and soon they were streaming out, thick with fatigue. She recognized him in the crowd, and she watched him walk up the broad avenue between the black, hangar-like buildings that seemed to fill that valley, then turn toward the security gate. He walked alone. He was wearing a blue factory uniform and a short jacket and carrying a lunch pail.

My father saw her standing across the road on the root-cracked sidewalk, and simply stopped. The crowd bumped and ground around him. She saw his shoulder jerk forward when someone shoved him and then he was walking across the cobbled road on which a line of canvas-covered trucks waited, halted by the river of men headed for the train station.

He stopped a few meters away. My mother saw him glance at the sandy patch of grass by the sidewalk, then up the valley. He nodded slightly, as though remembering something someone once said. She hadn't realized until that moment how much he loved her.

"Are you all right?" he said finally.

She nodded. "I need to talk to you," she said.

"No need."

"I know. Still."

He nodded again. She knew him. There would be no scene, no cinder-in-the-eye. He had his pride. He would make it easy for her.

"When did you get home?" he asked.

"Yesterday."

"I love you," he said. "Does that matter?"

"It matters," she said.

He smiled. A smile like a spasm. "But not enough."

"No."

My father nodded and then, setting his lunch pail gently on the sidewalk, unpeeled his glasses from around his ears and began wiping the lenses with his handkerchief. There was nothing in his eye. She looked away. One of the women holding the bowl of pills by the gate was checking the heel of her shoe.

"We still have to work together," he said.

"I know."

"Can you do that?"

"Yes," she said. "Can you?"

He picked up his lunch pail. "Is this what you want, Ivana?"

"Yes," she said, looking at him. "It is."

"You love him that much?"

"Yes."

"I see." My father put his glasses back on, winding them carefully around his ears. "I should go," he said. "You'll be all right?"

"I'll be fine," said my mother.

"Well . . ." He smiled, the way a man might smile while pulling a long splinter out of his arm. "I keep thinking I should kiss you goodbye."

She was well down the sidewalk when she heard him call her name. He was standing by a bench with two slats missing from the back. She'd known him well. "There's something you should know," he said.

She waited.

"I want you to know that I'll be here," he said.

"Don't . . . ," she began. "I don't . . ."

"I know you don't," my father said. "But I'll be here when he's gone." And he turned and walked away down the sidewalk.

That evening my father walked out of the Brno railroad station. He crossed the avenue to the trolley stop and took the trolley home to the corner by the butcher's, closed now, then walked up the hill to his parents' apartment overlooking the courtyard. And he woke at four in the morning and did it all again, backward: the unlit streets, the blacked-out train, the passengers groping for seats like the blind. And that evening when he walked out through the post and barbed-wire gate past the guards and the women with the vitamin pills he looked across the street, in spite of himself, to see if she was there, then turned toward the railway station with the others.

He couldn't stop the thinking and he didn't try. He thought about her when he walked up the square, where they used to walk together, or past the little tilting street that led to the Špilberk Castle gardens where they had planned their lives together. All that fall and well into the winter he worked his way through the briars that spring up in the foundations of love. He expected them. Rage? What was there to rage against? How do you fight for love? Or against it?

He saw her every few weeks. At meetings, on the street. They didn't talk much. It didn't matter. He could tell that this man, whoever he was, wasn't with her — that he was gone and that she was waiting for him.

My father didn't wish him ill. Anything but that. No, to kill the beast he needed it alive. Alive and well and living in bore-dom. Sitting on the side of the bed, pulling on its slippers; argu-ing at dinner over the price of the new furniture. Just let him live, he thought, and die on the field of days as other men do. He could wait.

In any case, it wasn't as though there were no distractions — the occupation made sure of that. The work in the factory was unpleasant, the daily ritual of seeding the bearings with steel dust bad on the nerves. The older factory workers — dutiful men, law-abiding traitors — hated him and his few comrades on principle: for being students, for being new, for interfering.

The world outside the factory was hardly better. Nothing was sure. No one knew how far things would go, or when they would be over. Some things stayed the same; others changed. The dik-tats printed in the newspaper or announced over the loudspeak-ers seemed to bring something new every day. The schools were to be closed on such and such a date. All radios were to be regis-tered with the authorities between the hours of ten and four. All persons of Jewish descent were henceforth forbidden from en-tering public spaces: theaters, movie houses, restaurants . . . Lis-tening to foreign frequencies was a crime punishable by death. Absurd. This wasn't war. This was disease. They were every-where you looked now: in cars, on corners, striding down the cobbles, like an infection in the body.

Appropriately enough, symptoms had begun to appear, like yellowed nails or brittle hair. To amuse himself, he noted their progression. In answer to the command form, for example, a for-est of gestures had appeared, gestures signaling not merely a rec-ognition of the status quo — for who could help but recognize it? — but agreement, willingness, above all, subordination: the dropped glance, the slightly bowed head, the careful smile. A bag or briefcase clasped like a child to the chest.

It was fascinating in its way. Faced with an individual who had complete power over them, most people would find themselves, almost unconsciously, wanting to please him. You could see them seeking out the right facial expression, the correct stance; like animals in the open, they would instinctively find the place between dignity and cowardice — and stay there. Not move. Draw their neutrality around them like camouflage. It was a kind of game. Validate the other's disgust for you without encouraging it; play the mongrel without incurring a kick.

Of course, this was the easy part. The challenge was in keeping public behavior from bleeding into private life, in keeping the two selves apart. And this was impossible. No one could accomplish it entirely. No one. Every hour you lived, from the moment you woke in the dark, you were reshaping yourself to survive.

It made for an interesting problem: the better you were at the role, the more talent you had for it, the more likely it was that you'd live — and the more likely that you'd lose yourself along the way.

Hate helped. In keeping things clear. But hate was a hammer anyone could use, and it served the others as well, and in precisely the same way.

And so he waited, and survived, seeing every side. Amused and appalled at the spectacle of men's predictability: at the shopkeepers who now refused to sell bread to Jews, at the children who made good money shopping for them.

That June, tired of his friend's constant questions, he told Mirek what had happened. He was sitting at the kitchen table, facing the window that looked out on the garden and the apricot tree, heavy with unpicked fruit. The whole south side of the house was overgrown with a layer of green vines, half a meter thick. When they bloomed once a year, as they were blooming now, the air inside the house seemed to vibrate as though it were alive. He looked down at the table: gray bees were landing on the small gray blossoms that waved and dipped over the napkin and the fork and the empty plate. "She'll come back," said Mirek. "She'll grow tired of him after they're together for a while."

"Maybe," said my father. And because he loved her as much as he did, he almost wished it could be otherwise.

HE AND OPÁLKA WERE THE LAST TO LEAVE. THEY STOOD next to each other watching Gabčík and Kubiš walk down the cracked sidewalk toward the avenue, passing through the long morning shade. Líba Fafek had disappeared up a side street. Valčík was already walking around the empty fountain, one hand trailing along the stone.

The air moved, a breeze bringing a breath of coolness. It seemed to come from the buildings above them: a deep, musty sigh, smelling of cellars and hallways.

Opálka picked up the battered leather briefcase which no longer contained the student papers and music sheets he had carried in it for fifteen years but a length of sausage in newspaper and three hand grenades, nestled in the dark like hard green eggs.

"So . . . ," he said.

"So," said Bém.

"We have a few minutes yet, we may as well wait here."

"All right."

"It's going to be a hot day."

"Yes, it is."

Opálka took off his hat and looked inside it, then placed it back on his head. "Are you all right?"

"I think so."

"Nervous?"

"Of course."

Opálka tried to smile. "For a few seconds this morning I couldn't remember the number of the tram to Vysočany. I've taken it all my life."

They turned back to look at the others. Kubiš and Gabčík were nearly at the avenue now. As they came to what appeared to be a stretch of broken cobbles, Kubiš gave his friend a small shove with his shoulder. When the other shoved back, he stepped neatly aside, making Gabčík stumble slightly.

"Boys," said Opálka.

"He seemed almost happy this morning."

"Kubiš? He's in his element. They both are, in their way. I've never been like that. I think too much."

"Most do," said Bém.

"A curse. I have to keep it leashed all the time."

"It's not all bad if it helps you see things."

"Think so?"

"Not really."

Opálka paused uncomfortably. "I should have asked you this before, but is there someone . . ."

"You mean in case . . ."

That's right.

"No. Not in the way you mean. Thank you."

"Absurd, isn't it?"

"What?"

"Thinking this way."

"Not as absurd as it should be."

"True."

"And you? You've made arrangements? For your family, I mean?"

"I have. Thank you."

Opálka pushed up the sleeve of his jacket to check his watch. "It's time, I'm afraid," he said.

"I don't mind," said Bém.

Bém had gone only a few steps when he heard him call. "Tomáš?"

He turned.

"One more thing . . . Do you like beer?"

Bém paused. Opálka was a brave man.

"I do," he said, though he didn't, particularly.

"We should get a beer sometime . . . when this is over?"

"I'd like that."

Opálka nodded. "All right," he said. "All right. We'll do that, then." And picking up his briefcase, he walked away.

By the time he got to the tram stop, walking in the shadow of the buildings, he was sweating freely. The suit they had gotten for him was too heavy. It was much too heavy. He would sweat like a pig. It didn't matter.

He waited in the shade, his back against the façade of a three-story building like a soiled cake. The crowds were increasing. Men carrying briefcases stood on the island, holding their hats in one hand, with the other wiping their heads with handkerchiefs. Boys in shorts dodged through the crowd. He couldn't help but look for her, even now. The thought that he might actually see her terrified him.

A sweet-faced matronly woman with calves like bowling pins walked next to a dark-haired young woman pushing a baby carriage. He knew these faces. Two workers in overalls passed by, one leaning in toward the other, the other listening intently until suddenly he exploded with laughter, throwing back his head as if shot. They knew nothing. None of them.

A tram. Not his. One hour and fifteen minutes.

What would the woman and her daughter say, he wondered, if he walked over and told them what was going to happen in Líbeň in just over an hour? Would they believe him? Would they turn around and go home and wait by the radio? Would they start screaming to the two soldiers looking in a shop window on the opposite side of the avenue?

He could feel the weakness rising in him like a wave: that familiar inner trembling, that doubt. He recognized it for what it was — fear, not of the leap itself, but of the seconds before the leap, of those moments on the cliff when everything could still be otherwise. And leaning against the building, feeling his legs going weak under him, he did what he had done with that fear ever since they were children together and quickly killed it, opening the tap of rage in his heart and feeling it flood through his veins like adrenaline, thinking of his mother's laugh coming up from the courtyard and the look on his sister's face the morning she came upon the jar of yellow butterflies dead in the sun and the winter morning two years ago when he had watched an old man kicked to death in a square in Brno because he had tried to board a tram without seeing them waiting. It had taken a long time. He'd watched through the frame of the tram window as one of them whipped the old man's face and back with a black riding crop in a fury so profound it seemed like a crack in the order of things. The old man had crawled about in the melting snow, first trying to pull himself up a lamppost, then grabbing onto the boots of his attacker, then toward the crowd which moved back like a respectful audience, and from somewhere in the tram a woman's voice had said, perfectly clearly, "For the love of God, someone do something," not because she expected it, but because she had to say it. No one moved. Bém noticed that the man next to him, a laborer dressed in overalls and a heavy black sweater, had bitten his lower lip; a thin stream of blood was running into the stubble on his chin. There was nothing to do. And remembering all this, Bém felt the sickness leave him, and when the tram came he walked across to the island and swung himself on and the doors closed behind him.

He could see them there, just before the road turned into itself and disappeared: Gabčík, his suitcase next to him, pretending to do something with the chain on his bicycle; Kubiš leaning against a telephone pole a few meters away, smoking. Even from that distance he seemed both alive and nonchalant, like a man waiting for a date while pretending not to care.

The fact of it flashed through his brain like a jolt of electricity and was gone. They were waiting for Reinhard Heydrich. Reichsprotektor. Obergruppenführer.

Forty minutes. The usual crowd. Heydrich's car would be leaving Panenské Břežany any minute. It could have left already. A tram pulled up to the stop before the turn and three people got off. If a tram stopped there during the hit, Kubiš had pointed out, it would be directly behind Heydrich's car. They had considered that fact. There was nothing to be done.

The scene was strangely peaceful. The trees on the hill above the turn moved tentatively in the breeze and were still. A car went by. Then another, the other way. Then two more. To the south, dimly, he could see the city. The air above the Vltava, or where he knew the Vltava to be, seemed softer, shot through with mist. A sort of calm had settled over things. A distance. The world seemed drugged, slowed.

No police to be seen. Nothing unusual. No sign. Gabčík picked up the bicycle and leaned it against a pole. A blue summer sky. Two small clouds.

He turned to look behind him. Through the shrubs that grew along the top of the retaining wall at his back he could see a row of small houses, their yards a clutter of fences and gardens and half-successful trellises and piles of brick. A woman was hoeing, working the ground with short, choppy strokes. An older, shirtless man was pushing a wheelbarrow. He noticed that the wall to his left was bulging a bit, the stones tilting out from the face, as if forced by the weight of earth above it. Someone would have to repair it.

Nothing. What would happen would happen. It was all right. He thought of her for a moment and she seemed very fine to him and very far off. He couldn't bring her closer.

He could feel himself sweating, the cold rivulets trickling down his back and sides. He took off his hat and wiped his forehead with his sleeve and looked toward the hill. Nothing. He felt the gun under his arm. Kubiš was still leaning against the pole. He'd wanted to be the one to look him in the face and pull the trigger. Didn't matter.

Another tram arrived. An old woman got off — he could tell by the way she walked, bent under the weight of the bags in each hand, by the blue kerchief on her head. It was half an hour from Panenské Břežany. He looked toward the hill. Nothing.

Sweat. Blooms. The smell of grass. No police. A man holding a little boy by the hand was crossing the street. Another tram was . . .

A flash like a spark of mica on the hill. For an instant he didn't realize what he'd seen. He glanced down toward the curve. Gabčík was kneeling on the sidewalk by the open suitcase. He stood and slipped something into his coat and kicked the suitcase shut with his foot and strode toward the curb as Liba Fafek's car appeared around the curve, a black open Mercedes, like a premonition of something, right behind her, both cars already slowing until the Mercedes seemed to have stopped altogether and there was Gabčík standing in the road ten meters away, throwing open his coat.

Nothing happened. There was no sound. Everything seemed to have stopped. He could see the gun in Gabčík's hands. He could see the driver, suspended, staring at the big man in the raincoat as though he didn't understand who he might be or what he could want. He could see the man seated behind him: the visored cap, the long, white face . . .

Suddenly everything accelerated. He could see Gabčík moving and jerking about strangely, bent over the gun in his hands as though talking to it. The gun! The gun had jammed! It was impossible. The limousine was picking up speed. It was simply going around him. Instinctively, helplessly, Bém began to run toward the scene even as he saw Kubiš sprinting up from the side and then a flash and a burst of black smoke and the limousine skidded to a stop. Two popping sounds. Another. Gabčík fell and was up, staggering toward the bicycle leaning against the wall. The man was standing up in the back of the car as though it were a chariot, pointing at him. Bém could see Kubiš running down the avenue. The driver was firing at him. Gabčík was on the bicycle now, pedaling madly down the sidewalk. People were jumping out of his way.

Bém slowed, then stopped. The man climbed out of the smashed end of the limousine as if stepping over a fence. He was alive. It was over. They had failed. The suitcase lay ten meters away. Kubiš's bicycle was still standing by the wall.

He recognized him. Even from this distance, he recognized him. That face. That long, curved talon of a nose. He was gesticulating with his right hand, ordering something.

A delivery van had stopped. The man took two strides toward it, raised his right hand as though snatching something off a high shelf, and fell to the pavement.

Bém began to walk in the other direction. Quickly, not hurrying. He walked past the bulging stones where he had waited. The shirtless man he had seen pushing the wheelbarrow had come down to the edge of his yard. There was no avoiding him. "*Viděl jste co se tam stalo?*" he called down to Bém from the top of the wall. Did you see what happened there? Bém said he thought the tram had hit someone, and walked on. Don't look back. He was grateful he'd put on the hat. Still, his abruptness had made him worth noticing. He should have stopped, gossiped a bit. Erased himself.

He came to the next road and took a right, walking up the quiet sidewalks, then down the hill past the school to another avenue. A tram was coming. He got on it.

"WE MUST THANK GOD FOR BLOOD POISONING," THE priest, Dr. Petřek, had said. He was standing at the bottom of the steps wearing a long coat with a fur collar. No, no, he wouldn't have any, thank you. Heydrich's wound, he said, had not been considered particularly dangerous. No vital organs had been affected; the bleeding had been contained. The German surgeon who had been rushed in had assured the authorities that the ten-centimeter-deep gouge was not fatal, that the Obergruppen-führer's life was not in danger. Petřek stroked his white, goat-like beard. The swine had counted their cards early, he said; the good Lord had yet to play his hand. The wound, it turned out, had been full of debris — bits of metal and upholstery from the car seats, leather and horsehair . . . But perhaps he would have just a little, no more than a finger's width — it *was* cold down here. In any case, a week later septicemia had developed and quickly finished the job, which proved once again that even when we thought we were free and clear and seemingly out of danger, the hand of the Almighty could smite us. And he drained his glass in a way that showed he was not entirely unfamiliar with slivovitz, and left them.

"That was a nice coat," Gabčík said. He was sitting cross-legged, cutting carrots into a can. No one had said anything.

"We must thank God for blood poisoning," Kubiš said, and farted.

On the evening of June 10 Petřek was back. Bém had slept badly the night before, struggling through dreams in which his father appeared to him in a threadbare suit and he saw his mother sitting on a small stone bench against a wall with his sister on her lap. Then it was dark, and in the dream he knew he had to meet her somewhere, that she was waiting for him, and he rushed through endless, unfamiliar cities, running up stairwells and down badly lit hallways, looking for rooms whose numbers were always out of sequence or missing, all the while knowing that the whole thing was absurd, that he was years too late but unable to bring himself to stop. He was in an industrial district filled with low brick factory buildings surrounded by high fences. Tilting cement embankments, pale and high as Sahara dunes, rose in his path, and he scrambled up them on all fours, like a dog. At some point he found himself standing on the shore of a vast river, and realizing that he would have to cross it, he bent to take off his shoes, and woke. The stone ceiling of the niche was inches above his face.

He rolled over to look into the main room of the crypt. A white square was shining on the stone floor. For a second he didn't know what it was, then realized that the moon's pitch had somehow caught the tiny window high on the north wall, that he had woken at the precise moment — perhaps the only such moment for a month, or a year — when everything met. Then again, maybe it had been the moonlight itself that had woken him, like a visitor moving about the room. He watched it narrow, parallelogram, rectangle, square. How beautiful it was. Ten minutes later it was gone.

The next evening, Petřek came down to talk to them, and nothing was quite the same afterward. He came without his coat, and they all knew from this that something had happened

— or told themselves later that they'd known — and they left what they were doing and gathered by the bottom of the steps. He didn't hesitate. At ten the night before, Petřek told them, the village of Lidice, about twenty kilometers west of Prague, had been destroyed. An act of retaliation. The inhabitants were registered; movable property was evacuated. At dawn, the male population of the town — 150 men and boys at least — had been herded into a barn and executed. Another 190 women and children had been deported, presumably to Ravensbrück. The town itself had been razed. Obergruppenführer Frank's orders, supposedly given to him personally by the Führer, had been to erase all evidence that the town had existed, all coordinates, all markers. Rumor had it that the stream that ran through the town was to be rerouted in its bed. It appeared the town had been selected at random.

He had thought about whether he should tell them, Petřek said, and had decided it was only right. He was terribly sorry.

Bém watched them as he spoke. Kubiš, who had been cleaning his gun, looked down at it for a moment, then brought it up to his face and blew on it as though blowing away some dust. Gabčík, who had been leaning against the wall eating a piece of bread, kept chewing. Valčík smiled and looked down.

He was sorry, the priest said again.

"Well . . . ," Opálka said. He shook his head.

"An inhuman thing," the priest said. "God will not be merciful . . ."

"Yes," Opálka said.

"None of you must think . . ."

"No . . . of course not."

"No one could have foreseen this."

"No," Opálka said. "You're right."

"We must pray . . ."

"Yes," Opálka said. "Thank you."

• • •

There were no rages, no tears, no flashes of anger. They didn't talk about it. They didn't know how. They took the blow like a short, hard kick to the stomach from an invisible opponent — from God, say — and went on. It was the only thing they knew how to do. They'd been chosen precisely because they could.

But he could feel it there nonetheless — a kind of sickness, a rot. These men — Gabčík, Kubiš, Valčík, and the rest — were still dangerous, they would always be dangerous, but now something had changed in them. Something essential. And because they sensed this, they grew still, careful. They didn't fight with each other, or even argue. A simple, instinctive civility became the order of their days. There was nothing false or forced about it. "I'll need those potatoes when you have them." "You want some more soup?" "No, I'm fine." It was pure instinct. Something was hunting them. Something they couldn't see, or fight. If they stayed still, stayed together, it might pass them by.

He tried to keep them numbers: 150 men and boys, 190 women and children. Numbers. Not unaware that this was exactly what the others had done in order to be able to do what they did. He didn't care. He had been to Kladno, only a few kilometers away from Lidice. He knew these towns. If he allowed himself to see the faces blinking in the lights, the marks of the sheets showing on their faces like scars, the men — enemies, perhaps, who had not spoken for years — now suddenly talking, asking each other what was happening, where they were going, as if nothing before had ever really mattered but had only been a long, elaborate game . . . If he heard them giving quick instructions to their wives or assuring their sons that everything would be all right even as the village dogs, barking, were being shot down one by one in the street, in the chicken yards . . . If he allowed this, something might give. And that could not be. Ever. They were numbers. To hell with them.

But some things could not be fenced off. They came through the walls. They were like a chemical change in the brain. Day by day he could feel it coming over him, a kind of slow, undramatic numbness, as though some invisible spigot had been turned the night Petřek had come down to tell them the news. It was like falling out of love: one moment she was still the woman you knew and thought you wanted, the next something had shifted imperceptibly and it was over. The world outside was receding. Or maybe he was the one falling away from it. Either way, he was unable to care in the same way he had before. The Beneš government in exile, the Resistance, the Wehrmacht and security police even now combing the city for them — all these seemed far away from him, strangely abstract. He told himself how he should feel, why these things mattered, and mattered supremely, but it was no good. He could remember how he had once felt, but that time had passed.

Hour by hour, day by day, as they made their meals or did their exercises or wrapped themselves up in blankets before crawling into their niches, he could feel the circle drawing tighter around them. Around him. Two things mattered now. The men around him mattered, because they alone, of all the people on the earth, carried the same burden. Because they understood. And she mattered. Because she didn't. Because she was free of it. Because he loved her.

She would be the rope into the well in which he was drowning. He knew this as surely as anything he had ever known in his life. There was nothing sentimental about it. It was simply a fact. Paper would burn. Day would bring light. What lived would eventually die. She would save him, and she would be able to do this because she was who she was. Because the gods of the arbitrary world had decided it should be so. Because her voice, her body — her very soul, if you like — spoke to him.

When he was twelve he'd spent two weeks on his uncle's farm near Jindřichův Hradec. One night he'd woken up to a sound — a kind of rhythmic barking, a forced *aark aark aark* — unlike anything he had ever heard before. The sound was coming from somewhere behind his uncle's barn. He tried to go back to sleep but couldn't, so he pulled on his pants and woke his uncle, and together the two of them went out to see what it was and found an old water cistern with the neighbor's cat drowning at the bottom of it. His uncle pulled it out with a rake, still making that awful barking sound — a sound he wouldn't hear again until he visited the seals at the London Zoo — and wrapped it in a shirt to keep it warm but it didn't seem to know where it was and it just kept barking until it died. If they'd fished it out a half hour earlier, his uncle had said, the thing might have made it.

Well, here he was. The analogy, and the image at the heart of it, gave him pleasure — he didn't know why. The absurdity of it. The stick-in-the-wound absurdity of it. It was the first thing that had given him pleasure in days. Here he was. Here they *all* were, swimming in circles in their own little cistern — God's little cistern — barking like cats. Eight cats drowning in a well. It sounded like a nursery rhyme.

She would save him. She was the rope, the rake, the steps appearing in the stone, leading up from the water.

THE MORNINGS ON THE TRAM ON THE WAY TO THE Language Institute in Líbeň were difficult for my mother. By late afternoon she would be tired and so less likely to think about things. She tried reading, but the movement of the car gave her headaches, so she spent the forty minutes simply staring out the window at the people coming out of stores or waiting at the stops, some hurrying by with bags or briefcases — businessmen, lovers, a little boy in blue pants holding on to his mother's dress with one hand while bouncing some kind of stringed puppet-like thing with the other . . .

In the first half of May, as the weather warmed, the half-windows in the tram would be pushed down and the air would come in — pillowy gusts smelling of petrol and leaves — until some idiot worried about her hair would lean over and ask the person under it if he could close the window a bit, and then May 27 came and human beings were lined up against walls and shot, and yet nothing changed somehow. People still went to work, if they had work to go to, and when the weather was warm, the half-windows were pushed down and the air still felt good in her hair. At times this seemed natural and right — what else did she expect? At other times — brief moments, usually — it seemed both heartbreaking and utterly mad as if, looking out the tram window one day, she had glimpsed a woman burning on a street corner, her dress going up in great black billows as she waited patiently for her tram.

She didn't bother trying not to look for him. Twice she thought she saw him — the hat, the glasses, that smooth, deceptively easy walk — and rushed out at the next stop, to the predictable disappointment. It didn't matter. On July 16, only six weeks later, she would take the train out to Žd'ár. She'd already arranged to take the day off. She would get out at the familiar train station and walk along the wall and the trees, past the little *hospoda* where she and her father had once seen the dwarf sitting on the bench, then take the number 9 bus to the bridge. From there it would be less than five kilometers to the crossroads. One year. He might not be there; she knew that. It didn't matter. He would be there eventually. And the forest — the mushrooms, the mossy icons, all the things they had known — would help. They'd make him real.

She didn't let herself think, after May 27, that he might have been involved. It was not something she could think about. There were many things that my mother could not think about. That he was dead. That she would not see him again. That she would not hear his voice again in this life. When she heard the descriptions of the attackers being read over the loudspeakers in Václavské náměstí that outrageously blue Sunday morning, the phrases echoing off the façades of the buildings, overlapping each other, she had simply stopped breathing. All around her the streams of people hurrying up the sidewalks or crossing the avenue had shuffled to a stop and frozen. Pantomimes of listening — the hand to the ear like a timid greeting, the slight tilt of the head: *At half past ten this morning, a failed attempt . . . anyone with information . . . two have escaped, one on foot, the other on a bicycle.* It was not him. It was not him. Nothing else mattered.

Every day she checked the newspapers for the lists of names of those arrested or shot for crimes against the Reich. Nothing. He had disappeared. It did not surprise her. If anyone could slide through, he could. She'd seen his way with the world — his competence, his carefulness. He had that aura about him, the aura of luck. When the bullet came, he'd be the one who bent to tie his shoe. She believed this.

These days she found it easier to think about the other one. He was safer somehow. She hadn't heard from my father, hadn't expected to. It was strange sometimes to think of him only hours away, going about his daily business. Getting on the 4:40 train to the factory, waiting at the stop in the evening for the tram to Žabovřesky . . .

Odd to think how different her life had been then, and how quickly it had passed. One moment you were taking the train to Vysočina or sitting in someone's living room passing around a tray of *koláče,* and the next someone had licked a finger and turned a page and everything had changed. You could leaf back and see yourself taking the train, sitting on the sofa, passing the tray, but now it was as if you were reading about a character in a book, a character who resembled you in every way, whose thoughts were familiar, who *was* you — but a character in a book nonetheless.

They'd talked endlessly. They'd made love. It was easy to think about — had always been easy. It didn't matter. Page after page. For a week or so that September they'd worried that she might be pregnant, but it was a false alarm. They'd talked about marriage. They could live with his parents until the war was over, he'd said, then move into a place of their own. He had been doing well at the newspaper before the war began; he could pick up again where he had left off. Nothing was certain, of course, he realized that, but Soukup himself had told him more than once that he could make editor by the time he was thirty. They could do worse.

His good-humored understanding of her had annoyed her those first few months, as did his failure to notice the men's names she dropped into their conversation like tacks, hoping to get the reaction she'd always gotten from men before. Eventually, as she had come to see that his humor lacked condescension, that his confidence was not really presumption, it bothered her less. Touched by his decency, by his obvious regard for her, unable, in short, to find a good reason *not* to love him, she listened to his plans for them. She wondered now what she could have been thinking. It would all be over soon, he would say, stroking her hair as they lay in some grassy corner of the Špilberk gardens, and then they'd share the bit of food they had brought with them — generally a slice of bread and a small green kohlrabi — and start back down toward the city.

She'd thought she'd been in love with him then. Which was not surprising. Good to look at, intelligent, funny, he'd seemed to be liked (or at least respected) by everyone who knew him, and when she let him take her virginity that night in the garden behind the second wall, it was not only because she liked his lank, dark blond hair and his thin, aristocratic nose but because she had begun to sense that his decency had little to do with weakness and a good deal to do with strength. It was not her fault. How was she to have known that love is not something to be measured out in spoonfuls, that decency has its limits.

There had been a calm about him that she'd liked at first, a refusal to be drawn in by the world, an understanding of things that was rooted in pain but rose above it. It was a quality she hadn't known in a young man before — most of the men she knew were children, forever preening or pouting, throwing themselves this way or that without knowing why — and if truth be told she hadn't minded living within the still circle it made. He wasn't dispassionate. When they'd rolled over his rimless glasses that very first night, crushing both lenses with a hollow pop like the sound of a flashbulb going off, he'd chuckled and shook his head, and then, pausing only to see if she had been cut, rolled her over him and back to the grass, his fingers tangled gently in her hair, and finished making love to her.

Afterward they'd found what was left of the mangled frame and he'd put it in his pocket and she'd led him out of the garden and down the barely lit walks, and he had joked about the vague shapes he saw ahead of them and tapped the path in front of him with a crooked tree limb as though he were blind. She could tell he didn't like this business of having to walk back down the sloping flights of stairs and through the half-deserted streets with his arm hooked into hers as if he had aged suddenly, inexplicably, but these things happened.

He'd taken it well. As he took everything. She'd expected it — and both admired and slightly despised him for it. A good man. She could think of nothing to dislike about him. And yet, if just once she had sensed some anger beneath his decency, his irony. If just once she had sensed the place in him where all his negotiations with the world ended, and the man began.

It was unfair, really. He'd loved her — possibly loved her still. She could list his qualities, and these qualities were substantial and real. Anyone could see them. In fact, if the two of them had been houses or cars instead of men, he might well have been the better of the two. And none of it mattered, because for all the things he was, there was one thing my father wasn't: he wasn't the other one. For this she couldn't forgive him. Fairness had nothing to do with it.

MY FATHER HEARD ABOUT HER OCCASIONALLY — FROM friends, from former schoolmates, even from her mother, whom he ran into one chilly April morning as she was crossing the street to the greenmarket. It was to be expected — Brno was a village of three hundred thousand souls, people always said, and it was true.

It had rained that morning, and low, fast clouds were rushing over the buildings, thinning to a clear, piercing blue one moment, thickening to rain the next. He saw her flinch when she saw him, saw first the quick, unpremeditated smile — she'd always liked him — then the quick desire to pass without having to speak to him, then the realization that it was too late. That it couldn't be helped.

It was good to see him, she said; he was looking well for these times. She was just hurrying to the greenmarket — not that there would be anything to buy. For two weeks now there had been nothing, just potatoes full of eyes, some garlic . . . Everything was so overpriced . . . She didn't know how people did it — well, that was not true, she did know, in some cases she knew very well, but this was not the time or place . . . And you, she asked him, your parents are well? He told her they were. And was he still at the factory as before? He was, he said. Everything was pretty much the same as it had been, he said.

Ivana was in Prague, she said, living with her uncle Ruda's family. She was working at the Language Institute they had there. "You should write to her sometime," she said, patting the sleeve of his coat, and for a moment he hated her for her stupidity and her kindness. My mother was young, she said. These things took time sometimes. She had cared for him very much, she said. And he smiled because he knew these things were true and because this was the joke of it, and he wished her well and continued on his way.

The world was full of jokes. My father appreciated them all. That he should have written that letter for Honza Kolařik that day was a joke. That he should have seen my mother's face as if for the first time that afternoon, though he had seen it a hundred times before . . . that was a joke too. That he should love her still, that he should realize only after she'd left him that he'd made a space for her — a space that he now carried around with him everywhere he went, like a cored apple . . . that was yet another joke, and a good one. And he was the punch line. She loved another — she'd told him so to his face — and yet he continued to love her anyway, to think about her, to worry about her, and there didn't seem to be any way out of it. That was the biggest joke of all.

In the first month or so he'd been just miserable and angry enough to let himself be talked into trying the usual schoolboy remedies: the bottle of slivovitz, the circle of friends, the long diatribes against women in general. For the better part of half an hour he'd sweated over a fifty-crown whore who had cried out in perfect time to the creaking of the metal bed as though she and the bed together made up some kind of mechanism, speeding and slowing down with his thrusts . . . ridiculous. Witchcraft. One thing had nothing to do with another. His friends might as well have recommended that he drink tea or eat a clove of garlic at midnight. It would have been no more absurd than anything else these days.

There were distractions, of course, some of them quite humorous. The factory was a distraction. They were hated there, ironically enough not by their enemies, the soldiers charged to protect the Reich's armament industry, but by the factory workers who had been there before the war, good Czech citizens like themselves. These hated them for being intellectuals, troublemakers, for interfering in things, for disrupting things. Carburetors or shell casings, it was all the same to them. Making the quota meant a Christmas bonus, an eighth of a liter of rum — everything else was politics. Idiots. They could be told they'd all be shot on Saturday, and they'd work like dogs to get out the required number of bullets by Friday. And betray anyone who tried to slow them down.

He was liked a bit more than the others, he wasn't sure why. Perhaps because his father had been a janitor, or because he knew one end of a screwdriver from the other, or because he didn't try to ingratiate himself. "You're all right, Sedlák," one of them had said to him a few weeks after he'd started there, "not like all these others with their Latin grammars jammed up their asses."

"Is that right?" he'd said.

"I can tell," said the man, whose name was Tonda Králíček, and who worked the lathe two stations down from him, his stomach in his blue worker's overalls pushed against the steel. "You know how to work."

And work he did, he and four of the others, adding steel dust to the oil while pretending to correct some small malfunction or measuring the gap of the blade with the micrometer, resisting the temptation to do more, to go faster. One broken machine could knock out the line for a day, a week . . . One tenth of a centimeter difference in the depth of the holding groove could make the casing too tight, and somewhere on the Russian front a shell would explode while still in the cannon. It had to be enough. Get too greedy, go too fast, and you'd make a mistake. Someone

— likely as not one of your fellow citizens — would notice something and then the process, unencumbered by any need for evidence or courts, would accomplish the rest with great efficiency. You'd be led out to the courtyard between buildings B and C, near where the bicycles were parked, and shot in the back of the neck. It had happened twice in the past month — a man taken out, a bicycle orphaned.

It was a peculiar game. You had to dance just right, though you couldn't hear the music and the steps themselves were unmarked, and every now and then, just to keep things interesting, your leg or arm would be jerked by a string you hadn't known was there. That February, for example, Králíček had joined him as he sat eating his piece of bread with preserves in the second courtyard, rotting his teeth, and they'd talked a bit. He lived near Blansko, Králíček said. He had two daughters and a son. He didn't give a damn about politics. If there was one thing he hated, it was these little interferers, snuffling their wet noses into everybody's business. That breakdown in the drill press in the second sector had not been an accident — he knew that — and they'd all lost three days of work. And for what? It was not as though they were treated all that badly . . . they should be grateful for having work at all. He had a sense the breakdown had something to do with the oil.

He had a *chata* in the woods not far from Blansko, Králíček said, just a little place near a pond. Not much, really, but he loved it like a baby loves its nipple, counted the days till the warm weather returned and he could start going up. "You like to fish, Sedlák?"

He told him he'd never been. It wasn't true, but he sensed that this was what he needed to say in order to keep up the terms of the relationship — a relationship based on the illusion of his directness, his unwillingness to pretend to anything. "You'll have to come up sometime, then," Králíček had said, "I'll take you," and in spite of himself, he had felt moved. Králíček, he realized, was not a bad man, and most of the horrors of this world were committed by men just like him.

It became this thing between them: he would take the bus up to Blansko and they would go fishing. His son hated fishing, Králíček told him, had never been much interested in anything besides playing with himself.

He shrugged. "Maybe I'll hate it too," he said.

"Maybe you will," Králíček said, and smiled.

He discussed it with the others, and it was agreed they would ease off for a time. Adjusting the settings of the carborundum bits was simply too dangerous; quality control could catch the discrepancy at any time, and the authorities made no allowance for accidents. The dust in the oil was better; it worked flawlessly, if slowly. And the dust was already everywhere — in their mouths and ears and shit; sitting in the latrine, he could see it glistening in the light coming through the hole in the pane, a fine steel rain. Králíček was a problem; they'd have to watch him carefully.

Nothing happened. The dance went on — the grand distraction, from which he couldn't allow himself to be distracted. None of them knew what to do about Králíček or the others, and a week later they began to seed the oil again, a fraction of a gram a day. And then one morning during the first break, Králíček waved him over to where he sat on his stool two stations down, his short legs in their blue overalls crossed at the ankles, and pulled an envelope from his chest pocket. "Take a look at this, Sedlák," he said, taking out a small stack of photographs. One photograph was of a one-room cabin with a metal pipe for a chimney; another showed Králíček sitting on a stool by the edge of a small pond holding a long fishing rod, his legs crossed at the ankle. Very nice, my father said. A third was of a big carp; the fish had been knocked on the head, and one of its eyeballs had bulged and swiveled upward, giving it a comical look. Králíček, who was holding it forward, had drifted out of focus; only his fingers, made huge by proximity, stood out clearly, pressing into the fish's scales.

"That's a big fish," my father said.

"There are bigger," Králíček said.

A week later, he was as dead as the carp in his picture. Rumor had it that he'd been caught smuggling food. And this too was funny, in its way — the way opening a vein with a pair of manicure scissors was funny.

The next Sunday, without knowing he was going to, my father went to the train station and took the train to Prague, where he walked around the streets for an hour, slapping his hands against his legs to keep them warm, then returned to the station and took another train back to Brno. There was no point in trying to find her. Let the comedy play itself out. If she returned, it meant that the other one was dead, and he'd take her back. He had no choice in the matter.

AFTER LIDICE, TIME CHANGED FOR BÉM. IT SMOOTHED out, unwound more easily. As if pain were a lubricant. He barely minded waiting now. It seemed to be the same for the others. A terrible patience had settled in, and if he recognized in it at times the resignation of snowed-in mountaineers who, having gone beyond their altitude, have quietly begun to die, he knew as well their reserves, what a moment's need could loose in them.

The coffins were ready. Everything was set. On the morning of June 19 they would be driven to a storeroom in Kladno in two funeral cars. The coffins would be uncomfortable, Petřek had said — after all, they hadn't been built for the living — but breathing, at least, would not be a problem. He and the others, he said, had discussed various possibilities, then settled on drilling small holes precisely every two centimeters along the edges of the lids. It had taken them the better part of an afternoon. The holes looked like some kind of decoration in the wood; touched up with paint to hide the work of the drill bit, they were almost imperceptible.

They would have to be ready by six, he told them. If all went well, they would be moved from Kladno to a gamekeeper's cabin in the forests of Moravia that same evening. If any complications delayed the transfer, there were provisions enough in the store-room to last them a week.

It was convenient to know the exact hour when you would be placed in your coffin, Opálka had said afterward, and the others, who would normally have been the ones to carry that burden, and who appreciated his effort, smiled politely and nodded. Not everyone had that luxury, they said. St. Peter by appointment.

He didn't think about my mother. Or rather, he thought about her incessantly but held her back, didn't look at her directly. She was his secret, the thing he had in reserve. If he indulged it, he'd use up its power; it was enough that she was there.

On the fourteenth the schoolteacher brought them kerosene and candles. The writer Vladislav Vančura had been shot, he told them. Others as well. The Germans were flailing, he said. The twenty-million-reichsmark reward had gotten them nothing; the bicycle was still in the display window of the Bata shoe store on Václavské náměstí. It would rust there. He could see no problem with their going out one at a time every few days for air. Kubiš and Gabčík, of course, were out of the question.

It rained that day, and they watched the clouds through the window on the north wall.

On the fifteenth Valčík put on his hat and went out for five hours with a gun in his pocket and a strychnine ampoule around his neck and sat in the sun on a bench in the Children's Park.

On the sixteenth they cleaned their guns and went over the procedure one last time: The signal if the cars were being stopped; the signal to shoot. Where to keep the strychnine so that it could be found quickly and administered by someone else in case one were unable to get to it oneself. And that evening Kubiš, while slurping his soup, looked up at them and laughed and said, "Christ, boys, less than two days," and the rest of them had shaken their heads and nodded. They were afraid, all of them, but that was all right. Fear they knew.

On the morning of the seventeenth, hoping to quiet the muscles in his legs, Bém went for a walk across the square and up Francouská Street and she walked out of a grocery store directly in front of him. It was absurdly hot for June, still and white, and he looked at her, at her hair, at the side of her face . . . She was looking into her wallet, counting her change, the net bag hanging from her arm, and he watched her tilt her head impatiently and push a strand of hair behind her ear with her left hand and then she stopped and looked up and stared at him for a few moments, and then, not even knowing that she'd begun to cry, the wallet still open and the bag swinging awkwardly against her side, walked straight into his arms. He hadn't been looking for her. Or maybe he had.

They walked everywhere that long morning as the heat built up in the squares and the leaves began to droop, at first following the busier avenues, her arm through his and her head on his shoulder, an atom of life in the crowd, then drifting north through the Vinohrady district along crumbling retaining walls and up endless cascading flights of stairs that seemed to sweat some kind of stone moisture in the heat, until they came to the huge Olšany Cemetery, where they passed through the wrought-iron gates and down the four worn steps and disappeared into the vast shade of that place, a forest of ivy and stone. And when they came to the end of a long path they stood very still and she felt the same arms, the same chest pressed against her breasts, smelled the same particular smell of him. "I didn't know if you were alive," she said.

"I am," he said.

She sensed it immediately, I think, in the paleness of his skin and the bones of his back and in the way he tried now when before he would not have had to try. There was a need in him now — they both knew this — and she wanted to tell him that she would fill that need, that he could draw from her for as long as he needed to. She didn't ask where he'd been or how long he could stay; all she wanted to know was how long it would be un-til it was over. They were sitting together on a white stone bench at the end of a row of garish marble slabs that gave the impres-sion of doors whose houses had disappeared. He had taken off his jacket and loosened his tie in the heat.

"A while," he said. "A few weeks." Dusty-looking sparrows kept spearing into the greenery, then flying out. "It's not quite done," he said.

"And the sixteenth?" she asked.

"I don't know," he said, "I don't know if . . . ," then looked at her and said, "I'll be there."

"Can you walk with me for a while?" my mother asked him.

"Anywhere," he said.

And so they did, down street after street, avenue after ave-nue, through deserted districts filled with warehouses and across a little bridge that spanned railroad tracks on which no trains could be seen in either direction, then up through the dusty vineyards and down again toward the river, burning in the midday sun. Just before two o'clock they stopped in a small *potraviny* store and bought a quarter loaf of bread and some soft cheese and she reached up and took a jar of preserved apricots off a shelf and they paid and carried them a kilometer or so to a small park near a building that looked as if it might once have been a museum of some sort and sat down in the shade to eat, but the cheese had begun to go bad, and even though he tried to cut off the bad parts with his pocketknife it was no good — the mold had gone through. He wasn't really hungry anyway, he said. My God, it was hot.

"Not quite the same, is it?" she said, smiling.

"No." He was lying on his back in the grass, the bits of pared-away cheese and the open knife next to him, and he leaned up on an elbow and looked at her. "It doesn't matter." She watched him tear off a blade of grass and begin twisting it around his finger. "There's something I have to tell you," he said. And he told her about the gun, feeling as if he were making it up to make himself more interesting, and she said it was all right, though in fact the word "gun," like a single clap, had set a flock of panicked thoughts wheeling through her mind, first this way, then that, and then he said, "So, should we go?" and he was suddenly standing in that way he had, just as he had that first night after they had come out of the wheat field with Svíčka and she'd seen him sitting back against the pine with his rucksack. He reached down his hand to her. "It'll be the same," he said, pulling her up to him. "It may take a while, I don't know how long — a few weeks, maybe longer — but it'll be the same again. Trust me."

"I know that," she said. "I do."

He indicated the little park they were standing in, the vacant lot next to it, the reedy weeds, the white, hot sky. "This doesn't matter."

"I know," she said.

But it did matter. The gun in the coat over his shoulder mattered. Their presence on every street or sitting in the cafés with their black boots thrown over their legs mattered. The heat mattered. Yet she knew there was nothing to be done. They had to walk. The red shoes were on — there was nothing else to do.

Just after three they crossed Libeňský Bridge, the Vltava flowing small and discolored below them, walked up a broad avenue with rows of small buildings on either side to a park with a stagnant fountain, and shared a lemonade. They sat on a stone bench and my mother told him about her uncle's apartment and her morning ride to work and how she thought she had seen him, and he listened and smiled when she said something funny and looked at her face as she talked, and she knew that he loved her, and that it would be just enough. She could feel it slowly bearing them down, and she could hear herself talking, talking simply to drown out its presence. They walked on, though they had nowhere to go, exhausted now, first left, then right, then left again, staying to the shade, wiping the sweat . . .

There was no shade along the bank of the Vltava, and as they hurried along the deserted cinder walkway they could see him, far ahead, sitting shirtless on a little stool between the shoreline bushes, the telltale rod sticking up like a scratch in the air. He was leaning forward, his elbows on his knees, motionless — a man fishing in an oven. They walked on, not talking now, bent on the shade of a stand of willows half a kilometer ahead, and as they approached she could see the fleshy shelves of his back, coated with sweat, the black rod protruding from a holder pushed into the bank. The river was narrower here, filthier. Pieces of what looked like furniture or bits of carpeting bobbed in the current; an automobile tire was wedged in the crotch of a tree.

It was as they were passing him, the sweat stinging her eyes, that my mother saw the yellow carp, the milk-white streak of its belly rising above the foam, its scales like rows of yellow coins or rotting armor, like a detail out of a dream of dying. Or so it would seem to her afterward. It floated just beyond the reach of his rod like an affront, and there was something terrible and funny about this. When she looked back from the shade of the willows she could still see him sitting there, his elbows on his knees, and she imagined she could see the fish, a spot of yellow in the shoreline foam, but knew she couldn't.

They went on. The sun had stopped in the sky. The fountains were dead. How long could he stay, my mother asked, though she hadn't meant to, and he looked away and said not long, a while, and for one miserable moment she wished he had to go so that they could stop this day, then knew it was the one thing in this world she wanted least, and that he felt exactly the same way. There was no help for it.

By seven they had made their way back to Vinohrady and the sun had gone behind Petřín Hill. A sluggish breeze moved down the avenues, then died. At a butcher shop they bought a bit of chicken, then a few stale *rohlíks* at a bakery that was closing, and walked on. On Žitná Street a group of four came down the middle of the sidewalk, and she and Bém stepped toward the buildings and let them pass. Two hours before the curfew, she asked him again how much longer they had before he had to go, and he looked at her and smiled a strange, pained smile. "I can't seem to leave you, can I?" he said. "Then don't," she said.

And she took him by the hand and led him back to Olšany Cemetery, carrying her shoes to save her blistered feet, and they found a gate that was open and a dark, overgrown place by the long back wall where the scraggy grass and dirt behind the row of trees and ivy were cool against her skin and he unbuttoned her clinging blouse and pushed up her sweaty skirt and entered her without saying a word, and the familiar shock of it, the desperate, unapologetic, hand-over-the-mouth ferocity of it, was enough to tell her that it would be enough. That she could save him. That she could save them both.

They stayed together that night, first moving even farther back into the dark of a small crawl space behind a row of overgrown monuments, then rolling her skirt for a long, thin pillow. It was very dark and they lay together, not touching because of the heat, talking as they hadn't been able to talk all day, and as she drifted toward sleep his voice would begin to fade, then suddenly grow louder, then fade again. Breaking the curfew was madness, they knew that. But it was done, and this place was as safe as any place could be; a patrol might come through, but there would be no dogs, and there were probably twenty kilometers of paths, thousands of monuments . . . No one would think to look behind precisely this set of stones, to crash through this particular thicket of vines.

At one point, it must have been well after midnight, she felt him jerk to attention and they lay very still as footsteps passed some distance away — a sound like knuckles tapping slowly on a bone — then disappeared, and sometime during those hours, reckless from fatigue, or love, he told her everything there was to know, where he had been and where he had to return in the morning and how it would go, and she felt, listening to him, that she'd somehow known it all along. She must give her notice at the Language Institute, he said — leave Prague. He knew someone who could get them over the border. They would meet on the sixteenth in the forest, just as they had planned.

And because they were young they made love again, just before the first leaves began to stand out from the dark, then dressed quickly, took a drink from the tap at the end of the row where visitors drew water for the flowers, and hurried out toward the gate.

The avenue was still nearly empty. She would walk him, my mother said.

It was a bit earlier than they'd thought. They waited for the tram for a while but none came, so they started walking down Vinohradská — walking tired, thinking about how they would manage it when the time came — then up Italská to Náměstí Míru, where a small knot of people stood talking on the corner, then finally down Anglická, past the shuttered stores toward Karlovo náměstí. There was some kind of commotion down by the square. An accident. They could see the barricades.

Bém had stopped. What is it? my mother said. A young woman was walking toward them, away from the square. Some kind of police action, she said. Something having to do with the church on Řesslova. The whole square was cordoned off.

She couldn't get him to move. She noticed they were beginning to attract attention. "Now," she said, taking his arm and whispering into his ear like a lover, "we have to go — now," and then he was walking fast, his head down, and as they passed each street like the spoke on a wheel she could see the barricades, the sentries, the security police with their black helmets standing in the low morning sun, and along with the nauseating throb of fear came the realization that he should have been one of them but wasn't, that he was here, with her, that he had escaped, that when the shot had come he had bent to tie his shoe, and they ducked into a small courtyard and my mother led him to a bench hidden behind the gate and held him as he sobbed, racked like a child, even as she noticed, over his shoulder, a father and a small boy with a white dog walk past them and out the gate, even as she heard the *pop pop pop* of gunfire, and realized with a kind of stunned gratitude that it was his love for her that had saved him.

IT WOULD TAKE TIME, MY MOTHER KNEW, PERHAPS A lot of time, but they would make it through — had made it through. The worst thing, the unsurvivable thing, had passed them by; now they could run. There would be no more waiting. He had said he knew someone who could get them out. And eventually, of course, the war would end, as all wars did. It had to end. The dead would be buried, the wounds would heal — or they'd learn to live with them.

She did everything. She managed to get them out of Prague to Jindřichův Hradec, from Jindřichův Hradec to Brno. She borrowed some money from her parents, found them a place, a two-room flat on the third floor of a building next to a printer's shop. It had an alcove for a kitchen and a window that looked out over the street, and there were a few pieces of furniture — a bed, a small table, a long white bookshelf with a few books in German and a Hebrew grammar . . . They had had to say they were married, of course, and when the landlady unlocked the door and showed them in, my mother had walked ahead, taking in the size of the rooms, the light, the bucket-sized sink, and she saw him watching her, and he understood what it meant to her and even tried to go along, turning a light switch on, then off . . . and when she had asked him if he thought it would be all right, he had smiled and said it seemed fine to him, a distinct improvement over their last place. A few minutes later, while checking the stove with the landlady, she looked up and saw him leaning against the wall by the open window, looking out on the street.

There was little meat to be had in the stores, but she managed anyway, making apricot dumplings one evening, bread and lentil soup the next, and they ate at the table by the window as the city grew dark around them. The evening breeze lifted the corner of the tablecloth now and then, and they talked about where they would go, what they would do. He had said he knew someone, she said, someone who could get them out. He would look into it, he said. They could stay here in the meantime, she said, until everything was ready. Yes, he said, it was the best idea. It was a very comfortable flat, he said — he liked it.

One evening as they ate, my mother turned to look out the half-closed window and saw the two of them reflected in the glass. He was looking at her. The light was almost gone but she could still make them out, sharing a table out there in the near dark, and even in the reflection she could see how much he loved her, the tenderness he had for her. He seemed to be memorizing her — and moved by this she turned from the image in the glass to the man sitting just across from her, but he had already looked away and was reaching for a piece of bread.

Three had died almost immediately. The remaining four had saved their last bullets for themselves. They'd tried to dig through the meter-thick wall to the sewers using knives and pieces of brick. When the fire hose was pushed through the small window on the north wall, they'd managed to find a ladder and shove it back out on the street. They had been betrayed by an informer, a partisan named Čurda, who later helped identify the bodies. The underground was being pulled up by the roots — men, women, entire families. Everyone they'd known. Everyone who had helped them.

My mother saw him looking at the pictures in the newspaper that morning — at the wet bodies on the pavement outside the church, at the close-ups of Kubiš and Gabčík. She was sorry, she said. On the roof she could hear pigeons cooing and then a quick flurry of wings. It was all right, he said. And for just that one moment, it was. And then he looked up at her with an odd half-smile on his face, as though he had lifted the paper to find he had no legs, and she said, "What? What is it?" and he said, "How would they have known it wasn't me? They didn't know it was Čurda when they died. They thought it was me."

She talked. She explained. They knew him, she said. He seemed to agree. She found work at a bookseller's and returned in the evenings and he was fine and she loved him and they ate their dinners together and he asked her about work and even smiled at the things that required smiling and day by day he slipped away — not willfully, not cruelly, but slipped away nonetheless. And she talked and cooked and held him at night and he did everything he could to help her and she said everything right and the reason it didn't matter was not because the others had died and he had not, but because he had been gone for sixteen hours when it began and because he would never know whether, as the water rose up their legs and the stairs began to disappear one by one, they didn't believe it was him.

And so together they staggered on, locked in love, until the morning my mother turned around at the tram stop for no apparent reason and made her way back to the flat next to the printer's and found the note on the table under the salt shaker and read the name and contact information of the man who was to have gotten them out of Czechoslovakia and underneath it, in the tall, disordered handwriting she had only lately come to know: Please don't look for me — I didn't have the strength to say goodbye. I love you will always love you. Forgive me.

And my mother refolded the note and put it back under the salt shaker and began the rest of her life.

IT WAS RAINING THE MORNING HE PARKED THE CAR BY the old town wall, unwound the stems of his glasses from around his ears, hooked them on the rear-view mirror, and started walking up the road from Žd'ár. No one had stopped him. He walked easily despite the rain, one hand in his trouser pocket, his head tilted slightly as though skeptical of the world ahead of him. Through the archers' clefts in the wall he could see the river, solid as pewter, a sooted steeple, a wooded hill, and for an instant he saw them there — bows tensed, fletching brushing their cheeks. Like children's figurines arrayed along the edge of a dresser.

At the wrought-iron gate he called to an old man dragging a tarp over an open grave, then pointed to some distant spot behind the bars and waited, his hand making a roof over the cigarette pinched between his fingers, calmly ducking his head every now and then for a drag, watching as the old man finished weighing down the four corners of the tarp with small heaps of brick, then shuffled, still partly bent over, past the cart half full of broken stems and small, muddy wreaths, and opened the gate, and he thanked him and walked on up the path — left, then right, then left again, putting as much distance between himself and the gate as he could — then stopped by a new grave and sank the knees of his trousers into the soft doughy soil. He brought the cigarette to his mouth in a big arc, sizzled it out carefully in the mud, then reached into his raincoat pocket and did what he would have done, had love and luck not interfered, twelve days before.

HE'D BEEN TRYING TO READ THAT MORNING, I'M SURE of it — first Sova's poems, then Horace, then Heine — fascinated by the way the fever seemed to charge certain words and phrases with a significance he couldn't quite grasp and suspected probably wasn't there. A warm, cloudy morning. Rain. His parents had both gone out. When the wind swung the window partly open my father wrapped the blanket around himself and went to shut it, and when his hand touched the wet metal of the latch, he shuddered.

He had hardly opened the new book when the frontispiece came out in his hand, and, irritated, he got up again and rummaged through the drawer of a desk that stood next to a tall black piano, then walked over to the dining room table with a squat brown jar and a pencil. He might be able to glue it back in. He wondered when they would return. The brush was too fat; it would glue half the page to the one after it. Dipping the point of the pencil just past the lead, he placed it across the mouth of the jar, opened the book to the missing page, then touched the gluey tip to the crease. A tricky business. Twice the book closed accidentally. Once he dropped the pencil on the table. He hated being sick. Heine had been sick for seven years, had written his greatest poems from the bed he would die in. It didn't make him feel any better.

The page went in badly. He pulled it out, dabbed at the glue in the crease with the tip of a napkin, then tipped it in again. Who knew when they'd be back. Everything took forever these days. He closed the book carefully, placed the Horace on top of it for weight.

Miserable weather.

He looked out the window and there she was. She was walking up the sidewalk, leaning slightly toward the suitcase in her right hand. She was wearing a long gray coat. For one nightmarish instant — perhaps it was the fever — my father thought that she was blind.

He wouldn't make her open the gate, walk up the path, knock on the door. He met her on the sidewalk in his slippers, in the rain, and even before he saw her face, before she collapsed in his arms and he half carried her down the rickety bricks that he and his father had put down when he was twelve, before he even got up from the table, in fact, he understood.

He saw it all, the arc and fall of his life — the sad carnival tune to which it would play — illuminated as clearly, as incontrovertibly, as if he had been hit by that hackneyed bolt experienced by characters in novels. He saw the gift, and the loss in that gift, and he rose from the table without hesitation or regret to shoulder the burden of his love.

ONE NIGHT WHEN I WAS FIVE OR SIX MY MOTHER WALKED out of the country bungalow we were staying in at the time. I woke to hear my father pulling on his pants in the dark. It was very late, and the windows were open. The night was everywhere. Where was he going? I asked. Go back to sleep, he said. Mommy had gone for a walk. He would be right back, he said.

But I started to cry because Mommy had never gone for a walk in the forest before, and I had never woken to find my father pulling on his pants in the dark. I did not know this place, and the big, square windows of moonlight on the floor frightened me. In the end he told me to be brave and that he would be back before I knew it and pulled on his shoes and went after his wife. And found her, eventually, sitting against a tree or by the side of a pond in her tight-around-the-calf slacks and frayed tennis shoes, fifteen years too late.

And I wonder if it was something in particular, the moon that night or the smell of the fields, that sent her out of my father's bed and into the forest, as though by simply walking far enough, deep enough, she might find him there, and herself as well, asleep in the moss, covered by a single blanket. I imagine my father closing the white-painted door of the bungalow and walking into the dark. Calling her name after he'd walked a bit farther from the other cabins. Listening to the far-off thrum of the freeway, two valleys over.

I wonder how he found her in all that darkness. And if he didn't say anything at all but simply took her back — for what else could he do? — holding her arm along the wood-chip path like an invalid crippled by grief. And if there was any way on this earth, in this life, she could not have hated him for it.

But I would wish it for her now — an endless forest, and twenty years till dawn.